WAITING JACKALS

IAN SANDUSKY

BEGINNINGS

They come in so many forms, in so many ways.

The sun had finally begun to rise. The road ahead lightened in shades of grey, finally releasing them from the night's stiff hold.

It had been the night, the only one he had ever known. Civilizations rose and fell before the morning's first rays penetrated the gloom. The world was falling to pieces around their feet.

And Carey Cardinal was running out of steam.

The company of military-men from the gas station were on the move, executing a full Australian Peelback. All men out, none left behind. Full speed ahead, no looking back.

The Canadian Forces had paid them no attention, though Carey and Keila were hot on their heels. The soldiers ahead moved like animatrons – never tiring, never slowing. Their heavy boots beat the pavement harder and harder, pulling out of the hostile zone. It was the last desperate move of a force without options, leaving their final line in the sand behind, the infected boiling forth to give chase.

The midnight retreat moved through six towns, all bathed in flames. Screams of horror stuck out of the mirth, but the empty howls of the infected overwhelmed all. The crackle of fires gutting subdivisions. Sputtering streetlights casting flickering bursts of illumination. Broken fingers. Yearning hands. Empty eyes. Snapping jaws.

It was better in the dark.

At least Carey couldn't see his desperation reflected in windows without the light.

Running beyond the brink of exhaustion, Carey and Keila followed. They didn't ask where they were going, and didn't oppose the flow. The soldiers were hope. Alone, the pair of frightened youth had none.

The hangnail moon jeered him from above. With every step, it catcalled at him to fall. The hangnail moon wanted blood. The hangnail moon was thirsty.

His lungs burned, the coppery taste of blood rising hot and sick in his throat. The human body had limits, and with every passing moment Carey knew he was nearing that wall. When he fell, the platoon wouldn't stop to pick him up. Hell, they wouldn't even turn around. Keila might fight to lift him, but she had taken more of his weight than she could bear.

He leaned on her when he faltered, steadying himself on her shoulder when blood slicked the road like black ice. Her piercing green eyes had lost their fire, but not their resolve. Carey only wished he could say the same. He was a puppet held aloft by a cruel master, some spark of the survival instinct making him a slave.

Carey wanted to lie down. Collapse on the road. Feel the pebbles and asphalt press into his face until the infected bore down on him, promising sweet release in their embrace.

New Braniff, his *alma matter*, the hometown to end hometowns, was left behind them in flames. His childhood home was nothing but a shell, his parents long gone, or—

Don't say it. God, please don't say it. Don't even think it. They survived. They got out. There's too much blood on my hands already. It's dripping from my palms and coating me with guilt. God, don't even think it.

Keila's brother was now nothing but a memory, his last spite to the world cast up on wings of ash from the gas station. Every deal with the Devil required a pound of flesh, and Roman had been their lamb led to slaughter. Survival had a price, but at what cost? At least it hadn't been the Taurus, still clutched in Carey's aching fingers, that had driven the point home.

The sniper that hit the younger Tindall was likely right in front of them, running from the city. He likely had no remorse, no shame in his actions. Roman was infected. Infected had to be cleansed. The only method: an injection of lead, delivered at hundreds of feet per second.

Though Carey hadn't shot the sixteen year-old when he stood, it hadn't been for a lack of trying. He could remember Roman's wild, feverish eyes, the pistol in Roman's hands pointed straight at his chest. The empty click of Carey's Taurus revolver rang off in his mind again and again, searching for the lone bullet in the chambers.

Tick. Tick. Tick.

But it wasn't Roman he thanked. No, Roman, infected with the virus or not, had wanted Carey dead. There was vindication in the madness brought on by the fever, the one that turned you into a walking monster, but it was hard to place.

Roman had held back the tide of advancing plague victims, hungry for their flesh. He had bought them time, a substance immeasurable but of more value than all the possessions of his days, stacked on one another until they towered in the sky.

Only Keila carried him when he faltered.

God, do I ever owe you.

I

The details of those lost hours sprinting in the dark careened somewhere deep down into Carey's subconscious once passed. It was as if the time spent fleeing from the approaching mass of broken bodies, crawling over each other for the first opportunity to tear his skin from his bones, simply vanished into the ether in hindsight. Only flashes remained, snapshots of horror.

Every surviving memory held the same common elements.

Pain. Desperation. Guilt. Keila.

Once the first rays of the new day began to creep over the horizon, Carey had finally torn his eyes from the boots of the well-trained men ahead of him to pass a glance at the flat highway behind. He expected to see the smouldering column of smoke where Roman had sacrificed himself for their lives, with the sightless eyes of the pack of infected close behind. It shocked him to see nothing of the sort staring him in the face with the cold first light of the April morning.

No twisted fingers grasping for his collar. No towering monument to Roman Tindall hanging in the wind. No blood-soaked wretches advancing relentlessly behind him.

Only the flat, curved road bordered by looming trees on one side, and a field of uncut corn to the other greeted Carey to the beginnings of his new life. No one cheered at his rebirth. No one even noticed. If not for Keila's fingers entwined in his, he may not have realized he remained among the living.

Ahead, the once-proud squad they trailed hung ragged with the renewed sun beginning to light the scene. Carey had expected to find an entire brigade of tall, muscular soldiers clutching over-sized weapons, boldly leading the charge west like a band of noble Crusaders pushing enlightenment towards the ranks of the godless. Instead, the company numbered less than fifty. They were short. They were tall. They were black. They were Asian. They were white. They were broad. They were narrow. There was only one constant across the decimated platoon - the tendrils of utter exhaustion threatening to overtake their determined thousand-yard stares.

They had seen their brothers-in-arms chewed apart by people they had once pledged their lives to protect. They had seen comrades fall, only to rise again as the enemy. They were shoved in through the Gates of Hell, only to have them slam resolutely shut behind. No clawing or begging would pry them open ever again.

Black planes passed high overhead, images of power above the ruined force below. They all flew north and none had passed back heading the other way. Carey, upon realizing this, felt the grip of guilt harder than he thought possible. *What if Roman was right? What if we should have gone to Coboconch? Would he still be alive?*

The leading pack of retreating infantry remained on a westerly track, but it did nothing to ease the straining of his heartstrings. Saying *I told you so* had no arrogant pleasure when he said it to one cremated at his own hands.

They moved onward as the sun rose. The silence wrapped firmly around the destitute horseless caravan began to break. Carey hadn't heard a word from the soldiers ahead or from Keila on his right for what felt like an eternity, but as the heat and light of the upcoming day burned away the night, so went the spell. Officers shouted, ordering soldiers to engage hostiles at the edges of the road who threatened to slow their progress. Hollow moans and short barks of controlled gunfire followed. Bodies fell across the pavement as Carey ran, the corpses fighting to catch his feet and make him fall. A few infected strayed from the endless pickets of corn, a couple of others from the shrouded wood, all cut down ruthlessly by men taught from the events of the prior day to shoot for the head. *About time*, Carey mused, the only coherent thought blossoming in the hurricane of panic filling his mind.

"Come on," he said softly to Keila, feeling her beginning to lag for the first time since they'd started.

It's my turn now. She looked at him, her pale eyes encircled with the dark purple of fatigue. Carey felt something click deep inside her via some strange bond of those linked by tragedy. She began to run again with renewed strength.

The road ahead curved gently to the right, but it was enough to hide the rough paved street from view by trees stretching their limbs across the road. A dread he couldn't place bred in his chest, the fear of the unknown more prominent after the dark clouding his sight had finally been banished to nothing more than a bad memory.

He looked again to Keila, making sure she hadn't disappeared in the minute since he last checked.

An unexpected hand grasped his sweater from the front and Carey cried out in dismay. The polished revolver in his hand popped instinctively upwards towards the breath he felt on his cheek as he jarred to a halt, turning his head to face the demon impeding his way. His index finger snapped the crisp trigger back in the guard, the action unbidden but not unwanted.

Click.

Carey stared into the brown eyes of the soldier before him, seeing the muzzle of the Taurus Model 85 dance beneath his stubbled chin. His gaze was cold, accompanied by a smirk at Carey's failed effort to paint the sky with his brain.

"Better reload that thing, buddy. And don't point it at me again," he snarled, spittle peppering Carey's face. "Didn't think you guys would last this long, but since you've made it this far, hold up a second. Destination's just around this corner and we're not gonna take any chances. You guys do something stupid that I think may ruin us now, and I'll shoot you myself. Oh and mine's loaded," he said, patting the black carbine slung across his chest.

"S-sorry. Rough day," Carey muttered sheepishly, fighting to avoid Keila's pressing gaze at his left. Nothing like trying to be the hero and walking out like a dick. Instead of laughing in his face at his best effort to slay the imagined dragon, she only gave his hand a squeeze.

Ooh la-la, Aaron crooned.

Shut up, was Carey's only response. It didn't feel so bad to be mocked by an imagined voice anymore. Hell, it was almost comforting.

The infantry sent a few of its members ahead, slowly moving forward in a crouch, guns trained upwards and ready for any victims of the illness that had run like wildfire across Ontario to stagger into sight. Carey found himself holding his breath as he watched, waiting for the sharp reports of rifles to signal his coming end.

The trained operatives slowly crept out of sight.

A moment passed. Two.

"*All clear. Base Alexander up ahead, Cap,*" crackled through the radio of the tall soldier he had almost lobotomized.

Fuck, I really do *need to reload this thing*, he thought as he white-knuckled the rubber grips of the revolver. Either that, or he needed to get some updated technology. He couldn't imagine fumbling with oiled brass rounds, skirting around the open cylinders as jaws snapped ever closer.

The force walked slowly forwards and the view ahead came into sight. It looked more like a slum-dog tent-city than a 'base' as the scout had called it. Regardless, compared to *The High Spruce Development* that had been his previous fortress, it looked like a veritable medieval stronghold in the centre of a flat, grassy field coated white with rapidly evaporating frost. It was difficult to discern at the distance, but large tan vehicles topped with long cannons surrounding the perimeter of what he hoped to be the island of safety.

Circling the wagons. It was a tactic born in the tumultuous pioneer days of the American West. Far from covered buggies drawn by steeds, these eight-wheeled monsters looked like all-terrain vehicles slammed together with a Sherman tank - all armour plating and armament. Their long black main-guns spat gouts of flame outwards intermittently, the concussive blasts echoing across the dimpled field. Towering structures rose above the camp with massive spotlights panning across the ground, but Carey couldn't place them.

Surely, this encampment hadn't existed for long. Although he had much faith in the wheels that drove the Green Machine, he doubted even the most motivated Canadian Forces unit could erect watch-towers this quickly.

Clear had also been a bit of an overstatement. Whoever considered the way ahead an open road had clearly faced teetering odds to cloud that particular judgment. Dark swarms of infected roved inwards, drawn like children to the tinkle of the ice cream truck's bell. They had dropped en-masse at the bid of unseen bullets, but there had to be at least a couple hundred bodies still tirelessly shambling towards the steel fences draped with concertina wire.

"Let's go!" someone bellowed hoarsely.

The squadron came alive as if a breaker had been thrown that gave them power. Instantly, the straggled company became one living organism, reacting without instruction into trained assault and support roles. They charged forward in unison.

"Time to go!" Carey yelled at Keila, springing after the column of soldiers.

They ran directly towards an opening between two masses of writhing infected and Carey fought the urge to shut his eyes like a preteen watching a too-scary movie. A staggering woman clad only in pink polka-dot pajama pants turned towards him on his right and his bowels clenched. He released Keila's grasp, shoving the near-empty Taurus into his pocket and drew the jet-black steel extendable baton from his jeans.

You've got this, Care, Aaron called from the depths.

Carey snapped his wrist downwards, feeling the telescoping segments extend to their full twenty-four inch length before locking home. He lifted it high over his shoulder like a batter anticipating a pitch as the woman raised stained hands towards him. Black, drying blood encrusted her chest and shoulders where it had wept from her neck in runlets. Something deep inside him felt sympathy for the broken soul. He flexed his arm hard, preparing to slam the ball tip into her skull, when her head exploded in a crimson mist.

"Fuck!" Carey cried. Keila yelped in surprise.

An equally vicious portly man behind her met the same fate before Carey realized what was going on. It was far from his mental will manifesting itself in some extravagant act of psychic force, they were high-caliber rifle rounds dropping the grey dogs around him like autumn timber.

"This is Fireteam 6-1 Echo advancing on your location — do not shoot! I repeat, *do not shoot* with those LAVs!" the Asian soldier behind him brayed into his shoulder-mounted radio as they drew closer to the fortified walls of the camp.

Shots rang out in the morning like sticks of dynamite, some from within the squadron's ranks, but the majority coming directly from the stronghold ahead.

"Roger, 6-1 Echo — supporting fire coming your way," a crackling voice answered.

As Carey drew ever closer to the encampment with Keila in one hand, the extendo in the other, the tower's identity was revealed. *Fucking cherry-pickers!* The looming structures were the reaching bassinets usually used for fixing hydro wires in cities mounted with high intensity searchlights, each with a pair of snipers perched within. It was ingenious — the ultimate repurpose that Carey could think of.

Pride for his nation's peacekeepers blossomed in his chest as they drew within metres of the high steel fence-line. It stood in stark contrast to a mass of horribly burned and disfigured corpses strewn across the moor to the left of the camp, each representing another of the Crown's many failures.

"Almost there, come on Kei!" Carey cried, clutching her to his side as they followed the soldiers through a gate leading into the safety within.

The Light Armoured Vehicles — a General Electric innovation — spat 60mm munitions once more, the sound deafening as they passed. Carey turned as he passed the coiled barbed wire flanked by infantry covering their entry, to see slews of infection victims drop like rain, having no reply to the lead foray. Men shouted. Husks of the epidemic wailed. Everywhere was sound, all of it oppressive. The stink of spent shells and shed blood clogged his nostrils, draining him further of his fading strength.

As the worst seemed behind him after what felt like a lifetime tiptoeing the balance between this world and the nether, a loud clattering erupted from the centre of the camp ahead. *Shit!* A harsh wind blew his hat clean off his head and pushed Keila's hair back in waves. A sleek black behemoth rose above the green canvas tents, its twin rotors spinning too fast to make out clearly.

Fuck me! Carey thought. *It's back!* For a moment, he was sure the attack helicopter was rising only to send Sidewinder missiles back down from whence it came as it had to the onramps of the 405, but before he could complete the thought, it was gone.

The chopper tilted forwards, accelerating forwards faster than he thought the feat of human engineering capable and vanished from sight. The hammering din of the chopper faded quickly into the distance, leaving only the dwindling battle outside ringing in his ears. Keila clung to his arm, pulling him downwards as she too began to succumb to exhaustion.

Carey took two firm steps forward before his knees began to give way. The will that had wavered but never fallen on the dead sprint to Base Alexander, finally began to crumble in earnest. The steel gate rattled closed behind him as the soldiers around them dropped packs and carried supplies on every side. Some fell directly on top of their rucksacks, panting and sweating, while others returned immediately to the frontline to aid the repulsion effort. Carey's own small backpack seemed full of steel blocks, every faltering step pleading with him to lie down.

"Come on," he said hollowly, trying to inspire Keila to move with him.

It was more than she could bear. She didn't open her eyes. Didn't speak. She only held his arm with both hands, face pressed to his broad shoulder.

A disfigured face crossed with scars appeared before Carey saw no more.

‖

The hours after arrival passed in a haze.

Disjointed images of military clothing and polished brass floated through the mire, signifying nothing and meaning even less. Carey was aware of strong hands picking him up, carrying him through the camp. With barely open eyes, he had seen Keila lying on a stretcher manned by two burly, rugged individuals looking old beyond their years.

"Identification, civilian," a loud, firm voice called through the clouds of sleep. Carey listlessly clawed at his back pocket with cold and clammy hands. He felt his wallet pried from his jeans, hearing the plastic cards in the leather folds torn from their resting places like rotten teeth before it was flipped onto his chest.

"Got it, sir," someone called from behind him. "The girl doesn't have anything in the way of ID, but how about that necklace?"

Her necklace? They're taking her jewelry?! Carey fought to roll to his side, but had no energy left to complete the action. *No!*

"Yeah, that's fine. Make it quick and get these kids over to medical pronto — check them over for bites and blood."

The voice was harsh. Graveled. Carey wanted to stand on his feet, fight for Keila's precious gold necklace and show these men he wouldn't be walked over. Instead of the heroic action, he managed only to turn his head before vomiting sour bile into the dust below. He choked and gagged on the bitter fluid, his stomach clenching like a rusty vice.

"Shit! Move them now!" the same soldier cried. Once again, he was moving.

Keila...

***

A white estate sat at the top of a broad hill as it had before. A moonless sky rolled with clouds passing slowly on celestial strings in some parody of an infant's comforting mobile. The same naked, pale bodies lay strewn along a grey cobbled path leading to the manor, lit only by a few misplaced streetlights with cold white bulbs burning reluctantly in the night.

Carey watched on as the corpses continued to bleed on the road from white, puckered lacerations crossing their throats, the clotted rivers of ichor flowing slowly downhill in the gutters.

The same wizened turkey vulture with glinting black eyes peered over the cooling bodies, searching for the perfect meal. It paced slowly on clawed feet, its black feathers dragging unceremoniously across the uneven ground.

There was nothing beautiful about the way it silently alit upon the bloated chest of a cadaver. It gazed deeply into the corpses still-open eyes, glazed and empty in the arc-sodium glare.

Once again, it slowly looked left and right before raising its callous, sharp beak above its prize. It plunged down into Carey's torn throat, ripping his windpipe from the unresisting flesh.

***

Carey awoke with a start, a weight on his chest flashing panic across his mind that the horrid recurring nightmare had finally manifested into reality. He panted hard, the light around him a strange deep blue. *What the fuck?*

It took a moment before it hit him — there was no carrion-bird perched on his collarbones — it was Keila. He was swaddled shirtless in scratchy wool blankets on a hard bedroll with his sister's best friend in his arms. Her supple figure pressed against his was comfort beyond words despite the rather unpleasant accommodation. The eerie blue light stemmed from sunlight filtering through the tarp that served as a makeshift tent above him. Carey breathed deeply before the beginnings of shame crept into his mind.

He had never done more than shortly embrace Keila in the past, so to find himself with his arms wrapped around her sleeping body was a shock. He began to pull away slowly, as not to wake her, before he felt her narrow fingers wrap around his wrist. She pulled his arm back around her, giggling quietly. *Shit.*

"Good morning, I think," she said quietly, no judgment held in her words.

He could feel the smooth skin of her back on his stomach and he felt a small involuntary twitch in his groin. *Uh oh.*

"Did you sleep well?" she asked in a small voice, not turning to face him.

"Uh — yeah, I guess so. I don't think it was so much sleep as it was a coma, but I feel a hell of a lot less shitty now, if that means anything," he stammered, cursing his brash prose at such a moment.

He considered telling her the truth, but after everything that had happened, he wondered if she'd simply laugh at his nightly terror before pushing him away.

"I'm sorry, I must've gotten a little cozy while I was out and mistaken you for a teddy bear."

He didn't know why he decided the rationalization necessary, but it was better than admitting he felt more at peace with her pressed against him than he had in quite some time. *Afraid of scaring her off, Cardinal? Sounds a little like someone has a crush!* Aaron mocked silently. Carey didn't dignify the stab with a response, mostly because he was afraid it could be true.

She giggled again, vibrating against him.

"No Care, I woke up and pulled you over. We slept through the rest of yesterday and it got cold once the sun went down. These blankets are thin and scratchy, but you're not," she said softly, finding amusement in the statement herself as he laughed.

He pulled her closer, pressing his hand against the slight curve of her hip. He could feel the narrow elastic of her thong underneath his hand, but he didn't move it. *Thank God I'm still wearing jeans. Thank God indeed.*

Keila rolled over to face him, her lips only inches from his own. In the cold blue secrecy of the tarpaulin abode, she was more beautiful than he could put in words. The smooth skin of her cheek was found by his hand, followed by her neck and shoulder.

"Uh, Carey — did you really sleep with your baton in your pocket? There's men around with guns, I doubt you needed to be that on-guard," she said with a laugh, smiling impishly at him.

Her breath smelled sweet and pure, nothing like the catshit morning taste brooding in his own mouth. *To be so lucky.*

"Well one can never be too careful, who knows if you'd turn in the night," he joshed.

He knew full well that the extendo was nowhere in sight let alone in his pocket, but he was thankful nonetheless for her immature assessment of the prodding mass. He leaned in a little, yearning for her lips on his before he saw tears leak from the corners of her eyes. He immediately regretted the offhand joke that had hit closer to home than intended.

"Shit, Care. He's gone. *They're* gone," she cried quietly, pressing her face into his neck, her tears tangling through his stubbled chin.

Carey had a moment of adolescent disappointment with the break of the passionate air, before the gravity of his loss gripped his heart as well. He pressed his hand against the small of her back and pulled her closer into him, the other running through her long blonde hair.

He had never been one adept at comforting those in need, but it was the only thing he thought he could do for her. Anger coursed through him at his impotent ability to reassure her.

"I know, but we don't know about all of them. Roman did something for us we can't hope to repay, but we need to be strong for him. We need to be stronger than we think we can if we're ever going to make it through. I need you here and you've got me to lean on. I promise."

The words flowed effortlessly over his tongue and past his lips. They leapt unbidden as if from a spring, nothing like his usual almost-hick paraphrasing.

He felt her frame wrack harder with sobs as she cried for a mother she'd never know, a brother she'd know no longer and a father she no longer knew anything about. Carey mused for a moment on his own parents before pressing the idea out of his mind. *Good thinking, boy,* Aaron agreed. *Won't do any good to have two emotional wrecks just yet. Keep it together for her.*

"R-Really?" she asked solemnly, raising her bloodshot eyes to him. Her tear-streaked face asked only for reassurance, nothing more. A sentiment expressing his undying commitment to her where everyone else had failed.

"I promise," Carey repeated, knowing he had nothing else to say. He held her in the gloom, breathing the same air. Mourning the same loss.

***

They stirred slowly from their fading slumber, finding their clothes waiting folded neatly beside the bedroll. He respectfully covered his eyes with the blanket when Keila rose to dress, fighting the hormonal urges to spy a glance at her leggy unclad frame.

Carey looked at the bloodstained t-shirt and hoodie awaiting his attention. He felt lost as he stared at the red droplets pasting the expanse of the v-neck tee, each one an unforgettable regret ingrained forever in the white fabric.

It's a fucking shirt. Put it on and get on with it, Aaron chided.

Yeah, yeah. I'm going.

The fabric smelled like sweat and soot, but he had no desire to walk around looking any more incapable of survival through a camp filled with the most battle-hardened individuals his nation would ever breed.

As he zipped his sweatshirt up the middle to cover the droplet-covered tee, he found no reassuring weights in the pockets. *Shit!* For one incredulous moment, he thought he had lost the Taurus Model 85 and extendable baton while he had been so pleasantly carried like a tuckered-out toddler to the tent. He saw them waiting for him beside his raven-black boots. It seemed almost a mockery, the way the revolver left with the spinerette open, the solitary brass bullet laying beside it. As if some soldier with a sense of humor desired to remind him that the gun had truly been a defanged cobra — dangerous to nobody but the handler.

Fitting the round back in the cylinder and snapping it smartly shut, he zippered the revolver back into his chest pocket, jamming the extendo back in his jeans before Keila could spot the lie.

My, that could have been embarrassing, he chuckled silently.

Carey pulled back the blue tarp more commonly used for covering piles of firewood than habitation, unveiling a would-be gorgeous day outside. *Would be, if the population of New Braniff wasn't so goddamned feral.* The sun hung low in the sky, indicating that it was indeed morning and they hadn't wasted two full days unconscious. Carey felt another pang of anger with himself, wondering how useless the infantry securing this position must think he was to require so much rest when they'd likely been running on fumes for days.

Drab olive-green tents sat at all sides, bordered by teetering towers of stacked unmarked crates. Carey couldn't see the cherry-pickers, burgeoning amazement at how large the camp must really be to hide such a high outpost. As if on cue, a low whine stirred to his right, revealing a bassinet loaded with two camouflaged men climbing into the sky. Carey kicked himself inside, but rolled with the punch. *Oh well,* he thought; *I bet this day's going to be filled with revelations. Hopefully, that's the worst of them.*

A broad-shouldered soldier clad in a very out of place desert CADPAT set of fatigues stood at the base of the crane, operating the ascension controls. A long, green plastic-buffered M16-clone was strung across his back, looking sleek and dangerous in the morning light. Paying the two civilians no heed, he diligently checked the meters on the running vehicle before turning off the keys when the swing-bucket reached its maximal height. Shots from above cracked loudly, joining those ringing out from other locations across the borders of the camp.

"Hey, sorry to bother you. We're new here and don't really know what's going on. My names Carey, this is Keila," Carey said, with a small wave of his hand. He felt stupid and out of place, like he was all of ten years old looking at this bear of a roughneck staring him down.

"Oh, yeah, came in with Echo din'ya?" he mused with a hillbilly twang. "You guys got lucky, you did — you know that? If it weren't for those sapper teams SEMTEX-ing the fuck outta that retreat, you'd likely be gettin' carved down with the rest of those bastards we're gunnin' down out there." The man spoke casually, as if he were discussing the results of a rather uninteresting football match rather than the beginning of the end of days.

"SEMTEX? I don't remember any SEMTEX," Carey tried, trying to sound macho and wise despite having no bloody idea what the hell SEMTEX was. "Nothing that looked like a SEMTEX anyway. You're sure doing a helluva job knocking them down past those fences, though." It resounded lame in his head, made even lamer when he tried to throw as much Northern Ontario drawl into his voice as possible. It sounded hokey, whereas the warrior in front of him sounded rugged. *Bastard.*

"A SEMTEX, eh?" he laughed. "No, son — I'm talkin' about plastic explosive. Those combat engineers you followed here rigged the gas-station they retreated through with a metric fuckton of the shit. They figured the fuses were no good when they didn't detonate, but I guess one must'a still been alright. Blew the horde of stumblers tailin' you straight up to the heavens. We saw the glow of the fireball on the horizion. It was like the big ol' Fist of God punched up through the ground over there, scattering the lot of 'em. Goddamned Sappers, they can always rig somethin' to save your ass. That was the night we tried chlorine gas on a mass of 'em out there — I'm sure you didn't miss the results on your way in. The living they were chasing keeled over, pretty quick too. The infected just looked scarier'n hell walkin' right through the cloud like the burns didn't hurt 'em. Took us ten goddamn hours to knock 'em down with the snipers after that one."

The soldier was miles away as he told the story, no longer amused at Carey's lack of military hardware and terminology. Carey had indeed seen the hideously maimed corpses on the way in, but it wasn't that little tidbit of information that twisted his balls just right. It was Roman.

"That wasn't a fuse, buddy," Carey spat, taking a step towards the man easily his size plus half again. Keila clutched at his arm but he paid it no heed. "That was a friend of mine — a *good* friend of mine. Hell, that was her brother. Her *twin*. He--" Carey stopped his correction dead in his tracks.

The infantryman simply shook his head, his attention no longer on Carey, turned instead to a puck of chewing tobacco he pulled from a pocket in his combat webbing. When he noticed Carey had stopped after a moment, he finally raised his eyes back to meet his glare.

"Nope. Sapper's said it was them. Sapper's don't lie, boy," the soldier drawled, packing his bottom lip with a pinch of the dark brown long-cut. He licked his fingertips, savouring every tendril of the shredded pungent leaf. "You sure are good at makin' a hero out of her brother for 'ya, but you don't know what 'yer talkin' about."

Carey could feel the blood rising in his face, but as soon as it struck him how mind-numbingly angry he was, it snapped away. *Good boy. What're you going to do, write the truth down on a piece of paper and jam it up his nose until he believes?* Aaron queried, speaking all too truly. He was right — Carey knew the truth, Keila knew the truth, and if this hick-ass tractor-jockey didn't want to buy into it, that was *just* fine. Petty argument had its place, but Carey would make sure that Roman got his own before he was through.

"Alright, fine. Guess I was a little misinformed," he conceded falsely, giving Keila's hand a squeeze as he mouthed the lie.

The loud reports from above continued. Carey watched a brass case spiral downwards, landing aimlessly on top of a large pile of ejected shells. It clinked as it rolled down the uneven surface, coming to rest near the foot of the monument to its fallen brethren.

"So the gas didn't work then, eh? Doesn't surprise me. I'm a little shocked you sound like you knew there were survivors near the group. How did you figure that one out after? No blood-rings around the necks or what?" Carey inquired, glad to feel like the conversation was entering a subject he felt well-versed in for once. He may have only been face-to-face with the empty eyes of the infected only a handful of times in his entire life, but since those occasions all stacked up in the few prior days, the fact he still breathed without wailing stood as the proof behind his expert status.

"Nope, gas didn't work," the Desert Storm would-be acknowledged, spitting a long trail of near-black saliva into the dust beside the wheel of the high-crane. "Cap thought it might burn out the infected's lungs or something like it, y'know; slow them down or at least put them on the ground. Didn't do much besides show us who'd already turned. We knew the runners in front were still alive, but one'a them had a clear bite wound on their neck. It was pretty easy to spot through the rangefinder and that marked 'em as expendable. It was a good opportunity for a lesson learned, at least. Fuckin' reeked like a pool round here for the next full day though."

Carey stared at the man who only half-grinned back as he adjusted the wet mass packed into his lower lip. *Expendable?* It seemed too much to take. Each concussive blast emanating from the picker matched the slow beat of his heart. *Expendable?*

"You're telling me that the one poor bastard who got nipped's life was moot, so you gassed them all?" Carey reiterated slowly, attempting to decipher the dumbass redneck's jumbled prose.

"Yup, you got it," he mused, spitting another jet and hitting the tire this time. "Cap's got a Scorched Earth policy with that one. One hot subject means a high chance of the rest of 'em bein' hot too. Too much exposure or somethin' like that. Cap's still not completely sold that the bite's the only way to catch this shit. Say's it's moved too quickly for such a slow delivery, but we haven't seen anything to prove otherwise. Yet. Regardless, soon as a group has one identified contamination, the whole lot's deemed hot an' thrown out with the bathwater."

It was a chilling statement to make, but even more disturbing how detached he remained as he frigidly described the cold-blooded murders of refugees seeking shelter in what could be the only place left. Carey felt Keila's fingers tighten around his own, but he made no silent reply.

"No shit, eh? Well, I guess you can't be too careful. You guys must be doing something right if you haven't been overwhelmed yet. Thanks again for taking us in, anyway. I'm not sure if we had a chance to make proper acquaintance earlier."

He lied through his teeth but he didn't give a fuck. He'd rather slap the tobacco out of this yokel's lip than give him a smile, but one of the two options would significantly shorten his lifespan. *Shit.* Keila stood at his side, her mouth a little agape at his blatant lie, but that was okay. If Keila needed to believe he was an asshole for a few minutes in order to keep her breathing a little longer, that would just have to be the way it was.

He put one hand out in front of him, grasping the soldiers hand in his. Carey had always thought that handshakes were a pointless action preformed by men in suits seeking respect for crushing each other's knuckles. It was a sanitized version of the Native American blood-binding ritual, where blood would flow from one man into the other via slits on the palms carved by rusty knives. As the usual corporate powerhouse could likely no more bear the sight of his own blood than he could a hot coal in the mouth, it had been cleansed and appropriated by the white man. *Typical.* Regardless, Carey grasped the nameless infantryman's digits in his own, looking him straight in the eye before turning away.

"Well, Kei — we might as well start poking around this place to see if anyone we know — FUCK!" Carey cried, his calm planning interrupted by a white-hot bolt of pain shooting down from the side of his neck.

"What is it?" Keila screeched, her eyes wide and glossy in the morning light.

Carey clawed at his collar, searching for the source of the brilliant agony spiraling upwards into his head and downwards to the tips of his toes. A glowing poker was driving itself through the skin of his neck into the muscle below.

"Fuck! I don't know! Ow, shit!" Carey yelled, oblivious to the tribal dance he was performing in the middle of the camp, searching for the unseen cause.

"Aw shit, hold still there, bucko!" the hillbilly-warrior behind him called sternly, sounding like an authority on a subject Carey knew nothing about.

Frankly, Carey M. Cardinal didn't give a royal *shit*, he just wanted it to *end*. All at once, the pain faded to a dull ache from its previous supernova quality.

"Gotta be careful around these sharpshooters, buddy. These things are hotter n' hell fresh out of the chamber," he chuckled, holding out a small tapered brass cylinder.

You've got to be kidding me. Carey examined the spent round that had fallen from the sniper above, evidently directly into the collar of his shirt. He ran his fingers over the wound, finding an angry painful divot just above his collarbone. It was a fresh brand, and burns aren't the most pleasant injuries to sustain. Despite feeling like he'd been stabbed by a shard of lava, he gritted his teeth, feeling foolish for his very unmanly outburst. *Oh yeah,* Aaron crooned. *You're the only guy I know that can get shot by an empty bullet. That's one for the history books.*

"Better get that one cleaned out, mister. Those shells are all full of shit, not much of which you should get inside yourself if you can help it."

Carey felt the heat again rising in his face and not just from the burn on his neck. *This asshole's loving it!* He balled his fists at his sides, trying not to claw at the feverish itch that had set in around the brand. Keila looked at him with wide eyes, the concern evident in her stare. She raised a quivering hand towards the wound, pulling his shirt down from the mark.

"I'm *fine!*" Carey snapped, brashly sidestepping her grasp.

It ached, deep into his chest, but the last thing he needed was to be some kind of charity case any more than he already was for squatting on military property.

"O-Okay," Keila said sheepishly, giving him a hurt, doe-eyed glance before looking away.

Nice one, kid. Aaron always had a way of stepping in at the wrong time, but he always knew what to say to get his point across. Carey closed his eyes for a moment, burying the pain deep below the surface. When he opened them again, he was as composed as a priest giving sermon. One cool customer. He turned to Keila, searching for the words to reassure her place in his heart, but found none.

"Let's get going. See if we can't get the lay of the land, yeah?" Carey said quietly, breathing a little heavily despite himself. "Thanks for the help, buddy," Carey quipped as he walked back towards what he thought must be the centre of the crudely thrown together shantytown.

Many things stunned Carey Cardinal in his short twenty-two years as an inhabitant of the Planet Earth, but few things moved him the way the strange land he found himself hiding in did at present. As he walked slowly beside Keila, not knowing where exactly to begin, the precision of the Canadian Forces he had held so high began to falter. Tents held together on all sides, with zip-ties and duct tape. Trucks sheeted with drab olive green tarpaulins serving as rest areas. Crates upon crates with unmarked contents stacked at every juncture, warm to the touch from the April sun. Most of all, he was struck with a sense of comfort.

Comfort. It was a bizarre feeling, but it held firm just the same. The human species survived long enough in the wilderness to become the apex predator on the planet by the virtue of one ingrained trait — adaptability. Throw a group of city-grown men into the wilderness and while some may die, others will happily feast on the corpses if no other food is available. Toss some accounting executives onto a deserted island and they will form a government to better regulate themselves regardless of how futile it may seem.

It was what kept you from losing yourself completely in the face of adversity, and it was unavoidable as breathing.

The snaps of gunfire that had once made Carey jump in surprise tuned into the background as easily as birds softly cooing in summer trees. He didn't hear the whine of engines running from all sides. He didn't smell exhaust fumes mixing with burnt gunpowder and rotting corpses when he should have been gagging from the stench. Soldiers toting implements of death and destruction were as unremarkable as old men sitting on a front porch in a small town, swilling lukewarm beer and talking about days gone by.

It was a sense of regularity in a place that shouldn't be, but there it was. It looked him in the face and taunted him to break its stare, lest it dissolve back into chaos and fear at the blink of an eye.

In that moment walking aimlessly next to Keila, something shifted deep within his chest that took only a fervent heartbeat to place.

He was alright. They were *safe*.

It may be temporary, but his own survival had been secured. His needs were met. While striding through the refuge, his mind moved backwards through time of its own accord to the last place he had sought shelter. The last place he had thought himself hidden from the world.

The basement. The small room of poured concrete, secreted away within the foundation of the home he grew up in. The place reporters on the television told you to retreat to when bad weather struck. Every family's stronghold in the storm.

The place he had abandoned his own.

"Dad," Carey said, barely audible.

Keila turned towards him, coming to a halt to face him, chin raised to meet his eyes. *Neil.* It was if his consciousness had reached a milepost in its own unseen agenda and the page had turned. It sat in the forefront of his head, refusing to be ignored.

Dad.

There were no white papers fluttering in sight as they had been after September Eleventh. There were no corkboards littered with the sheets, each pleading for lost loved ones to be found and returned to dinner tables with empty seats. The only poster tacked alone on a solemn grey wall was in his heart and it bore his parents names.

Neil. Roslyn.

It was the juncture he hadn't anticipated, but the crossroads loomed before him.

He knew there was only one way to go.

His mother and father had put themselves on the line, going to bat for their only son against impossible odds. They were the only reason he had gasped his first breath and the only reason he continued to breathe in the warm April day when so many others had met their last. The debt of any child to their parents is beyond any monetary worth, but Carey owed more than imaginable to his own. And he intended to begin repaying it immediately. Hopefully, by some divine grace, in full.

Carey stared into Keila's green eyes, recounting days spent in the backyard under the willow. Days when he had pushed his sister in the mud and his father had treated it like murder. Days when his mother had brought out lemonade and dry cookies he had never really liked, but she had always claimed were healthier than chocolate chip. Days when they had filled a stupid little turtle pool with water but felt like it was an amusement park instead of an overgrown cheap green plastic dish. Far from feeling like good ol' nostalgia creeping in, each memory another line on a ledger, scrawling out an invoice well past due.

"I know. We have to," Keila mused softly, seeming to read his expression and the thoughts underneath.

He hadn't been close with her in his adult life, and even those whom he had been with were never all that good at picking cues out of his sharp features, but she knew exactly what was on his mind nonetheless. She had ridden the tide with him hand in hand and some bonds ran deeper than the time spent forging them.

Carey nodded, breaking her gaze, his eyes instead alighting across the puffy white clouds drifting in from the east. It was good to have an aim, to have direction amid such disorganization. Only one question remained — *how?* It was if he had been given a monumental mission without the benefit of a briefing. He watched the cotton-ball clouds with disdain, their wistful cajoling across the sky his antithesis. Unlike them, he had a destination. Much like them, however, he was lost on another plane without signposts.

"Maybe we should ask someone?" Keila asked, looking around the sheltered landscape again.

Carey turned the idea over, composting the its validity. If his previous interaction with military brass was any indication, he knew he'd have a better chance of getting information by finding an Irish snake to interrogate, but it was a start. A reluctant one, but a start nonetheless. Carey spied a soldier dragging a crate of ammunition to one of the cherry-pickers, but found no courage in reserve to approach him.

It was an unwanted concept, but lay beneath the glassy surface of his consciousness like a lamprey eel coiled in the lowest submerged cavern in the lake of his mind. To ask would beget an answer.

The answer wasn't always what you wanted to hear.

To ask the man lugging the mold-formed plastic box across the ground would make it real, for better or for worse. The outcomes would no longer be beings made of smoke, given life by mirrors. They would either be living, breathing entities, or festering husks laid out in the dirt. One or the other. Each equally likely, but only one would crush him. Only one would tear his heart apart with every beat. *God, don't let it be that one.*

Carey snapped back to the outside world to find Keila had left his side, already approaching the laboring infantryman. *Shit!* Apparently, he had forgotten he wasn't the only instrument his quest had at its disposal and was happy to plod on without him if the need arose. *Getting egotistical in your old age?* Aaron crooned. *Oh, come now — without you, my head would be a balloon,* he fired back, finding amusement in the exchange despite the insanity of the conversation.

"Hey there, sorry to bother you, but has anyone else come through here lately?" Keila stammered. He applauded her courage.

The man looked up from the crate on which he had been fixated, letting it down gently. Carey could imagine the clinking rattle of a hundred thousand coming deaths jarring inside the confines of that box and shuddered a little at the thought.

"I'm not sure what you mean, sugar... Echo came in a couple days ago, but before that it's just us from Kilo and Quebec units that holed up here originally. Who you looking for?"

He sounded irritated to be disturbed, even more so by someone who so clearly fit the description of a sheeply civilian.

"No," Carey interjected. "What about non-army people? Any of them make it here when you set up camp?"

He felt awkward and silly asking the question, but couldn't help himself — to be eloquent was something he had never excelled at and certainly not at a moment such as this.

"We had a few tag along with us when we dug out of New Braniff, but not many. Most thought we were the bad guys or something. We stopped trying to 'rescue' civ's once one of our guys caught two rounds to the throat by some blue-collar dumbfuck trying to gas up his sedan," he answered gruffly, seeming to blame Carey and Keila for the death of his compatriot because their wardrobes didn't comprise of camouflage and ballistic vests.

He could identify with the guy's resentment — if he had been on the other side, he doubted he would have bothered trying to save anyone other than his closest loved ones, let alone some idiot planning to take his Roadmaster to freedom. Carey doubted the modern warrior toting the ammunition even knew what became of his *own* family and cringed with guilt at proceeding.

"Alright, thanks. Any idea where we can find them, then? The ones that came in with you, I mean?"

"Mess tent. It's feeding time. Right over there," he gestured with his left hand, wiping sweat from his brow with his right. "You wanna give me a hand with this bitch, though? It ain't packed with feathers, after all."

"Sure," Carey agreed, grabbing the handle to the rear of the crate, instantly regretting the choice. He wasn't a small lad by any means, but the storage unit felt like it weighed at least as much as a tractor.

***

The mess tent was a green canvas beast, designed to house an entire platoon of men for mealtimes. It stood mostly empty, only a few tired looking infantry gracing the long picnic tables sitting inside. A haze of smoke filled the tent, cigarettes smoldering in soldiers' hands fuelling the cloud.

It struck him as strange in a society that so frowned upon second-hand smoke health effects, but Carey doubted any of them cared. Long-term complications were no longer really a concern, he supposed, when simply seeing another sunrise wasn't promised — something that may kill them in twenty or thirty years didn't prove all that frightening when ravenous infected pressed in from all sides, day and night. It would be futile to nurture a clean and pure vessel only to have it torn apart two days later by teeth and hands.

Christ, just be glad they ain't fuckin' on the tables, boy. Hell, Carey wouldn't be surprised to see piles of cut cocaine piled on the rough benches in lines awaiting inhalation by exhausted troops, given the circumstances.

Regardless, the bluish clouds obscured vision in the dimly lit tent, forcing him to wait a moment for his eyes to adjust to the gloom after the harsh light outside. A lone soldier stood at the door of the tent, a large-bore carbine in his hands, his finger only slightly off the trigger. His features were steely, cast in bronze, a silent sentinel in the room. Carey wondered whether he was on guard as the first line of defense against an incursion, or if he was there to hold the line if naysayers decided to get physical. Either way, Carey knew he was more Doberman Pincher than man; one to be treated with much careful respect and distance. Carey at once thought of the revolver in his pocket and was struck with amazement that not only had it not been confiscated from him upon arrival, but willingly given back to him without question while he lay asleep. *They take my driver's license, but not a handgun?* A blessing of trust or survivalist flair — he wasn't sure, but it was slightly reassuring nonetheless.

He scanned from left to right, finding only one table of civilians. His heart leapt at the sight of street clothes, only to drop back into place when he realized neither of the pair perched in the corner were whom he sought.

At once, his eyes met the wide, seductive brilliant green of the girl farthest from where he stood. Her hair was as black as a raven's wing, her features pale and noble. Striking. She could have easily been the most beautiful woman Carey had ever seen in the flesh, but his standards were a little skewed in light of the recent events   anybody without a beard was like a supermodel in these parts.

The large, tanned man sitting beside her lit a cigarette, inhaling deeply, but Carey barely noticed him. She didn't blink or look away, peering deep into his soul from across the makeshift room. A small smile lit her lips as she pulled a silver lighter from the chest pocket of her gleaming leather jacket without looking; a practiced, reflexive movement.

"They're not here," Keila concluded, snapping him back to reality. He was ashamed to admit that he had completely forgotten his purpose once the raven-haired siren in the corner had sung to him, a pang of guilt reverberating again deep in his stomach.

Got no time for hunting your folks, but plenty for thinking with your junk? Tsk tsk, Aaron chided and Carey had no response. He was lost in her features, a world away in her gaze. He shook his head as she reached across the table to snag a butt from the muscular man's pack, feeling the cobwebs loosen but not come free entirely.

"Right, well someone should know something if they've been here," he muttered.

Feeling a little dizzy as he regarded Keila once more, seeming homely in comparison to the woman who had spoke volumes without opening her mouth from across the room.

Nice. Real nice. The burly man he had bounced with — his mentor and substitute father figure — hit a nerve with that quip.

Did I really just judge her?

How surreal, that he could pass high school-esque rulings on the girl who had selflessly driven him onwards when he felt he could move no longer. That he could be even considering how she looked, when she herself was beautiful beyond measure in her own right. *Get your shit in check, Care. Now's not the time.* He addressed himself like a tutor with a trucker-mouth, refocusing on the task at hand.

"Sir, do you have a moment?" he asked the automatic-toting guard by the door. He was answered only by a cold glare above week-old stubble. *Guess so.*

"Are there any more non-military personnel in the camp?" he asked, a trace of desperation evident in his words. "If they're not here, where could we find them?"

"Nowhere. If they aren't here, they likely aren't *here* at all. You asked to see the records to see if they even made it to Alexander?" he replied after a moment of examining the evidently undisciplined youth before him. His voice was like iron, booming in a quiet way.

"Records?" Carey asked, astounded that such a fledgling institution as the camp could have developed such a thing already. It was like being told that a small thatched roof hut in a third-world country had high-speed internet running on twigs and roots.

"Captain Meyer has set it up, it's a little crude, but it works. PIEs, mostly." The man spoke as if Carey was an especially dimwitted student struggling to answer what should be an easy question, giving him a sidelong look expected in either scenario.

"P-Pies?" Carey felt like it was some rather unfunny joke at his expense, *a la* 'let's fuck with the civilians'.

"Not pies like your mother baked, idiot. PIEs. Personal Identifying Effects. P. I. E. Sound it out, skipper. Government documents or unique personal shit. Got a whole trunk of them somewhere, the Captain will know. I can find out for you out of my infinite good grace, since you've caught me in an extra-jubilant mood. Don't get your hopes up, though. We took pieces from everyone we escorted to Camp Robinson before setting up shop here, so it's not an exact science." He laughed a little, coughing near the end, a smoker's wheeze rounding out the triad.

Hilarious, Carey thought, wanting more to slap the callous prick in the mouth than chuckle along with him.

"Be careful, though, we never took pieces from anyone who died between here and there. You may not want to open that can of worms, but it's up to you."

The soldier adjusted the carbine in his hands, fidgeting with the strap across his shoulders, no longer looking at the young pair beside him. He returned to his statuesque pose, showing no emotion; displaying no fear. *That went well.*

"I don't know," Carey began, already ashamed of the words as they left his lips.

You don't know if you want to find out the fates of your own Ma 'n Pa? Cold, dude. Real cold. He licked his lips, his mouth filled with cotton balls. *Some things can't be undone, boy. Keep it in mind,* Aaron cautioned from the deep. It felt like the ol' Korean Bear had finally tired of sarcasm and digs, thankfully moving on to constructive advice for once, at that.

"I do," Keila said as solemn as a prayer. "And so do you."

Carey stood there in the hazy tent staring at the canvas, knowing she was right. Wise beyond her years, and right.

Carey nodded once more and turned from the tent towards the bright day outside. As he strode through the canvas archway serving as the entrance in Keila's wake, he swore his back felt warm. Maddeningly hot.

Some stares are more felt than seen.

III

A large plastic storage bin sat before them on the dirt.

It reminded Keila of an enormously oversized Tupperware container, but she doubted there was going to be any leftovers found inside.

Daddy, please.

A guard had opened the padlock with a simple silver key, kindly allowing them to peruse it at their own leisure after reading them the riot act for consequences of theft from the records — none of which seemed pleasant.

Neither Carey nor Keila moved as they stared at the crate, lid still resolutely shut. *Oh Care, what are we going to do?* She looked at him, feeling closer to him than she had to any other male unrelated to her in her entire life. The sway of his blonde hair under his black cap seemed calculated by a higher builder, designed to make him her savior. Deep down, she knew she had equally, if not more than, repaid her debt to him since he had saved her in the small apartment.

Somewhere beneath conscious thought, she knew that without her, he would have been left in the dirt shortly after leaving New Braniff. He would be wandering aimlessly with glazed eyes and outstretched hands, feeling nothing. And that made her glad. Glad in a way getting straight A's in school never had. In a way kissing boys in the stairwells at her high school had only begun to touch. Keila didn't know much about love, but in some blushing way, she felt she might begin to learn sometime soon.

Love? Get a hold of yourself, Kei! She bit the inside of her lip as she considered the statement. *Love.* Was it love for Carey or just the want of the familiar? Was he her knight in shining armour, or just the next best thing because he knew her last name?

Keila found herself lost in thought, as helpless as one tasked to measure the number of drops in the Pacific Ocean. She missed her best friend, safe and sound somewhere in Spain. She felt a chord of jealousy. Why should she lose so much while Tarryn —Carey's sister and her only confidante — comfortably rode out the storm?

You don't know what Carey's lost yet. Nor Tarryn. Save your judgments for later. Keila sighed.

It spoke the truth, but it didn't make it any easier to bear. She missed her father. She missed her brother. She missed her old life.

Does this really matter right now? She supposed not.

Roman.

Carey stood beside her with his arms folded across his chest, one hand absentmindedly scratching the stubbly beard that had set firm in earnest in the last day or so. He didn't meet her eye, but she didn't mind. Keila and Carey danced around each other without stirring, each wondering who would make the first move. Each wondering who would find loss. Who would find favour with the gods.

Keila mused at the injustice of it all. *Why?* Her mother had been robbed from her in a time before she had memories. Her father had held back the sea of hate that had threatened to burst into the Cardinal's basement; allowing the trio of Carey, Roman, and herself a chance at a continued life. Her brother had sacrificed himself in a fiery blast only days ago after becoming infected in a final bid to save her. As she stood in the space between the tents near the centre of the camp, she found herself immobilized with guilt. *Roman. Dad. Mom.* Only one of three titles could be punctuated with a question mark, and that was Bennett. Her father.

Keila hadn't even said goodbye as she had fled through the basement window, pulled out by Carey's strong, waiting hands. She hadn't cast him a backward glance letting him know she'd be waiting and praying for his success. She hadn't thrown any tender words into the fray to give him courage in the face of a swarm of countless searching hands, each seeking to drag him downwards into a place he could never rest; never escape. *Am I the product of three lost souls?*

Keila stared at the plastic box, wondering whether she could accept the fact that her father had truly committed the ultimate sacrifice for her, if that was in fact the case. A single tear rolled down her cheek as she looked back to Carey's strong shoulders, spying the angry crimson brand half above his collar. A whitish pus was already forming within the ridges the spent cartridge had scalded into his skin. She reached again up to his arm, seeking to give him comfort — both in the physical sense for his sustained hurt, and for the obstacle that sat so complacently in the dust at their feet. Carey's head whipped towards Keila as her fingertips made contact with his black sweater, a feral snarl twisting his lips.

"Don't!" he growled, his eyes wild and animalistic, showing nothing of the caring, brave soul she had traversed the bowels of Hell with her to this hour. He raised a fist sharply, no trace of recognition in his gaze.

She recoiled in fright, a small yelp escaping her mouth as she pulled away. *Who are you,* she asked silently, pleading him to see her for the friend, no — *lover* - she desired to be. For a moment, they stared at each other, Keila cowering in fear as Carey's knuckles quivered uncertainly, poised to strike at any moment. A soft breeze blew through the camp, blowing her hair around her ears, carrying the sound of muted rifle cracks and distant groans on the wind.

His features softened from spite through to confusion until he dropped his glare, staring at his feet while rubbing at his neck with the hand that had almost struck her down.

She waited a second before relaxing, letting her posture drop its defensive nature. She wondered what she even knew of him beyond the previous days, finding nothing in her past to ease the pain of the cold gesture. *Why, Carey? Why?*

"Let's just do this," Carey muttered, shaking his head from side to side like a bull disturbed by a horsefly.

With that, he leaned back a little, kicking open the lid sharply with his heavy boot. At once, dazzling points of reflected light shot daggers into her eyes from the confines of the container. She raised a hand to shield her face before realizing the source — an enormous pile of dog tags. Ominously, there were only one half of the pair she had spied across the chests of men in army action movies, none of which were attached to long chains — only small loops of beaded links held fast onto the miniscule stamped-aluminum plates.

As her eyes adjusted to the sharp gleams, the contents of the crate presented themselves in shocking clarity.

"Oh my *god,*" she gasped, the piles of items overwhelming her with both their multitude and diversity. The sun beat hot on her neck, beads of sweat rising on her forehead as her eyes picked over the box.

A significant stack of driver's licenses and Ontario health cards bound with a thick elastic band sat beside an aluminum pie plate stacked high with glinting jewelry, shining arrogantly outwards. A few cell phones set beside their batteries along with a leather-banded watch graced with Mickey Mouse's deliriously grinning face.

What really struck Keila to the core was the brown plush mass sitting in the centre. Its glossy, sightless eyes peered out of the darkness, sewed into the face of the well-worn teddy bear laying on his back. It seemed an uncomfortable pose for even a stuffed toy, but in its textile face, Keila saw another. The visage of a young child, torn from their only fleeting memory of a better time for purposes of 'identification' by soldiers speaking roughly in large words the toddler couldn't understand. She saw tears streaming down the teetering girl's face, her blonde pigtails messy and unkempt with a mother, now infected, no longer around to maintain them. Her breath choked in her throat, itching and burning as she gasped. The girl had looked exactly as she had in an old picture from kindergarten her father had taped to the fridge so long ago, her tiny arm draped around her twin brother's shoulders with a beaming smile on her face.

Just when the vision threatened to overwhelm her completely, Carey cried out quietly, his hand shooting into the pile of jewelry to emerge with a small gold band. It was narrow, obviously designed for a finger of the fairer sex, encrusted with small diamonds in a shallow channel cut into the glimmering surface.

"I-It's my mothers, I'm sure of it," Carey mused in a small voice.

She could hear the struggle to believe the words in his tone, though he had left no doubt in his statement. He turned the band over in his hands before holding it out to her in his palm, pointing to the inner space, reserved for contact with the finger of the wearer.

"Look right there, see? *RGC—NAC.* Rosslyn Geissler-Cardinal, Neil Allan Cardinal. My *mom.* My *dad.*" He regarded the small gold ring with wide eyes, looking more like the toddler from her vision than the competent man she thought she knew. "It's her eternity band. Ten diamonds for ten years of marriage. She never took it off."

Keila knelt at his side, her knees uncomfortable on the hard earth. A noxious brew of emotion bubbled beneath her breasts. On one side, she was gripped with a delight for Carey, knowing that he had so quickly found a link to his past — and future — with minimal effort. He had a lead on which to pull, a thread to follow wherever it led. That same gushing care, on the other hand, had a deep rot seated within it, one she didn't want to acknowledge even in the secrecy of her mind - jealousy.

That he should be so blessed yet again while she was left to fester in loss and grief. *He* hadn't lost his mother. *His* most cherished kin hadn't thrown their life away in a fireball for their benefit. *He* had a chance of finding his parents while barely trying, while *she* found nothing at first glance to point towards her own. She shook her head hard as Carey had after his moment of seeming rage, banishing the thoughts to a place where childhood nightmares and fears languished in their depravity. She needed to focus now and she didn't need any more Karmic burden at a moment such as this.

"That's great! Hopefully Neil left something behind too," she said softly.

She left out mention of her own father to avoid feeling more selfish than she already did. She waited a second for him to inject a comment to give her hope, but it never came. A twinge of anger mixed with sadness rang in her heart, but she stuffed the unwanted thought down beneath the surface too.

They sat for an hour, picking over the contents of the crate piece by piece. When the stack of identification cards passed without the face of Bennett Tindall gazing back at her, she steeled her will to place him with one of the other objects in the box.

With every trinket, macguffin, and once cherished item, she found herself searching harder for a memory linking it to the man who'd reared her alone in the world; for some binding thought to tie each passing piece of confiscated *shit* to the bespectacled father who hung in limbo in her mind. It was like waltzing through a well-trodden bone yard where every grave had been exhumed to lay out in the moonlight, turning forth the worst in her as she struggled to find the right headstone. The coffins came as gold lighters, tiepins and adorned pocketknives. The crypts revealed themselves as wallets and engraved flasks.

Finally, they began to tackle the most personal of the effects—the glittering mass of precious metal and stones. *Something. Anything.* She passed a gold watch across her fingertips and found herself unable to remember if her father had ever even so much as worn a timepiece, let alone this particular one. She plodded through chains and bracelets, none of which screamed names to her that meant anything. Keila screwed her eyes shut as she placed a thin gold chain to the side of the box. It was the one she had worn since her father had bought it for her elementary school graduation. It made her feel like she too was cooling on a slab, long expired along with many of the owners of the items in the crate. It was deadwood.

Carey slowly raised a plain, thick nuptial band to his face, turning it over in his palms as he had the eternity band, which she noticed had now found a home on his smallest right finger.

"I... I think this could be my dad's," he said quietly, no conviction in his words. "It's plain. Spartan. Just like he was," he continued, speaking from a million miles away despite his perch on the dirt beside her. His blue eyes scanned the azure sky as he lost himself in thought. "He didn't usually wear it because he was worried about it getting snagged at the machine shop, but maybe... maybe he put it on before leaving the house?"

It sounded to Keila like he was more interested in selling himself on the theory than he was her, but she remained quiet nonetheless.

Carey remained lost in memories as she continued to trek through the heap of meaningless links, reaching the end without finding a single reassuring object. *No!* she thought, refusing to believe she had been thorough enough. *It's in here, I know it!* What 'it' was, she had no idea, but the idea that her father had failed to make the camp, when at least his compatriots had passed through, was too much to bear.

Soft footsteps met Keila's ears from behind before the voice played into the scene. It startled her as she swiveled in place to face the source of the words.

"Carey. I've been looking for you."

IV

Carey was deep in the realm of forgotten thoughts, desperately seeking one where Neil's ring finger showed clear and true through the haze of well-passed time. The presence behind him snatched him from the dreamworld like a fish on a hook into the alien landscape above when they announced themselves.

"Looking for me?" he answered as he rose to his feet.

He couldn't place the voice as he turned to face its owner, knowing it to be strangely familiar but out of place, like hearing an old friend shout while visiting a distant city. It was like silk, too pure to be one he was associated with well.

Carey turned about-face, expecting recognition to flood him with nostalgia, instead finding only recent memory able to place the pair standing between the tents before him. Her raven's wing hair and noble features gave her identity away, but it didn't explain why she was looking for him. It was the siren from the mess tent with her *compadré* who would look more at home on American Gladiators than coming to greet him.

"Yeah, you," she replied in the same smoky tone, sultry despite the asexual nature of the response.

Why the hell are you looking for me? Need directions to the latrine? Carey had no idea who the gorgeous woman or her *amigo* was, let alone why they were so hellbent on making his acquaintance.

"I'm sorry, why?" Carey half-mumbled.

The striking young woman staring at him was more intimidating than a gnashing pit bull on a rusted chain. She muddled his thoughts and clouded his mind. Her tight black leather pants may as well have been painted on, accentuating the curve of her hips and thighs. It was absurd, how frighteningly sexy she stood on the ragged grass in thick-heeled boots. She looked like a superhero drawn by an adept hormone-drunk teenage boy with a thing for bikers in comparison to the rest of the uninteresting scenery.

"What's that supposed to mean? Would you prefer I didn't?" she asked, a trace of venom dripping from her voice.

The large man with the bleach-blonde spiky hair behind her barked a laugh. It did nothing to help Carey's already judgmentally low opinion of the juice-monkey.

"I thought you'd be as glad as I was to see a familiar face in this hole, but suit yourself," she ended curtly, turning her back on him.

Carey couldn't help but notice the way the warm sunlight shone off the curve of her ass as it began to bounce away from him. *Hate to see ya go, love to watch ya leave. You really gonna let her walk away?* Aaron laughed, reminding him there was more to life than nice rears and tight pants. *Shit.*

"Wait, I didn't mean it like that!" Carey cried, dumbfounded.

She stopped dead in her tracks, turning back to him with an impish grin on her face. As he examined her features, many things crossed his mind, but one stood out from the rest. *Eyeshadow?* The dark makeup on her lids mocked the severity of the situation, but he bit his tongue. He'd almost lost this unknown sage once and he wasn't about to do it again.

"You really have no idea who I am, do you?"

Her words hung in the warm April air, staring Carey in the face. *Oh my god.* Her identity swam from the ether, tied to one of the driver's licenses he had passed over. The name had seemed familiar, clanking a gong in his subconscious but the picture sparked no reaction. She looked nothing like the sixteen-year old girl on the license and had certainly had a dye-job since they'd last met, but it was her. *No shit, fancy that.*

"I knew you were just too stuck up to talk to me before, ya prick!" she said, poking him good-naturedly.

Memories of his glorious night in St. Albins flooded back. Sweat. Lipgloss. Heat. Perfume. Blonde hair. Touching the highest peaks while writhing between the sheets. Warm summer air filtering through the window screen from the night outside.

Fuck me.

"You got a lotta gall, Cardinal. Whatever. I don't blame you not wanting to introduce me to your girlfriend. She's pretty; looks nice. Besides, you never called like you said you would."

She gestured to Keila as she spoke, looking her up and down with an evaluating glance. Carey could feel the heat creeping into his face. She had a lightning wit even now, able to cut you to the core if you fell from her grace. Able to use that same razor tongue in other ways if she fancied you.

"Oh, no. She's not my girlfriend, she's my neighbor. Er, was my neighbor. We came here together from New Braniff."

He could feel the perspiration forming beneath his armpits and kicked himself for not including a stick of deodorant in his survival kit. He wondered how bad he smelt and how awful his unwashed, unshaven face must look to the unblemished vixen standing with her hand on her hip beside him.

Oh yeah, shoulda got that Noxema and left your baton at home, boy. Good thinking. If I wasn't dead already, travelling with you around women would be my first choice of ways to die.

"Um, sorry to interject if this isn't my place, being just a *neighbor* and all," Keila said, the poison dripping from her voice. "My name's Keila. Carey and I came from his parents' house a couple of days ago. We were lucky enough to find some army guys leaving the city who brought us here." Carey wanted to believe she was naïve enough to believe the words she spoke, but her initial stab in his direction informed him otherwise. *Whoops.*

"Morgan," Carey's trophy-lay replied, offering a long-nailed hand.

She didn't look much different from the night he'd acquired the Glenfiddich. If anything, the change of hair colour served to accentuate her emerald green eyes, making them pop from afar like two lagoons in a sea of her perfect skin.

"This is Kerrigan," she continued, casting an aloof wave at the gargantuan man standing behind her like an apprehensive bodyguard. Carey offered his hand. Kerrigan met it with a slapping low-five instead.

"Pleasure," he said gruffly.

He was clearly older than the three, leaning more towards Aaron's previous age than his own. He looked like one who'd lived the hard life, a fact which Carey assumed the many tattoos covering his exposed arms attested to. He didn't spot any barbed wire or spider web prison-style ink, but figured beneath the cutoff shift he'd be certain to find some if he dared look.

Carey looked to Keila, but she refused to meet his eye, instead examining the pair she'd just met. Her brow wasn't furrowed in a contemplative expression, but Carey doubted her wheels were idle in that blonde skull of hers.

"Kerrigan and I were just outside St. Albins, partying near the border the night this shit went down," Morgan continued. Her voice sounded to his ears the way the single-malt had tasted. The same scotch he had blown his laughable life-savings on shortly after having her. "He was working security at the club I was dancing at. Good thing too. If he hadn't twisted my arm into coming out this way to see so his family, we'd likely still be there. Or buried somewhere close to it."

She spoke of her near-missed death with such offhand casualness that Carey wondered if she even realized how close she had come. It was confidence, pure and unbridled, edging on the realm of cockiness — unbearably so. He noticed Kerrigan standing behind her instead of at her side like a good boyfriend should. He wondered whether the fellow bouncer, well older than he, was just another one of her human wallets, doubting he was anything to the contrary with each passing second.

A boyfriend would cling to her, regardless of the circumstance, proud to show off his golden goddess to anyone who would look. She had reveled in the attention on Thursday nights in The Stallion, so that was the obvious answer. A leopard didn't change her spots, and this leather princess didn't look much like a panther.

"Look, Care — I know we're all pretty messed up from this, but I'd like to catch up a bit with you if you have the time. It's been a while and it feels good to meet a... 'kindred spirit' in this place."

Her eyes closed slightly as she spoke, her seductive gaze nothing but deadly. He began to agree, to say that right now would be a *super great* time to chat, converse and undress, before an unfamiliar weight on his right pinky stopped him dead.

He glanced down to his hands, aghast that he had forgotten once again his purpose in the newly-created Purgatory. *Mom.* The ring snagged on his littlest finger brought him back. *Rosslyn.* The decision was clear, pushing through the murky lewd thoughts flooding his mind, pushing them back down into his pituitary gland from whence they came.

"I'd love to, but listen — I can't. I might have just found a lead as to where my parents are and as crazy as it sounds, I can't do anything but think about them until I chase this down." It sounded as hopeless as he felt.

Carey bent down, slamming the lid on the records crate, clasping the lock once more on the box that had given him an ounce of hope to follow. Keila opened her mouth to speak, but shut it as soon as the bolt clicked home. When he peered back to Morgan, she was already walking away. He didn't call out to her, he didn't even whisper. He simply watched her stride behind the tents before looking back to Keila. Sweet, sweet Keila.

He took her clammy palm and walked from the storage unit, hoping he'd made the right choice in opening Pandora's Box.

***

Carey sat in a small, dimly lit tent with an empty mind. He should have welcomed such inner tranquility, but it was more disturbing than ever.

Instead of the vast expanse of his inner world resembling a Zen garden, complete with raked white sand and polished stones basking in the sun, it was a darker place. It was the blackest night he'd ever witnessed, more reminiscent of a dead vulture's eye than a veritable paradise. There were no pearly gates. No golden doorways. Just one big empty plane in which he sat, begging for reasons to rationalize his anguish and finding none.

Carey sat on the canvas cot in the medical tent, staring at his feet, hearing nothing. His initial queries about the woman who'd raised him from the get-go had been promising. *Seen her around,* they'd said. *Oh yeah, passed this way recently,* they'd said. *Should be around here somewhere,* they'd said.

No one had said a word about ashes.

Sometimes there really were things that couldn't be taken back, no matter how much he longed to remain ignorant to the wisdom he'd once begged to hear. Sometimes the truth was something better left alone, to be covered over with the silt of ignorance and time. *Fuck.* He hadn't been ready to hear the words from the man with the medical degree; Carey too high on his own feigned promise to truly consider the gravity of the information he could receive.

Rosslyn Geissler-Cardinal: female, Caucasian, age fifty-two, had indeed graced the confines of Base Alexander. She had passed through the rolling steel gates to the safety within, her eternity band pried from her clenched fingers by the Captain of the base himself in the early hours procluding the establishment of the defensive position. She had been alive. Her heart had beat. Electrical impulses had crackled from neuron to neuron in the soft, grey tissue of her brain. She had been alive.

She had been alive.

A few directions at the hands of helpful military men around the camp had led Carey and Keila to the small tent bearing large red crosses on the outer face, where he had expected to find his mother calmly recuperating from her journey. In the short minutes that had passed from being pointed to the location and reaching it, Carey had allowed himself to write the oral thank-you letter he would dictate to the matriarch of his family. The heartfelt words meant more than any spoken in his entire twenty-two years. They were truthful. They were gracious.

They had remained unspoken.

Carey sat at the foot of the cot, not meeting the eyes of the combat medic across from him. Keila was perched somewhere behind him, but she felt a hundred miles away with the onset of reality.

She was already weak, the medical officer had said. *She was a fighter, your mother. She'd been wounded by a car taking a run at one of our initial barricades — a case of wrong place at the wrong time, that's all son. When she was carried in, she already had some serious internal bleeding from the accident. My staff and I did all we could to save her, that I can promise you. We worked on her even after I got the order to send my staff to man the walls against a coming incursion.*

His eyes had glossed over as he continued, staring at the canvas walls.

I put this entire base's livelihood on the line because I thought we could do it. I did it because she was a mother. She had fought so long and hard; she was so brave. I stayed with her after we'd done all we could, I didn't really care if I got reprimanded or not — I've lost so many boys to the infection here, I didn't want to see a woman of that spirit lose a battle to a conventional injury like that. She had a chance, Carey. We gave her a chance, and I hope you can with time learn to forgive me for my failure.

Carey had wracked his brain, looking for holes in the story through which is mother's continued life could fall, finding none.

No escape hatches. No secret passages. It was plain as a brick wall and equally as futile to fight. *I was almost here,* he thought bitterly. *I was so close.*

I made sure she was comfortable. I gave her double-rations of Demerol to ease her pain. I gave her my own blanket that night to keep her warm. I wish I wasn't the one to tell you this. May God have mercy on my soul, because you don't know what you ask.

Carey had bit his cheek, the soft skin beneath splitting between his teeth as he steeled himself for the reception of the inevitable.

When I woke at first light, she was cold. I cried at that moment, that much I can tell you. No one should pass from such common injuries when we have such worse opponents out there to fight. No one should feel that kind of pain in an age when we have the technology available to stop it.

I made sure she was the first in line for cremation, Carey. I washed her and closed her eyes. She looked beautiful. She looked calm.

Carey had expected to fall from his seat, arms outstretched in a pose reminiscent of Christ, screaming through his tears to a God who refused to listen. He had expected to feel a sick ache so deep in his stomach that he would vomit and fall into a coma, stirring no longer. He couldn't have been more wrong.

Instead, he sat not in the tent, but back in the centre of that lightless abyss, unmoving. His mother had passed. His mother had moved onto a higher plane than this.

His mother was *dead*.

No one had said a *word* about ashes.

"Cremated," Carey muttered, knowing the definition of the word well. *Burnt until nothing remains but powdery white cinders.*

His uncle had chosen the same way to rest, his mother picking an ornate little urn in which to store the remains nicely on the mantle. His uncle, a man of few words but much promise and accomplishment in his life, reduced to a mere decoration, the only touchstone in of human memory to the fact he had ever existed.

"Yes, cremated." The bespectacled combat medic spoke softly and evenly, reassuring him that his mother hadn't been laid out in the sun to rot. "Shortly after the fuel-truck arrived, we set up a small crematorium. Captain Meyer isn't allowing us to use it any longer, as he wants to conserve the fuel for the generators for the spotlights. Callous *bastard*," he spat, making no effort to shroud his frustration.

Carey acknowledged him with a nod, but said nothing. He felt Keila shift closer behind him, but she kept her distance. She must have learned from her last attempt at contact. He wished he could take it back, but really had too much filling his head to pay much heed. *Mom.*

"Listen," the medic continued, "I've debated this from the moment you came in here and I'm at a loss. You've already had your hopes raised when you should have been cautioned, and I don't want you to be traumatized by bad news any more than you already have. You've been led on false hope to receive what I can only imagine to be the last thing you wanted to hear. I fear it will lead you down the same road, but I don't feel as if I have an option outside of a valium cocktail."

Carey's heart stopped dead in his chest, his eyes finally rising to meet the speaker's.

"Your mother wasn't alone."

Keila let out a small gasp behind him, the first sound she had made since entering the destitute medical ward. The medical corpsman shook his head in a gesture of futility, wrenching his hands together in his lap.

"An older gentleman carried her in. Tall, like you. Grey hair. Real large fellow."

Dad! Carey knew it in a way he couldn't describe, the same way a mother can pick out her offspring's cry in a sea of squalling infants. The blackness around him lightened from all sides, the blue hour of his mind where daybreak emerged from the darkness.

"She was in a bad state when he brought her here. She barely recognized him, kicking and thrashing at him, insisting he was a stranger bent on taking her away. I had to do some fast-talking to convince the sentries she wasn't infected. The sickness seems to affect the chemical balance of the mind in much the same way in the initial stages. I haven't been able to work it down to an hour-by-hour formulation just yet, but-"

"My father," Carey interjected. "You were talking about my father." Even though the words were only rooted in one man's first-hand account, they made his chest swell, his heart reinvigorated. *Dad!*

"Oh yes, your father as you say," the doctor continued with an embarrassed expression gracing his features. "She was in a bad place by then, son. Her thrashing was making it worse, stirring internal injuries in ways that could have been immediately deadly. I asked him to wait outside the tent while I sedated her to examine for bites."

He hesitated as Carey glared at him to continue, daggers from his eyes all but material in the gloom of the tent. The silence pressed on for a full minute. Carey bounced his knee impatiently, clenching his fists as he waited for the doctor to finish his story.

"Well... he wasn't there when we went to retrieve him, son. There was a large-scale mob of infected pressing in at us from the west, you have to understand. We were still fighting for survival minute by minute - we didn't have a chance to identify who was leaving. So many ran to Camp Robinson that night. So many never made it."

Carey sat dumbstruck, unable to process what he was hearing. *My father* left? *Just like that?* It was beyond comprehension that the man who had loved his mother for so many years would just cut bait and run at the twilight of her life. That he would fight to save his own skin after nearly giving his own life for his family. That was Neil, but that behaviour *wasn't*.

There had to be a reason. There had to be. Carey knew the man he had called 'Dad' better than that.

Deal with the fine details later, Care. Your dad may still be alive. You still owe him. Double now, for missing this. Careful, Aaron advised. Just one seven-letter word, spoken as purely as Carey had ever heard.

"Look guys," the medic continued, "You two better get over to mess. You need to eat something to keep your strength up."

"Dinner?" Keila asked in a small voice. He had almost forgotten she was there, her silence like a mouse in the walls. "But it's only three o'clock at the latest, isn't it?"

The question sounded trivial and unnecessary, the beginnings of anger gripping Carey's fists. *Who fucking cares, Keila? Do you really give a shit?*

"Yes, you're quite correct, my dear. Fuel is running low, so we work on the sun's schedule now. Its schedule says eat, so you'd better pay it heed. This is nearing the end of the day for much of the force that has been up since before sunrise, hence the time for our meal previously enjoyed in the evening."

"I'll give you some time alone here; privacy hard to come by around these parts, but I certainly hope to see you in the mess tent soon, alright?" The medic rose and walked from the ward without looking back, leaving only Carey and Keila in the dimly lit canvas room.

Carey heard her rise from behind him to take the medic's previous seat across from where he sat.

"Guess it's just you and me against the rest, eh?" Carey tried on for size, attempting to sound brazen, but coming off depressed.

Leave the dramatics to those who care, boy. Speak your mind, Aaron advised, seeming to find his sarcastic niche once more.

"I don't know what this means about Bennett, but I think we have something to go on. If we can find my old man, he'll know where yours is and that's all there is to it." Carey spoke quietly, seeking to once more reaffirm the bond between himself and the girl he'd unconsciously been pushing away.

"I'm so sorry about your mother," she blurted, tears leaking from the corners of her eyes. She leaned forwards towards him, her hands on his knees. "I wish we could have been here, I mean if I had run faster maybe we-"

"Stop," he said gently, yet sternly. "What's done is done, let's just let it lie." He hated the way the statement tied into the final resting place of his mother, but it was the truth. "We'll do it together, even if we only walk out of this with each other. No matter what, we'll always have that." It sounded melodramatic even to his own ears, but it struck a chord deep within his heart. Keila slid back beside him on the cot, tucking herself under his arm.

Oh, how the mighty had fallen.

V

Although he sat barely speaking, the world around him opened up in volumes. The mess tent was crowded with the sentry rotation coming in from the frontline as the reserve string headed out to man the posts. Carey had never imagined eating while thousands of mindless murderers sought to find his present location to tear him limb from limb with their teeth, but some things defy even the most basic logic.

The small MRE's — Meal Ready to Eat in the military world's obsession with acronyms — came from the back of a large truck armed with an imposing padlock. He supposed the last thing they needed was a deranged soldier who'd lost the will to live eating himself to death if the moment struck, but it still seemed a little like overkill given the circumstances. Hell, two soldiers manning the distribution of the small packets keeping their sidearms drawn was a bit much as well. He had taken his allotted drab brown packet and sauntered into the mess hall and found a table in the rear corner.

The petit zein-wrapped bag was immeasurably small to feed a relatively large male as he, though the wrapper stated the contents contained over eighteen-hundred calories per serving. *Christ, what's this filled with — pig lard?* The contents were dismal. A piece of gum. A plastic spoon. Cocoa powder. A foil package claiming to contain 'chicken teriyaki,' which he seriously doubted would be palatable given its feel under his fingers. He sorted through the items from the package, finding particular amusement at an energy bar emblazoned with *HOORAH!—OOH-RAH!* on the packaging. *Morale boost? Desperate, desperate times.* He chewed listlessly at the bar, finding no trace of promised apples or cinnamon, but plenty of cardboard subtlety.

The tent slowly filled with the haze of cigarette smoke as infantrymen and women lit up after finishing their prescribed rations. Carey found himself disinterested with the food. He hadn't eaten anything in easily over forty-eight hours, a point he had never reached without some form of nourishment, but he wasn't all that hungry. The bottle of water that came with his meal, however, was a welcome sight. He quickly lapped up the contents of the plastic container, relishing every drop that tickled his throat. It breathed new life into his spirit. *Ahhhh.* He could have been a commercial for the benefits of H2o, the way he slurped the water with such obvious delight.

Upon finding the bottle dry, he approached the soldiers manning the truck for another only to be turned away. Apparently, he had just unwittingly drunk his share of the stock allotted to him for the night and no more would be dispensed until first light of the next day. *Fuck!* Carey thought, reclaiming his seat on the well-worn picnic benches. He wondered which unlucky park had been salvaged for parts to bring the wooden planks to this location.

Keila pushed her bottle towards him gingerly, offering a sip of her own water to quell his dry tongue. *Oh Kei.* He accepted it, only rinsing a little through his mouth, not wanting to take away too much from her paltry stock. She, unlike him, had torn voraciously through her rations, devouring every last morsel in the package. *At least one of us has an appetite,* he thought, pushing the untouched remains of his own towards her, which she happily accepted. He carefully wrapped the rest of the HOORAH! bar, placing it in his pocket to stave off a hunger he was sure would strike him sooner or later.

Part of him wondered how she did it — how she managed to eat when her only remaining parent could be one of the moans in the distance. Could be ended by one of the shots incessantly ringing out from above. It was an unending symphony of noise, punctuated by crescendoing explosions and muffled concussive blasts reaching their ears from far away violence in action.

Sitting across the table from Keila and Carey, were Morgan and Kerrigan. They'd sauntered over shortly after their arrival, picking the only seats in the place not occupied by gruff-looking roughnecks. Carey had at first been secretly overjoyed to share the space with Morgan, but the emotion had quickly faded with the passing minutes.

A mood crept into the scene that he was surprised to witness. It was overwhelmingly *awkward.* He looked around the table as the four made small-talk and shared minor details of their respective journeys, all operating on an unspoken agreement to keep the mood light at dinner service. He tried to place it, first examining Kerrigan. Kerri-Kerri-Bo-Berry. He spoke little, most of his comments highlighting particularly gruesome events he'd witnessed on their trek to the camp. His description indicated he found them humorous. It was appalling, but Carey kept his poker-face firmly rooted, not wanting to turn things sour so quickly. After dismissing his attention from the huge jock's stupid repartee, he determined Kerrigan wasn't the source of the feeling. He may have been imposing and overwhelmingly crude, but he wasn't making things feel squirmy. He had no open relationship with Morgan, who with the passing moments Carey also dismissed as the one making things awkward.

She had been his perfect night, after all. She had been what he'd always aspired to have and in some dark, perverted way still did. She made no lewd comments, spawning breath-held silence. She made no defamatory remarks that insulted the mood. She simply chewed her shitty issued food and tossed in her mind when appropriate.

And finally, folks — he hits it. The GIRL! Everyone, a round of applause! Aaron catcalled. It *was* Keila. The fact that she sat next to him across from the leather angel — or devil, he wasn't sure — was making him undeniably uneasy.

He felt in a way he was in the process of atoning for the sins of that world in this implicit middle-ground, but he regretted nothing of the evening they had shared between the sheets of her tiny red bedroom. It was simply like Keila was being exposed to a part of himself that he would have liked to have sheltered her from, a part that in this new life with her he would have liked to have left well enough alone.

Carey drummed his fingers on the table, knowing something else lay beneath the surface. So what if she knew his past, there were so few links to it remaining that it was completely irrelevant to this new path he trod. Why would she care? Why would he care about what she thought? She was his childhood neighbor, the girl who used to give dolls avant-garde haircuts in the basement with his sister. She certainly wouldn't leave him to die in the wilderness upon discovery of his trifles with the opposite sex in the past, especially after all they'd been through together. Especially not because of the bond they shared. *Bingo,* Aaron mused.

The bond they shared. The emotions he held for her. The —
dare he think it — love they had begun to cultivate. It hadn't
passed too far into romantic territory yet, but he would be a fool to
think that it wasn't coming up ahead on the road, just past a few
more hurdles. *Shit, love?* Carey hadn't even thought of the word in
relation to a woman outside his family in so long that it was as
foreign as a beat played by a three-armed drummer in sixths. *Love?*
Four letters he had long felt he could do without after leaving his
previous *amour* without a backward glance. After he had grown
tired of being half of a whole instead of a full. After he had left her
without explanation.

Despite the odds, the two vowels and two consonants mocked
him despite his best efforts to tell them to piss right off and leave
him alone. *Why fight it, boy?* Aaron's question hung in the fetid
space of his head, daring to be answered. Finding none, he turned
his thoughts more towards Keila and away from the feelings
bubbling inside him for her.

*What if she feels the same way, would that really be so bad? Would
that really top off as the worst thing that's happened to you this week?*
No, that could possibly be one of the *best*.

The thought dissolved as he found himself lost in Morgan's
green eyes she discussed some unimportant topic with Keila
jovially, paying him no heed. *Ah, I see* Aaron remarked. *Thinking
like a high school boy again, are we? Don't want to ruin the chances of
claiming your prior prize? You never cease to amaze me, kid. At least
grow a set and admit it.*

Carey shook his head. *Fuck you, asshole.*

The more he tried to avoid and downplay the revelation, the
more it insisted to be heard. *Linked.* The word blinked like a neon
sign with a faulty ground line in his mind. *Inextricably linked.*
Some bonds ran deeper than want. Some ran deeper than lust.
Some held firm even when you were scared to acknowledge their
presence in the first place. It may not have been blooming love
centered deep within his soul, but he felt some seeds had been
planted without his knowledge. They could be carefully cultivated
and tended to, sprouting tendrils of affection and desire. Or they
could be left alone to die; husks in the dirt. Either way, they could
never be removed any more than Carey could bring himself to tear
out his own throat if the need arose.

As he slowly came back to the world outside, the one walled on all sides by desperation and faltering hope, he caught Morgan staring at him with heavily lidded eyes from across the table. They were the deepest green he'd ever beheld as she examined him closely with a small grin before breaking away. *What was that?* Well, maybe a little attention from the noir beauty wasn't all that bad. Not all bridges had to be burnt in his wake, after all.

As the light outside began to dim, the tent slowly emptied. Soldiers exchanged cigarettes, flasks and handshakes as they retired from the mess. Carey wondered if they slept or whether they would simply lie with their eyes closed through the dark hours, musing on the fates of their friends and loved ones. He wondered if any would see the faces of the infected they'd condemned to death flash before their closed lids, each one screaming *father, mother, brother.* He shivered a little, hoping he wouldn't suffer the same symptoms if that was the case. Barbra, the old woman he'd smashed the life out of in the spirit of survival, dwelled not in his thoughts. He certainly hoped it would stay that way.

The four collected the waste from their respective meals, dumping it into a large, burnt oil drum for disposal. They stood at the doorway of the tent in silence. The falling night came unapologetically to swaddle them in fear until the sun rose again. He hoped.

"Well," Keila gently broke the silence, "I'm going back to the records crate for a second look. I know I missed something in there."

Carey thought about questioning when Bennett would have passed through the camp without Neil to protect his frail frame, but stopped himself. To be unconditionally supportive took biting one's tongue, and callous remarks would get him nowhere promising anytime soon.

Those comments would surely come out if he went with her; he knew it in the same way he knew himself. Exhaustion was beginning to rear its wrinkled head, already turning him surly and all around unpleasant. He knew going with her would be more of a detriment to her search than a helpful hand.

"Okay, I'm gonna go try to catch a little sleep. I'm not sure how well I'd fare if I waited until full dark to give it a shot. I think the heebie-jeebies would keep me up all night."

He tried to keep it as light as their dinner conversation, but he could tell Keila was reluctant to accept his withdrawal. They hadn't been apart since leaving New Braniff and he doubted she wanted to begin flying solo. *Spread your wings and soar, little bird — I need some rest.* As if on cue to mock his words, the bank of generators sitting in front of the fuel truck hummed. Spotlights sprung to life on the cherry-pickers surrounding the camp. *Now what's your excuse, boy?* Aaron laughed.

Shut up, Carey retorted.

"Alright," Keila conceded quietly, turning without another word.

At least that went well, boy. Idiot.

Carey nodded silently to the remaining pair, taking his leave. As he plodded back towards his tent, he felt the weight of the day press heavily on his shoulders, accentuating the existing weariness threatening to strike him down where he walked.

Carey was fucking *spent.* He couldn't believe that only hours had passed since he'd learned of his mother's ceased lifeline. It all felt so surreal, like he was reading his lines from a script written carelessly by a sadistic playwright.

As he pulled back the tarp that served as the entryway to his sleeping quarters, Carey was shocked to see the bedroll neatly made awaiting his embrace. *She made the bed?* It was the same vein of normalcy that stunned him at every juncture; that someone who had witnessed the horror Keila had in the previous days would have the wherewithal to make the bed after rising like a diligent child performing daily chores. It was also undeniably sweet. She never once asked for thanks. Hell, she never even asked for recognition. *She really does care,* he thought, reeling in the moment. He pulled off his boots and crawled on top of the rough blanket.

I should have gone with her. She had so selflessly supported him with every endeavor, even when he had unintentionally placed the sanctity of finding his own family seemingly high above her father's whereabouts. *Poor, cranky old me. Really had to have that nap, didn't I?* The least he could have done was stand fast by her in her moment of need, to be the rock to cling to if the need arose. What if she again found nothing in the records? What if there were no disguised signposts in the crate to give her a fighting chance of finding Bennett? What if she realized he likely was bloated and pale on the moor somewhere, a jacketed slug lodged deep within his plagued brain tissue?

Carey breathed a deep sigh, rolling onto his side. *Well, shit.* He resolved to be a man instead of a selfish boy.

He lay in the gathering night on the bedroll, hands linked behind his head. Images of his mother and father danced in the darkness, his vision filled with inconsequential memories. They slowly spun in circles in his vision, windows to a time long passed. He looked through the peepholes to that wondrous place when things made sense, if only in hindsight.

Where superheroes were real. Where everything had a rhyme and reason walking hand in hand down a sunlight pier on the Atlantic Ocean. Suddenly, pushing them aside, a short-statured balding man with thick jowls appeared in the centre. He gazed at Carey with pleading eyes, begging for redemption of a life that never went the way he had intended. Bennett Tindall, lamenting not only the loss of his one true love, but the children he had sworn her memory to safeguard against the rain; now also gone. It was the saddest goddamn thing he'd ever seen, the man whom age had not treated fairly, for whom fate was always seeking to toy with in a twisted game of mouse and puma. To know a single glimmer of hope existed as to his continued heartbeat, as small as the faintest star in the sky, it was there. Keila was searching for the roadmap to the barely-there spectre of a destination, filled with the fires of hell as her driving force. *Fuck.*

The vision faded, leaving Carey only with the tarp walls of the makeshift tent for his eyes to play over. As ridiculous as it sounded in his own head, he felt at home. He felt *safe.* He knew that the thin blue material wouldn't hold back an angry six- year old with enough resolve, let alone a swarm of teeth baring down on him where he lay.

His spine quivered with the thought, the ruined bodies piling on top of him while he desperately writhed to get away, jaws tearing through his sweater to reach the flesh beneath. It was horrifying, but it was reality.

No matter how many times he closed his eyes, it would come back when they opened. It was the environment he had been unwillingly thrust into and despite all his kicking and screaming, he was here to stay. *Fuck,* Carey thought. *This is it.* It was an odd time for the revelation to strike him, but it came slinking quietly into his mind nonetheless.

This is it.

How long would it take to find a cure? Did one already exist? How would they distribute it, because that first plan didn't seem to manifest. Would they be able to weather out the tides of infected in a camp held together with zip ties and duct-tape? The methods they were using worked well, but what about when the ammunition ran out? Was it worldwide?

The last question hit home in a way he hadn't intended. Worldwide. *Spain.* Where Tarryn was. Carey had been holding Tarryn in a locked box in his head, high above the tribulations of Southern Ontario. The States definitely had a problem on its hands, but what about Europe? What if Tarryn was hiding in a closet, infected scratching at the door, begging for a mother she didn't know had already passed on in a billowing cloud as her corporeal self dissolved in the flames?

He rubbed at his hair with his hands, pushing his hat from his head.

Tarryn had to be alive, the same way he had forced himself to believe his parents had been safe and hidden from the turmoil outside when he'd left St. Albins. *Had been.* That was a rather traumatic memory to recall, if there ever was one.

His parents, along with the Tindalls, had been doing just *fine* without him there. They had established a sanctuary in a world going to the dogs. They could have remained under the infected's radar indefinitely, knowing the kind of surplus food and water his father liked to horde in the downstairs pantry. They had space to move and fresh air whenever they wanted it. It was a survivalist's dream, minus the guns, ammunition and freeze-dried food.

All of it had come crashing down at his arrival, dragging the pack of trailing virus sufferers shambling after him like a parade.

If he had only stayed in St. Albins. If he had only been shot by the officer who had let him go. If he had only been blown apart by the sidewinder missile of the chopper. If he'd only broken his neck when he'd leapt blindly from the overpass. *If only.*

A dim rustling startled him from his thoughts. The bottom edge of the tarp serving as his doorway trembled lightly before peeling back. *Oh my god.* He had wished for the opulent eye to steer away from him if it meant those better suited and deserving would survive, but he never dreamed it would all come crashing down so quickly.

"Shit!" he muttered, scooting backwards on his ass as he fumbled with the zipper keeping his revolver from reach.

One shot, boy. Make it count.

The tarp rustled loudly, pulling back farther and farther with every passing second, the anxiety gripping him like a vice. The zipper marred into the fabric tasked with shielding it when not in use, Carey cursing the makers of such a fruitless feature. The tarp silhouetted an unbelievable figure as it gave way to the outside. The snag pulled free and Carey plunged his hand into the pocket. He grasped the handle, feeling its ridged rubber grips beneath his fingers and cocked the hammer with his thumb.

"Care?"

He stopped dead, leaving the pistol where it lay in the confines of his sweater. It sure as hell wasn't Keila.

"Morgan?" he called out tentatively, knowing full well who was making the incursion to his haven. *Uh-oh.*

Carey lingered for a moment longer before dropping the hammer down slowly to its resting place, softly on the firing pin.

"None other — can I come in?"

He was stunned that she'd actually posed the question, asking like a male attendant entering a girl's public bathroom. Could she?

He supposed. Keila wasn't going to be back for a while, if their first multi-hour fondling of the records had given him any indication. Besides, what was the harm in a little conversation?

Consider carefully, Aaron stated plainly, no trace of his usual prodding wit.

It scared him in a way that the imagined infected couldn't — could it be that he truly had something to lose besides his life? It was a puzzling premise, but he decided it was one that could be examined more fully at a later date.

"Sure, next time let me know you're coming," Carey said softly, feeling like Keila was listening to him from afar, hearing every syllable. *So I don't put a slug in your gut.* Who knew, it could save her life someday.

Comical, get back to the point at hand, bud. In two seconds, she's going to be in here. You. Her. Alone. Good idea? Your choice, but I guess it's already made.

Aaron had a point. Carey noticed his groin twitch involuntarily as he jammed his hat back on his head and smoothed his hair to the sides beneath it.

"Oh, I will. I'm glad you're already thinking of a next time." Her voice was a liquor of the sweetest variety, the strongest honey mead ever created.

Shit, she's good. She even knew what to *say* to crank him into overdrive. She revealed herself in full, allowing the tent-flap to fall behind her, shielding the outside world from view. In her leather outfit, she looked like a porn star from a skin-flick with a biker lead-up. Even in the low light, her viridian eyes bore straight through him to the ground below like sodium lasers.

This isn't good. This isn't what you're supposed to do. His subconscious could rant all it wanted, but it wasn't running the show. The subconscious was inferior to his conscious, after all.

"Mind if I lay down with you and talk for a while?"

It was plain, it was blunt and with no trace of the oozing sex appeal her body exuded. Even if he had wanted to, he'd be powerless to say no.

"Sure, come on down," he said quietly, motioning towards the patch of wool blanket beside him.

Her eyes never left his as she eased herself down, hovering over him for a moment before relaxing fully on the bedroll. She lay on her side, facing him while propped on her elbow. Her leather jacket was unzipped slightly, revealing her to be gloriously nude beneath the cowhide coat. It rattled his heart, eliciting a response that Keila had never stirred.

Fuck me, she's gorgeous. Her black hair tickled his ear a little where it fell close enough to touch him, but he didn't dare tell her, lest she move further away. Even though their bodies remained separate, her heat radiated across the narrow expanse between them, warming his frame.

"Pretty crazy, huh," she mused. "Who'd have thought that of all the boys to meet at the end of the world, it's you. The one that got away. The one who refused to call me back."

No contempt tightened her voice, only a strange sense of dejected longing that he didn't know she was capable of. *The one that got away?*

"You called me? When?" Carey asked, barely able to contain the excitement in his voice.

She had called me?! He couldn't remember ever procuring her number after their one-time romp. He had assumed she wanted a fling and nothing more and thought a girl of her caliber wouldn't want a nobody like him. He didn't have money. He looked alright, but he wasn't a muscle-dummy with a shiny tight shirt. But *she* called him the one that got away? *Shee-it.* It was like he had just been told that he had won the lottery, but had missed claiming his ticket before expiry. *Fuck!*

"Of course I did. You put your number in my phone at the bar, but after that night you never picked up. Not once."

Carey wracked his brain for any mysterious missed calls he might have received, finding none.

"I probably put in the wrong number, but how come you never asked me in person at the bar after that? You saw me on shift enough and I would have been more than happy to correct my mistake, to say the least." He wasn't sure if he was trying to talk smooth or if that was just the fitting statement for the moment, but it came off like butter on a hot frying pan. *Crackle crackle.*

"I'm not one to chase boys, Care. You should know that. I figured I just wasn't your kind of girl, y'know, the strong ones? Figured I scared you off and let's just say I don't take rejection well." Her eyes half closed as she spoke and he knew it was the truth. It had to have been the wrong number, she wouldn't just put one over on him like this, not after everything she'd been through.

"Where's Kerrican tonight?" Carey questioned, trying to shift the topic away from his failure with the opposite sex.

I almost had her! It was maddening to think — dwelling on it would only depress him; that he knew.

"Kerrigan?" she corrected. "I dunno. What do I care? We snuggled together last night, sure, but he's not my man or anything. I already told you that. I wanted to be here with you, so here I came." As she spoke, she pulled back the cover and scuttled underneath. "Come under, I could use a hug. Plus, I don't want you catching a cold."

It was a little chilly, the frigid air easily finding its way through the voids the tarp didn't cover. *Okay, what's the harm in a little cuddling. It's not like I'm married or anything,* he thought.

Keep telling yourself that, Aaron chimed in. He pulled his side of the blanket back, admitting himself to the warm realm beneath the fabric. She extended an arm over his shoulder, pulling him close and squeezing him tight. Her body pressed against his, her breasts soft against the hard muscles of his chest. *Christ.* It felt better than he could have imagined. It was like finding a heartfelt letter written from a long lost friend buried in a box of brimstone.

As she slowly pulled away from him, he left his arm beneath her neck and she didn't seem to mind. She rested her head on his shoulder, drawing her taloned fingers up and down his chest.

"You can't deny it, some things are just meant to be. I mean, what are the chances of you and I meeting up again? A thousand to one? A million to one? Even lower? But here you are and here I am," she spoke, breathing onto his neck. Gooseflesh erupted over his entire body, tingling through every nerve. "I've been with a lot of guys, I won't deny that. I've seen every single one of them walk away, starting with my father, but I've never been one to cling onto a memory. Still, I think every day of the night we shared in my bed."

He pondered for a moment what she meant, but for the sake of his already over-excited nervous system, assumed she meant the *time* they'd shared as opposed to the alternative.

"Here you are and here I am," she repeated. "I think in some way, I've always been yours. Whether you like it or not, something's pushed us together. I know you and Keila have a thing..." she paused, clearly waiting for him to interrupt her.

Keila wasn't a subject he wanted to dive into at the moment, feeling even the mention of her name was tainting her spirit despite her ignorance of the situation.

"I never thought you'd be the one to cradle me when I needed it, no matter how much I wanted it. We could have been something, you know that?"

The words struck him to the core. *Could have been something.* Coming from such a tigress, it was hard to believe the thought had even crossed her mind, let alone to disclose it to him in the flesh. Carey merely nodded, looking deeply into her eyes, not knowing what to say. Not knowing what she needed to hear.

"Sometimes, you just need to know you're alive. To know your heart still beats. To know that everything you've done hasn't been a waste. You know that, Carey?"

In her gaze, he finally placed it. *Hunger.* It was beyond desire. It was beyond lust. It was beyond need. It was *hunger.*

"You can't fake a waking dream. You can't trick the mind into believing a fantasy when it's really happening. You know how that works, don't you?"

Carey found himself nodding in spite of himself, pretending he knew exactly what she spoke of despite being as lost as an elderly woman in a post-modern fashion market.

"I'm glad you agree."

With that, she was on top of him, the blanket peeling back from her naked legs.

No pants? Jesus, that's a nice trick! She tore open his sweater, her eyeshadowed gaze hot with want. She unzipped her jacket, her tanned breasts supple in the cold blue light. She leaned down to him as she pulled up his shirt, fidgeting madly with his belt while kissing his neck. Her lips were soft and moist, driving all rational thought from his mind. His hands met the small of her exposed back, her tight muscles underneath pulsing her hips against his. *Oh my god.* Her skin was soft and firm, deliciously smooth to the touch beneath his rough fingertips as they played over the curves of her hips, powerless to her embrace.

Keila.

Her face jumped into his mind, as unwelcome as a cockroach in a punchbowl. *Keila. I can't do this.* His hands moved lightning fast from her waist to her shoulders, pushing her back. She sat up, straddling him, grinding her smooth frame deeper against his jeans. She licked her fingers and tossed her hair.

NO!

It took a full ten seconds before he realized she was there, holding up the sea-blue tarpaulin from outside. Keila stood there, mouth agape, watching the vixen push against his groin, hidden by the itchy wool covers.

"Keila, no!" he cried, roughly pushing Morgan farther back.

She planted her hands firmly on the ground, ignoring the intrusion. She kissed his neck once more as Keila dropped the tarp, her footsteps trailing quickly into the distance.

"Ah, who doesn't love an audience, baby?" she moaned, licking his earlobe. Her voice was breathy, seductive.

Through the haze of his transgression — his betrayal — he let it take him away for a moment longer.

"Love gets loud sometimes!" she cried, pulling once more at his belt.

He almost didn't hear the siren ring out in the night air.

VI

Carey first thought the sound was the ringing in his ears, having been found by the girl he thought he *could* love in the arms — hell, under the *straddle* — of another. It took him a second to realize the repurposed air-raid alarm was being raised, acknowledged fully in his mind by shouting troops rallying their sleeping brethren to arms all around him.

"Oh fuck it, ignore them!" Morgan pleaded, the desperation in her voice unmistakable. "Just fucking do it!"

He pushed her off him fully, rolling her back onto her side before freeing himself from the blanket.

"What the hell does that mean?" Carey asked, confused and rattled to the bone.

Oh god, what's happened. She sighed heavily, pulling her pants back on quickly while shaking her head.

"Incursion and major. Big swarm approaching. Means we all have to head out to the frontline to help. They've got a lot of badass guys here, sure, but they don't have enough bodies to put guns on all sides," she muttered, zipping up her jacket.

From the pocket she drew a small, silver, boxy-looking gun more reminiscent of a chromed Zippo or a 1950's imagining of a raygun than a sidearm. She put a firm hand on the back of his head and kissed him hard, directly on the lips. Pulling away slightly, she looked at him with fire in her eyes.

"Don't you fucking die on me now," she breathed, quickly rising to her feet. She brushed the tarpaulin out of the way as she left.

What have I done.

He struggled to pull his boots over his feet, the leather folding and the insoles bunching in his haste. His head ached deeply, his forehead hot. *That's what you get for getting heavy with another woman and getting discovered, you idiot,* he thought. His head was light, dizziness gripping him as he wrestled with his boot laces, fumbling awkwardly with the thin cords. The siren was louder than the gunshots he had grown to ignore, swelling forth from the very earth beneath him.

As he tightened his boots, his thoughts went back to Keila. She must be thinking the worst of him, of that much he was sure. *But I didn't do anything!* he thought, whining like an insolent child. He knew better. It wasn't what had happened, but what it had looked like and with no witnesses to clear his innocence besides the part-time stripper grinding against his jeans, he doubted that air would be cleared in the near future. Especially not when there were infected clawing ever closer over the moor to siege the entrenched encampment. *I'll just tell her,* he thought. That's right, he'd level with her. Spill his bloody fucking guts. Let her know everything, from the night he had held so dear, all the way up to her shocked face hovering outside the blue tarp sanctuary. Full disclosure, nothing less than what she deserved.

She deserves it? Why, I thought you 'weren't married' to the broad. At least you were busy mentally arguing with yourself to the contrary only an hour ago, bud. Aaron's tired words through his mind spurned forth an image Carey would never forget.

Keila stood on the beach with Carey in a different time, laughing and smiling like high school kids playing hooky for a little thrill. They were collecting driftwood from the edge of the surf and stacking dry branches in a massive pile. They were creating an ad-hoc masterpiece, a work of art without a signature. Keila had just added the final piece, a small sand-dollar to the peak of the mound, bringing the whole together. Hand in hand, they stood back, grinning at what they had created, when a bright light grew near. It was a torch made of reeds, crackling fiercely in the otherwise starless night. It was thrown beneath the monument to their shared acquaintance, immediately engulfing the tinder in flames, creating a funeral pyre for their love that shot a hundred feet in the air. Keila shrieked and ran, leaving Carey all alone. Almost alone, anyway. Morgan cackled as she wiped lighter fluid from her hands, the silver lighter gleaming harshly with the towering inferno. The flames desire, the ashes his future. *Great, smoke and mirrors, eh? That one's all you, bud. Forgive me, but I believe you were going somewhere.*

The vision broke, his right hand aching. He looked down to find the revolver clutched in his palm, quivering violently. *Fuck.* He dropped the hammer, seemingly cocked of its own accord, back against the firing pin. The Taurus was dangerous in itself, but it was his own mind with that kind of armament readily available that scared him.

He slapped the release knob, setting the spinerette free from the frame. A single primer cartridge stared back at him, the rest of the chambers as hollow as he felt. *God, what I'd give for another four.* He slapped it back to where it could be of his benefit, the one bullet possibly his only means of defense outside of hand-to-hand range. And he did *not* want to get that close. Ever again.

Carey tucked the revolver into his pants pocket, the closest thing to a holster he could stomach. The thought of tucking it in behind his belt-buckle drew forth horrible crime-scene images of gunshot wounds and he had no desire to experience a shot to his most prized selection of anatomy.

The extendable baton came forth from the other side, compact and yearning for action. *Hold on, little buddy.* Charging out like a knight on his day off held little appeal, so the extendo remained telescoped into the handle, requiring only a hard twitch to make battle-ready.

Carey zipped his sweater as he considered his arsenal, wishing he had found a Vulcan Cannon, perhaps an A-1 Abraham main battle tank hidden where his wallet should be. *Good thing you're not just relying on your wits, boy. Then you'd really know what an unloaded weapon looked like.*

Har-dee-har-har. Another gem.

The commotion outside grew louder with each passing moment, the siren fading away. Footfalls stamped the hard ground all around him, the shouts of comrades preparing for war sweeping him up in fervor. He pushed back the flap, finding the spotlights blindingly bright as they panned about from above.

Shirtless men clad only in ballistic vests, helmets and fatigue pants stormed past him, clearly roused from their sleep but never found unready for the bloodshed soon to come.

He ran after them, not knowing where else to go. There was a lot of perimeter to cover, but he had no intention of being alone.

The main gate came into view, slid ajar while a soldier barked orders, alternating between a radio handset and a megaphone. The back of one of the many olive-green trucks hung open, the canvas tarp covering it pulled away to reveal a veritable stockpile that would make a redneck drool.

As he drew nearer, he joined the queue forming, moving quickly forwards to an infantryman tearing rifles from the racks for distribution. The firearms were startling replicas of those in a videogame Carey had loved as a child. He recognized the black frame, but not the green stock and grips. Still, it was undeniably an M16. *No way.* He had never fired a gun in his life in the real world, as adept at banishing electronic evils to their maker with his old Nintendo 64 growing up.

As he reached the front of the line, a buttstock and a magazine flew carelessly into his waiting hands. He fumbled with the black clip, crossed around the middle with a strip of red electrical tape, almost dropping it into the dirt.

"Don't do that now, these bitches are fickle," a gruff voice said from behind.

A heavy hand braced his back, guiding him through the gate. Had to be the soldier with gold bars on his shoulders and a thousand scars on his face he had spied before collapsing when he'd reached the camp. He was sure of it. In the harsh glow of the arcing floodlights, he looked like he'd been sent to Purgatory long ago, only to carve his way past Satan's own to rejoin the ranks of the living.

The purple lines crossing his face were intimidating, but reassuring as well. Anybody who'd seen what this guy had knew what he was doing and Carey was glad to have him at his side regardless of his brash tone.

"C7 Assault rifle, take it with you over there," he continued, pointing to the back of a LAV at the perimeter beyond the fence. Carey couldn't help but notice the soldier dressed more for the desert than for a *soirée* near the Prairies.

In the cold light, she stood waiting for him, dressed in more black than the Grim Reaper himself. *Are you fucking kidding me?* Morgan smiled at him for a moment before jamming a magazine into her own long-gun, completing the action by pulling a level with a loud *click* as if she did it every morning after she brushed her teeth. She caught his amazed stare, giggling slightly at his reaction.

"Hit a range in Vegas when I was down there for a feature dancer gig — good thing eh?"

She looked like the bride of Ghost Rider in her biker *chic* garb, draping the shoulder-strap around her neck. All she needed were a few hand grenades and a bandolier and she'd be a fitting match for Stallone in the jungles of Vietnam. The firearm in his hands made him feel like the most rugged man to grace Ontario as he strode towards her, its oiled steel under his fingertips.

This charade lasted all of ten seconds before he tried to hammer the magazine into the receiver in perfect mirror image of the death-dealing vixen, succeeding in doing nothing more than pinching his finger against the frame and missing entirely. *Shit.* His hands fell to his sides, already conceding defeat. His head burned even hotter, the beginnings of a migraine creeping in above his spine. *Oh, you blushing beauty, you,* Aaron mocked.

"Like this," she said letting her own rifle dangle from her shoulders as she expertly fitted the clip into the gun, turning a ten pound piece of shit into an implement of destruction.

"That's better. This end goes towards the thing you want to die, remember," she added. She pointed to the muzzle as she turned to lean her own on the back of the Light Armoured Vehicle, striking the pose of a marksman.

Well, shit, Carey conceded, wishing he was as comfortable in the role as she was, trying not to question her source of authority on the subject.

"Don't worry," the Captain continued, sniggering a little under his breath at the exchange. "You don't have to be an expert to hit a target with this configuration, kid. The loadout has a tracer every third round, so if you point and shoot you'll see where you're firing and be able to adjust accordingly. We've got lots of ammo, so don't worry about being a little trigger-happy. Ammunition reserves won't do us any good if our line breaks anyway," he added.

His eyes became distant before snapping back to Carey, who nodded acknowledgement.

"The rest of the rounds are incendiary, so don't worry about going for the heads. Try and hit the closest stumblers in the centre of their mass to mark them. The snipers will work clean-up duty from there. Don't try to be a fucking hero, kid — there're no heroes here. The ones who were brave are the bleeders in uniform coming this way, not the ones with the guns."

Carey nodded once more, affirming he had comprehended the words, even if he didn't understand how in the name of the Holy Ghost the man in charge expected him to carry out his duty. As the scarred warrior walked away, Carey turned back to Morgan, her tanned skin white as milk in the glare of the spotlights.

"This the same as last time, you think?" he asked, seeking reassurance that this had all been done before.

That the ones in his place had been able to fend off the tide and made it. She nodded, looking out to the killing field on the other side of the personnel carrier. It looked like an abandoned driving range in the dead of night, the green grass sprawling before them, untouched by golf balls lazily resting about. It elicited a misplaced feeling of tranquility, the way the expanse rolled from sight, the light penetrating no more than a few hundred feet out into the brooding darkness beyond. A few tangled hollow screams alit on the wind headed their way, the coppery smell of blood just detectable in the cool air.

"Yeah... well, maybe not so many," she breathed. A peel of gunfire echoed out from above as if on cue when the pack came into the wash of the floodlights.

Three near the front went down, crumpling as their heads exploded into a fine crimson mist exaggerated by the moment. It rained scarlet over the horde before six more shambled over the bodies of the fallen.

"Here we go, Care. Remember what I said," she said. Any other words she had intended were lost in the bark of the LAV's main cannon.

Tongues of flame shot from the muzzle, licking the shadows away as huge sabots hammered downrange. As if the conductor of the orchestra had begun swaying his wand in time, the rest of the forward-based vehicles answered the call. Deafening explosions on the moor ripped holes in the expanse of bodies shuffling in an almost calculated line. So far away, but still too close.

Even though they walked on broken legs near half a kilometer away and closing, he shivered as the vast openings torn by the cannons filled as quickly as they formed. Morgan dropped to her knees below the steel plates of the LAV, motioning for him to do the same. He dropped to his ass rather unceremoniously in a heap, bracing his spine against the rough rubber of the vehicle's mud tire.

This is fucking insane, he thought.

It sounded like every teen's dream, to be able to manifest all the hate and angst brought about by an 'unjust' society into a killing rage. The reality, on the contrary, was exactly the opposite.

Carey didn't feel like a proud warrior as he crouched in the dust, trying desperately to control his bladder despite its best attempts to release. Men would fall. Men would die. Men would rise back up, jaws snapping when they transformed into the very enemy they had given their lives to fight. It was ludicrous to believe that the hundred or so rag-tag militia could stand like a rock against the festering surf. It was just so goddamn overwhelming.

With each shot, the LAV rocked behind him, jarring him forward on the balls of his feet. His balance meagerly prevailed, only marginally holding fast while some part of his subconscious very much desired to lay face down in the dirt and for it all to just go away as he closed his eyes.

He peeked under the battle vehicle, careful not to allow the steel plating to rock into his forehead. He caught a glimpse of the forward-most bleeders, seeming frail and weak on their own, barely able to maintain basic locomotion on their trembling legs. Alone, they barely made his stomach clench anymore, especially not at the distance from which they shambled. What stole the breath from his lungs was what couldn't be seen. A mass, darker than the surrounding night that drew ever closer, just out of the spotlight's valiant attempt at banishing the blackness enveloping the scene.

As he turned his head back towards the camp, the lights inside dimmed, leaving a few brave twinkles of handheld torches bouncing among the tents. *They really want to conserve fuel. They really think it may take that long.* It was a stark realization — a gallon of water on the already-smoldering fire of hope in his chest, leaving only meekly glowing coals struggling for heat beneath.

His eyes searched the row of miniature tanks, looking for a snatch of blonde hair to reassure him, something to let him know that his anchor to this life hadn't abandoned him completely. Nothing. *Oh god, Keila. What have I done.* The glare of the spotlights dazzled his vision. Large blue spots hung in the darkness, making him panic when he rose with Morgan to look downrange.

"It's our turn," she muttered, the fire in her ocean eyes still very much ablaze.

She raised her weapon with the concentration of William Tell preparing to shoot the apple off the head of his only begotten son, staring down the sights into the horde beyond. Taking her cue, Carey raised his own rifle to port, bracing himself on the back of the LAV to quell his quivering arms.

He held his breath as the muzzle found its mark over a ragged woman in blue jeans and a white sweater, the notch-and-post sight twitching wildly between her breasts. His heart pounded wildly in his head as his brain begged for oxygen. His finger found the small trigger inside the infinitely large guard before snapping it back crisply.

Plink.

No hatred spewed from the weapon. No testament to his survival went spiraling out into the fray to meet his adversary. Only the slap of the firing pin dinging harmlessly off the receiver. *What the fuck?*

"Cock it you dumbshit," Morgan advised roughly, his incompetence throwing off her coming shot.

She jacked back a lever with a sneer, cycling a round into the action of his rifle before cracking off five shots in rapid succession. Without a moment to blink, four seeming walking corpses recoiled as bright spots of flame painted their chests. The sharpshooters above got to work cleaning up her mess; five infected falling by the end of the ten-second repartee.

Carey stood in the cool night air, feeling incredibly impotent as soldiers around him reloaded LAV cannons and a massive howitzer-looking contraption with a square buffer around the muzzle. They didn't even watch the action as they carried out their prescribed duties, firing nothing of their own arsenal at the juncture, merely biding their time until the order fell.

Carey looked downrange as more of the black cloud came into view. *At least they make it hard to miss,* Aaron mused as the countless ruined lives drew closer. Once again, he jammed the buttstock into his shoulder, clutching the C7 tightly as he lined up his shot on the same soccer mom from hell, peering down the sights into her throat. Morgan's sheer display of killing talent relaxed him. He pulled the trigger.

BLAM!

The shot rang out, his ears ringing with the sound as he lowered the rifle to reap the results of his effort. *Nothing.* The brunette continued hobbling over the uneven earth, but blissfully too far to visualize her jutting teeth snapping hungrily for his frame. *Goddammit,* he thought bringing the rifle to port once more.

BLAM! BLAM! BLAM!

He poured fire into the crowd, a veritable riot-level swarm pushing ever closer to the position of resistance. He saw no flaming beacons open across stomachs from his own hand, though through his peripheral vision saw many from Morgan's careful aim. The fireteam's longrifles above clattered endlessly, the LAV's growing quiet beneath the din.

Women's skulls opened up like dropped cans of beans, pouring blackened blood onto the grass as they toppled. Two children were blown four feet backwards into the outstretched arms of what could be their infected parents as high caliber rounds made contact with their fusing bones. All the while, he plinked uselessly into the pack, wishing he had spent more time in Boy Scouts and less time reading cheap drugstore novels in his youth.

Every so often, a large beam of light would spray from his muzzle, looking more like a science fiction B-movie laser than a NATO slug, tracing the path of his shot into the unseen darkness. *Shit.* The soldiers next to him shouldered their own issued service rifles, joining him and Morgan in the marking siege. At once, luminescent flames burst forth on all sides as shots made contact, each unlucky victim falling shortly thereafter. It reassured him a little to know he wasn't the only one at bat for the camp any longer, excluding the feminine terminator at his left.

I bet Keila wouldn't have been a crack shot. I bet you'd even have to comfort her. Wouldn't that just be a burden, Aaron chided, reminding him of his shortcomings lest he forget in the fray. His head ached now, burning like a thousand suns beneath his temples. He shot more wildly, taking less time between trigger-pulls to line up his aim as his eyes squinted against the pain.

After an eternity — likely no more than five minutes in reality — a patch of inferno emerged on the fat man in his sights. The balding fuck didn't even look down as his skin boiled in the flames, seemingly immune to the agony as his arms rose higher in the pursuit of flesh. Within the blink of an eye, he was headless.

He keeled over like a rotten tree in a violent windstorm, his arms folding beneath him as he fell.

One for twenty? Not bad. You might even get a medal at this rate. Carey stared at the obese corpse down the moor. *Fuck off, Aaron. I'm busy.*

The kill filled him with pride, his confidence peaking despite his previous failed attempts. Like that, he was off. Two. Three. Four. Marked for death, his quarries swiftly met their ends. He barked a reckless laugh as the rifle rocked in his hands, not feeling the bruise developing on his shoulder in spite of the recoil pad pressed there. He was the Angel of Death and all he chose would be struck down. That was, until he pulled the trigger a fifty-first time, met with a mechanical *pop* instead of a sharp report.

"What the fuck!" he cried, his implement of destruction emasculated in his limp hands.

He pulled the trigger again, hearing only a metallic *clink*, no more dangerous than a fierce scolding by a vehement complainant. *It's empty, you didn't break it. Relax,* his rational mind soothed, quelling his fears that he had somehow destroyed his only real line of defense against the nearing crowd.

He toggled a small lever by the magazine, pleased to see the steel rectangle drop into his outstretched hand. He sighed, glad to finally figure something out for himself without guidance. Carey found his satisfaction short-lived, however, as he stared at the empty mag, the only one issued at his time of reluctant enlistment. *Shit!*

Panic swelled in his throat. He looked wildly from left to right for a solution. A beast of a man caught his eye, leaning on a pile of sandbags between two soldiers.

Kerrigan. Carey would have recognized that swagger a mile off, the way the old bouncer shot from the hip in three round bursts, conserving ammunition seemingly beneath him.

Maybe... he barely allowed himself to think it, lest his hopes drop like stones into the endless abyss. Despite steeling himself for the let down, five warriors along, there she was. Keila looked nothing like he would have imagined with a firearm clutched in her dainty hands. He would have expected tears. Hesitation. Fright. He viewed neither, only an exceedingly youthful-looking civilian determined to live, hammering bullets against her adversaries.

She let out a primal shriek as her own weapon ran empty, casting aside the empty magazine. *She's really doing it.*

"*Keila!*" he cried, knowing she'd never hear him over the harsh din of the battle. "Keila! Over here!"

She turned away, rolling out her shoulder, not hearing his words. She moved like she'd been doing it her whole life, as if she'd been born with a magnum in her crib. She stuck a hand high in the air. Carey followed her stare, finding his panic abate as he found what she sought.

An infantryman crouched over a large crate, lobbing clips underhand-style like softballs to soldiers on the line as they raised a hand. *Clever,* he thought, placing the empty mag on the LAV before raising his own. Upon catching the distributor's eye, a fresh clip sailed over to him which he deftly caught, bringing back his sense of purpose.

Slapping the magazine home — remembering this time to cock the rifle — he fired back into the fray, revitalized and refocused on turning the tide. With each fallen member, ten more staggered over the corpse. It was like fighting a hydra, where each fallen head would spawn two fanged maws in its place.

We're fuched, he thought, spewing rounds feverishly into the horde. *We're absolutely fucked.*

"This is pointless," Carey breathed.

Morgan turned in spite of the noise to face him. She reached a hand to his face, tenderly caressing his jaw for a moment before pushing him back to face the LAV.

"This isn't pointless, this is how it's done. This is how we did it before and this is how we're going to do it again," she answered sternly, waving to the line of shattered people halfway across the killing field. "Just keep shooting, or put a tracer in your head now. It's not going to get easier, but it *will* end. Just *shoot*, Carey!" she cried, her muzzle flashing once more into the pack.

He stopped thinking.

Carey leveled his rifle on the LAV and shot. And shot. And shot until his rifle clicked empty. Reloading, he joined the repulsion once more. *Don't fucking quit on me now, boy* Aaron called through the haze, a trace of pride glimmering in his inaudible voice.

As glints of the infected's glazed eyes shone in the hard floodlights, swaying slowly from side to side, the Fist of God came crashing down when firmly entrenched soldiers crouched in machinegun nests opened up. The front ranks of the bloodstained assaulters fell like rain, stacking oozing bodies en masse.

"Yes!" Carey cried, stopping his own battle to witness the carnage fully.

As the automatic weapon crews paused to change the ammunition belt, the wave of bleeders rose and marched over their fallen comrades with unsure steps. *Not now*, Carey thought, opening up with his C7 once more. *Not fucking yet*. Although they tripped as they fell over the jumbled heap, the infected stood once more, dripping holes gaping in their broken chests. He fired left and right as he swept the crowd, marking bleeder after bleeder for death.

The darkness inside begin to take over as he watched his triumph die and the spotlights grew dim, reflecting his inner downfall. Flashing twice before fading out entirely, night overtook the battle.

Carey panicked once more, every feminine cry in the night no longer the infected only a few hundred metres away, but Keila losing her own fight. He blinked hard, his blood chilling as his night vision refused to fall into sync. Loud shouts carried over the crashing discharges and moans. He hoped it was an aggravated lieutenant ordering the generators refueled as opposed to the alternative, where the repulsion had failed on the opposite side of the camp.

I'm going to die here, Carey thought, his head swimming with boiling heat. Somewhere in the dark, as he dropped to his knees, cradling the rifle, he found comfort. The extinguished spotlights removed the ice-picks driving into his eyes. He no longer saw the hanging jaws and sightless eyes. He wouldn't know his end as it dragged him under the LAV any more than he could remember his birth into the world. He would feel teeth break his skin and it would be over. It would be *over*. No more fighting. No more running. No more concern for his safety and no more shitty MRE's.

Carey rose to his feet, lifting the rifle's strap from his shoulders to lay the C7 on the back of the vehicle he felt before him in the blackness, gently so as not to scratch the paint. Morgan's firearm continued to crash. She shrieked, a bray fit for a warrior princess full of the hate of a thousand lost days. He was lost, alone in the dark despite the men calling rallying cries and words of encouragement.

This is where it ends, he thought. *This is where I end.*

Out there, somewhere lost in space, Carey wandered the lines between success and failure, his only company the moaning all too close on the lightless moor. What brought him back wasn't a startling image of his father, guiding him by the hand to the world of the present. It wasn't his long lost friend Aaron with a snappy remark, cutting him to the bone. It wasn't Keila rushing blindly down the ranks to his side, bringing him hope. It was a natural human function, as ingrained as breathing. It was so simple, so small, so inconsequential. Such a mundane ritual of daily life. It forced his survival instincts to take over, snatching the rifle back into his hands and squeezing the trigger.

Carey had to piss.

The pressure of his filled bladder banished every wistful thought on the subject of his mortality. Life wouldn't just *end* if he was bitten. He wouldn't keel over, roll into the dirt and lay still. He would rise again as they all had, inbred with a hunger that could never be quelled; with an urge to murder more basic and terrifying than any creature could match. The signal of his system to excrete waste was all he needed, the catalyst his subconscious sought to push on.

I'm not finished.

Carey screamed as he flung rounds wildly into the dark, shouting spiteful curses every time a scorching brand hovered in the dark. With the black air of the April night caressing his face, the lights came on. The horde was close now, no more than a hundred metres downrange. The glistening ichor streamed from their throats, the yearning hands brokenly reached out for him. A loud concussive blast rang out in the night, the earth opening up beneath their feet before he realized what was happening.

As if coordinated by the skillful hand of a higher power, the entire field under the writing mass erupted in fire and flames, tearing apart the pack from the source. The ground fell out from beneath them, as if Hell had chosen the rocky locale for a feeding frenzy.

"Sappers, you glorious fucks!" a gruff voice called out down the line. A cheer rose from the exhausted forces. As the fire raged on, no ravenous sleepwalkers came any closer. No stumbling infected crossed the fifty-yard line before they fell.

"CEASEFIRE! EVERYONE CEASE FIRE!" the Captain called over the loudspeakers. It left nothing but the wails of the burning grey dogs to break the silence left under the din of the roaring inferno cast in a line. Smoke rose in black billows, raining ash and debris.

A black figure leapt into Carey's view. His startled hands brought the assault rifle to port before the muzzle was smacked down by a massive palm from behind. The gun was wrenched from his hands as he spun round in a daze to face the intruder. The Captain stood before him, tossing the C7 to the ground. Expecting a punch, he winced, closing his eyes before a large arm wrapped itself around his soldiers.

"Look," the scarred leader advised softly, turning him back to the killing field.

The Reaper he'd sought to defend himself from walked slowly out onto the grass. He joined other soldiers similarly dressed in hazmat suits marching towards the row of fire.

"Mop-up crew. It's over, kid."

The calming grip around his shoulders reassured in the way a child depends on his father to safely remove the boogeyman from the closet. His vision swam, grey fog pushing in on the edges.

"Fuck," Carey cried weakly, knees buckling as his legs gave way beneath him. Only Captain Meyer's strong embrace kept him from spilling to the ground below.

"Shit!" Morgan cried aghast, "Medic! We need a medic!"

Carey tried to speak, finding only a tongue made of stone. Fuck, he thought as his fevered mind swam into the dark waters of the endless abyss.

As his bladder finally let go, the last thing he heard before the light left his eyes was Keila screaming.

"Carey! You promised!"

VII

The cold wind blew through the window of his pickup truck. It pushed softly falling droplets onto his smooth cheek. They chilled his flesh, unapologetically dropping in runnels down his collar.

Carey's eyes glanced around through the windshield, watching the mist grow and fall over the smooth glass. It was dark, just barely light enough under the moon to see by. The lights usually painting the Horseshoe side of Niagara Falls were dim, the falling water only a parody of its former glory. It ran at barely a trickle over the escarpment where thousands of gallons would usually run in a suicide deluge over the edge. It was as if a celestial hand had turned off a faucet somewhere far up the Niagara River, laughing as it spun the dial. He barely blinked as the surreal scene registered in his mind. He was back.

It was the place he'd almost ended his life to follow his mentor. It was the place he had last felt the icy hand of death wrap around his own, leading him to a place he couldn't return. He had been weaker then, but his own mental fortitude hadn't stayed his trigger finger. It had been the first time he'd heard Aaron whisper up from the depths. The last time he'd been alone.

Carey closed his eyes and reached out with one hand, searching and finding purchase in his cup holder. It was the same lukewarm Tim Horton's coffee, one cream one sugar. It was mostly empty, but he raised it blindly to his lips and drew the rest of the swill in one fell swallow.

It was heaven, the way it played across his tongue, faintly warming the hollow recesses of his mouth. He knew if he ran a hand across his face he would find no beard grown since the rise of the infection. He hadn't had one then and this wasn't the present.

He tossed the cup out his window, not bothering to open his eyes to see where it fell. He had finally come full circle. They didn't give out tickets for littering here.

"I wondered when you'd get here," a soft voice played around his ears.

Carey leapt in his seat, his eyes jarring open like barn doors thrust inward by the storm. As he turned his wild-eyed gaze to the passenger seat, he saw a black shadow. It was one he recognized instantly, forcing his stare away from the spectre seated beside him.

He sat in Aaron's seat, but his pseudo-father figure was nowhere to be found.

It was Roman.

"Shit," Carey gasped, tasting stale coffee and sour panic trickling down his throat.

"It's not so bad," Roman mused, the acrid smell of cigarettes in his nostrils as he stared back over the Falls.

Carey refused to meet his eye. He knew what it meant. Roman had gone off on his own to save his sister and what he thought to be his worst enemy and had taken his own life for the benefit of others. Unfortunately, the Holy Book of the Christians had no provision for noble suicide. It was all a sin. The worst sin. The unforgivable sin.

To look at him equaled acceptance of where he was. It may have looked like a spot he was accustomed to sitting, but it was far from Southern Ontario.

Roman had gone to Hell. Carey had just joined him.

Breath hitching in his chest, Carey thought back to the last time he'd been here. Aaron had sat beside him, the image of his dying day. Clotted hair had sat in matted locks around the exit wound of the shotgun blast responsible for his end. The grisly parody of the man he'd grown to love as family. He was dead.

Although Carey refused to look at Roman, he knew it would be the same way. His voice still held a semblance of childhood innocence, much as it had been near the final moments. It was untouched by twenty-two cigarettes chain-smoked to stave off the pain of infection raging up from his ankle. When Carey had looked into Aaron's eyes and seen nothing, courtesy of a twelve-gauge slug, he could only wonder what a monumental explosion could have done to the young Tindall.

"It's over, isn't it?" Carey commented, shaking his head.

A soft chuckle lit from the passenger seat, but it was enough to know the truth. Roman hadn't been overflowing with tact in life, but in death the renegade twin possessed even less. *Laughing in the face of the recently dead.*

Tarryn, he thought, his younger sister's face dancing before his eyes as he stared at his lap. *I'll never get to see you again.* Losing his parents — one permanently, one indefinitely — had been a tough pill to swallow. Wandering off the mortal coil without sharing an embrace with his sister was like trying to chew broken glass.

His mother and father stood with his sister on a grassy knoll in his mind, waving but entirely out of reach. They had gone to a better place, put out like the end of a candle without a sin on their conscience.

If only Carey could say the same. By errantly returning as the prodigal son to his family home, two bloodlines had been completely extinguished. Keila wouldn't last long without him, that much was for certain, regardless of their last standing. They had leaned on each other in their worst moments, but now she would fall into the dirt without a single shoulder to support her.

Staring at his hands he could almost see the deep sanguine red coating them. They were filthy, bathed in crimson hues from unseen accosting sins. He was responsible for the ending of the Tindalls. He was responsible for the extinction of the Cardinals. If not for him, they may have still been safe.

He *deserved* to burn in this Hell or the next.

As he stared at his blood-coated palms, a single wisp of smoke soared into his eyes. They stung, bringing fresh tears from the depths of his sockets.

"Dead men don't cry, buddy."

Carey snapped up, resolved to his fate, prepared to take in the grisly scene before him. Roman was dead and he was too. Time to face facts and stop pissing about. He'd done more than his fair share of *that* little evil enough in his days alive.

He took in the young man sitting beside him. Strawberry-blonde hair hung out from beneath his hood in waves, no trace of blood in their strands. Two hazel eyes met his own, sparkling defiantly instead of the hollow sockets he expected to see. A burning cigarette jutted like a white exclamation point from his lips, creased upwards in a grin at the corners.

"Expecting something else?" Roman cackled, apparently drawing great pleasure from Carey's confusion.

"Y-You're alive!" Carey cried, hands jumping to Roman's shoulder. They met hard, sinewy muscle underneath the black hoodie. He had expected them to go straight through the apparition.

"Don't mess with the merchandise!" Roman mocked, slapping his hands away. "It's bad enough I'm in this shitbox of a truck, I don't need you crinkling the duds on me now!"

Carey's head spun, dizzy dust-motes crowding out his thoughts as he searched for a reply. He blinked twice as hard as he could. Roman didn't disappear. He didn't even flicker.

It was a bittersweet moment. One half of his sanity prayed for him to fade. For the whole scene to dissolve and leave him in the darkness before the real world spilled back around his shoulders. It would mean it was all a dream, a silly apparition borne of battlefield stress and a poor constitution for bloodshed. It would be something to be laughed at when he finally again spoke to Keila. He knew she'd love to hear of her brother's recent endeavors, no matter how fanciful the circumstances of their meeting.

On the other hand, it gave weight to the world around him. It gave the earth gravity and put oxygen in the air. Somehow, someway, he was here. It wasn't a pithy charade to be dismissed at first light like a child's nightmare with a glass of warm milk. He was sitting in his old Ford F-150 near a trickling Niagara Falls and Roman was sitting beside him. A tangible, physical person sat beside him, as opposed to a man made of moonlight and smoke.

What does it all mean?

It was a painfully simple question, devised of only five short words with the proper punctuation at the end. Five one-syllable words that asked something deeper than he could truly grasp.

Carey thought back to the raging battle before. Shambling grey dogs had pressed in on the edges of their last fallback position. He'd shot more rounds than there were stars in the sky on a cloudless night. He had cut down mothers, brothers and children in cold blood, thinking only of his own skin to save.

But what if there's a cure? What if you just extinguished their hope in order to save your own?

It was another question pressing in on his sanity, but one for another day. He thought back over the events of the siege, dwelling on any time the vicious infected had gotten close. He found none. No teeth breaking his skin. No fluids spiraling through the night into his waiting open mouth. Nothing he could think of that would have left him open to the leathery wings of the sickness.

Roman had been infected.

It was true. It was one of the only things he knew, but as he turned his gaze back to the fresh-looking youth beside him, he found no trace of blood welling through his skin. No wild eyes begging to tear him to shreds with his fingers and jaws.

Is this where they go?

It couldn't be. This was a place for the peaceful. A place for the dead.

Then?

This voice was not his own. Although Aaron was far from the confines of the slate-grey pickup, it was a relief to hear his gruff prose spiral through his mind. Then what? It didn't matter.

"You done with your saunter down memory lane there, Carey?"

Roman puffed another cigarette, offering the matching pair to Carey from delicate fingertips. It hung in the twilight air like a sleeping dove, threatening to alight from the space between his knuckles at any moment.

Carey slowly reached out to take the butt. As his fingers closed on it, he felt the dry tobacco inside crunch and crumble slightly. Just like he was used to. There were no smoke and mirrors here. The cigarette was no more made of moonlight than his former compatriot's shoulder. Compatriot, conspirator, they were all one in the same in this place.

Placing the filter between his lips, he patted his pockets. No lighter. Roman merely chuckled again at Carey's fruitless search and flicked open his Zippo. It was gold, with *Annabel Mason* inscribed across the front in filigree. The spark caught the wick without hesitation, the flame merrily dancing up to meet his cigarette.

Carey inhaled deeply, relishing the light burn as it enveloped his lungs before blowing out the smoke in a bluish haze.

"Where'd you get that?" Carey mused, remembering Roman's beat-up yellow Bic lighter from the trip leaving New Braniff.

"I'm not sure," he replied slowly, his brow furrowing in concentration. "It was in my pocket when I came around here. You've been asleep for a while. Thought I'd finish the whole pack before you woke up," he added, tapping his ashes out the window into the mist.

Carey laughed, extending his hand across the bench seat.

"It's been too long," Carey said as Roman grasped his fingers in a firm handshake.

"It has," he conceded, blowing smoke around the cabin.

"This is it, isn't it?" Carey asked, trying to sound casual. The cigarette relaxed him, but it wasn't about to quell his fears in full.

"What do you mean?" Roman asked without a care in the world, seeming happy to merely puff his Belmont Mild's and relax in the truck. It must be easy for one whose life had already passed by. Entirely.

"This is all there is, isn't it? You don't have to lie to me," he added, feeling Roman knew more than he gave away. Ghosts found pleasure in speaking in rhyme, content to keep him guessing.

"Is this life?" Roman asked, brow again crossing in confusion, as if he couldn't grasp the concept laid out before him.

"Yeah," Carey replied.

He hated giving such closure to the question Roman offered, but there was no other way. It was a black and white scenario with no time for shades of grey. The stopwatch was running out and the sun was hitting the equinox.

It was time.

"I hope not," he said, opening his hands as he tapped his cigarette on the floor.

Carey felt a twinge of frustration blossom at the corners of his mind. Not only was the graveyard oracle dodging his question, he was ruining some damn well-kept floor mats. Carey took another long draw of his cigarette before releasing his quivering fists from his sides.

"You hope not?" Carey repeated, finding no adequate response to such a hazy answer. *It WAS or it WASN'T, god dammit!*

Roman merely reclined in his seat a little and looked at him down his nose. Instantly, he was a sage in a forgotten land, far older than his sixteen years.

"If this is the end for me, I hope it isn't the end for you," Roman replied evenly, taking his time to bite off the end of each word. "If you're dead, then my sister doesn't have much hope, does she?"

"Speak honestly!" Carey cried aghast, sick of the circular game.

He flicked his cigarette butt out the window, the tobacco burned down to the filter. It careened lazily in the mist, landing in a puddle with a tired fizzle as its eulogy. Roman merely shook his head and offered his pack once more, a solemn smile meeting the corners of his lips.

"You're not dead, Carey," he said after a moment, the pack hanging precariously from his fingers over the armrest. "I suppose I can't be a little jealous not to say the same"

The careful, calculated speech sounded nothing like the boy he dragged under his arm through the streets of his hometown. Nothing like the *child* he had slapped about the face to keep from screaming. Nothing like the youth that had sacrificed his life for him.

Carey sighed, the last thought hitting home, before taking another cigarette from the pack. *Why the hell not.*

"I'm sorry, Roman," Carey said quietly around the smoke pursed in his lips,

He leaned in close to the boy become a man, baptized by sacrificial fire, to light his second cigarette. As he inhaled and leaned away, he caught a glimpse of Roman's face before gazing back at the windshield. It wasn't an expression of contempt. It wasn't an expression of hatred. It was concern.

"You didn't shoot me, Carey," he said, leaning back once more. "Be sorry when you have something to apologize for."

Carey mulled the words over in his head. A cold, slimy snake writhed in his gut. *Having a few regrets for Keila?* Aaron crooned. Carey had no idea what Roman was privy to, but it wasn't a subject he felt like broaching at the moment. Not here, not now.

"You're the one in charge now," Roman stated.

It wasn't a question.

"I'm not sure I follow," Carey answered honestly.

"You're the one who has to watch her. You're in charge of her fate."

"I'm trying, Romes."

"You better do more than *try*," Roman snarled, baring his teeth at Carey.

His eyes were wide, lids peeled back from harsh irises. His lips pulled back to his canines, he was nothing more than a feral grey dog beside him. Then it was gone. Roman merely shook his head again, grabbed a cigarette from his pack, lighting it with the smoldering ember.

"I'm sorry," he offered, a slight colour rising in his cheeks. *The Tindall Flush*, Carey thought.

"No, *I'm* sorry," Carey spilt, feeling the words no longer held back by his best effort. "I wasn't there for you when it all... you know, came down. I left you in the dirt, shot through and bleeding from that sniper and I let you fall. I let you *fall*," Carey continued. Bitter tears formed at the edges of his eyelids.

Roman patted his leg and gazed out the window. His palm was warm, his fingers too hot to be dead.

"It was the last thing I could do for her," he mused softly. "It was the last push I could give you two in the right direction. Consider it payment for my sins. Let's just hope whoever comes after this ends takes it for the same. I've been here too long, seen too many faces."

The gravity of the statement lit a fire inside Carey's chest. It burned so hot he didn't feel his cigarette sizzling the edge of his ring finger, dropping half from his grasp.

"You've seen others?" he asked, trying to keep the excitement from his voice. "Anyone you knew?"

It was too much to contain himself. He needed to know. He needed to know *now*.

"Some," Roman offered, meeting his stare once more, though sharing none of his enthusiasm. "Time flows strangely in this place. It's hard to keep track of the days. Sometimes it's a white void, other times my high school homeroom. It's difficult to piece it all together — what's real, or what's catching me dreaming."

Carey grew impatient, selfishly caring little for the boy's own post-life fantasies. He had information. Information Carey *craved*. Carey *needed*.

"My parents," he blurted out, unable to hold back the words any longer. "Have you seen them? My mom? She... she died too," he admitted, the words too heavy in his mouth.

"I'm sorry," Roman offered sincerely, half turning in his seat to face him.

In the gloom, Carey could just barely make out the knots in his forehead as he grimaced. Maybe the medicine was difficult to swallow, no matter how distant they had been.

"Apologize when you have something to be sorry for," Carey said, voice hollow. "She's gone now. There's nothing that can be done about that."

"Doesn't mean it hurts less," Roman said distantly, cigarette trembling between his fingers. "You know I saw them, before I went."

Carey felt like a freight train had crashed directly into his sternum, driving the wind from his lungs.

"You did?" he cried, imagining his parents shambling over the twisted chain link fence as the infected boiled past the gas station so very long ago.

"Yeah," he continued, not meeting his eye. "My mother cradled my head, my father helped me with the grenade. The rest is kind of foggy, but that's been etched in my mind ever since I left."

Carey's breath once again passed through his throat, slowly, hitching slightly. *It wasn't them*, he thought, the relief bittersweet. It left him no closer to his father. It left no breadcrumb trails for him to follow.

"And mine?" he asked, once again feeling more self-centered than a brat crying for attention.

"No."

It meant nothing. Held no significance. Somehow, it was almost less than kind, less than what he wanted. For Roman to have seen his mother would have meant she too was a troubled soul, bound to this place, unable to pass on. That also meant Neil could have swum along with her into the after without a backward glance.

He sighed, feeling the cool burn of the tobacco deep in his chest. *What's the point.*

"It's probably for the better," Roman said quietly, as if reading his thoughts. "Everyone here seems kind of... lost. Like they've just woken up from a deep sleep but fight to remember the dream. Someone was asking for you, though..." he trailed off, brow once again furrowing in frustrated concentration.

"Who?" Carey prompted, only half caring.

It wasn't his parents. It wasn't his dead dog from ten years ago. It wasn't his sister — the living didn't tread these waters.

"I can't remember," Roman conceded, tossing his hands in defeat. "Someone big, older guy. Kept calling me 'broheem' or something, but it was a while ago."

"*Aaron*," Carey cried softly, surprised at his own elation.

He remembers. He was actually out there, something more solid than a nagging by-product of Carey's conscience. It made his guidance more wise, his comments more probing. Roman only looked confused before shrugging his shoulders, shaking his head slightly.

"Doesn't matter," Roman continued, "I doubt I'd even recognize my own reflection these days to be honest. But I'm glad that you're with her. Keila, I mean."

"I'll do my best," Carey said weakly, feeling slightly faint.

His head was spinning, as if he'd been sitting in a truck full of exhaust fumes instead of smouldering tobacco. His mind swam into a fog. It took all he had just to keep his eyes open.

"It's slipping away!" Roman cried faintly. It sounded like his voice was coming from the other end of a sewer, warbling at the edges.

A cold wind blew in the window at that moment, carrying a mist that shouldn't be into the cabin.

The last thing Carey remembered was Roman's cigarette hissing with the moisture before extinguishing entirely.

The ember glowed no longer.

VIII

The mud slogged around his ankles, finding every opening to saturate his boots.

The moonlight filtered through the trees above him, washing everything in faint speckled light. As he looked to his left, the rock hanging half in the swamp became the egg of a giant partridge, the shadows playing over it in turn.

I'm losing it.

It had felt that way ever since he'd emerged from the tomb — that place underground where he'd been trapped, begging for air as the crimson arms of the infected pressed in. He'd almost remained there forever... or at least as long as the sickness would take to blossom through his system like putrid roses.

It had been dark, smelling of cedar and rotten dreams. He had watched so many go out before him, leaving only he and one other beneath the dirt and concrete. It had once been a place of dreams, but it too had fallen along with the rest of his memories. The proper ones, anyhow.

Images passed across his vision in the dark.

Broken arms with the fingers still yearning. Teeth stained with blood, some fresh, some stale. Lips peeled back in horrid grimaces, missing in places where misplaced bites took the flesh of the owner. A man with glasses, hair pasted to his forehead with sweat as the illness ran through him like a bullet, changing him. Making him one of *them.*

He had lopped that man's arms off with an axe before he turned. The man hadn't been unconscious yet, but he hadn't screamed. Hell, he hadn't even twitched voluntarily as the iron ripped through his flesh and cartilage, tearing the limbs from his body like green branches from a willow.

It hadn't stopped the change. His wrist had been bitten. Barely a graze of teeth, just enough to break the skin. It hadn't mattered. He came around bleeding like a pig at the slaughter, eyes just as red and blank as those outside the underground sanctuary, quickly becoming a trap.

The man's glasses had fallen from his face as the creature rolled onto its side, fighting for its feet. Its bottom jaw ground against the hard cement as it used its own face for leverage, legs coming under it in the hazy glow of emergency lights.

It had only taken one whack with the axe he used to cut wood before it stopped moving. He had given it forty more to make sure it stayed that way.

An unseen bird startled as he slogged through the marsh, taking his time to be careful, calculated. It made him cringe, grind his teeth. Even then, he worried the infected would hear it. The enamel of his molars wearing into tiny fragments and pasting his tongue.

He stopped to listen, struggling to keep his jaw from clenching harder. A moment passed, with no sounds more threatening than the soft ripple of water against dead trees and crickets slowly drowning in the mire.

It hadn't been long since he'd left her. She'd been his lifeline and had taken his ticket out of this world.

She was supposed to be his wife, the one he clung to in good and bad. And she had left him. She was supposed to be the one he would ride this storm out with somewhere far from here. Far from the soldiers with faces as blank as the dead. Far from the search lights and generators. Somewhere where they could trap rabbit, make stew and sew quilts where none of these *fucking* zombies would claw at his throat. And she had left him.

When he'd noticed she was there in that underground shithole, she'd already been close to death. Her breath had been slow, her face pale. Cold sweat had slicked his palms from her forehead as he carried her out with one arm, cleaving the infected out of the way with the other.

He was going to be her knight in shining armour. He was going to be the one who rescued her and nursed her back to health. She would've learned to be thankful, in time. She would've loved him the way she should have. For such a rescue. For such a new lease on life.

Instead, she had served a higher purpose, one he couldn't quite put into words. Sacrificial lamb? No, that wasn't quite correct. She had held off the teeth of the rabid for him, but it wasn't quite that romantic.

He hadn't wanted to leave her back at that military base. She had been too kind to him for a fate like that, but at least she would be safe. He hadn't thought she had much time left, but if anyone could've helped her that late in the game, combat medics could've used their worldly charms.

She had been going cold by the time he left her at Base Alexander. When he kissed her on the forehead before he left, her skin felt like old, wet leather. *Used up.*

As he walked now through the swamp, boots sticking in the clay, one of *them* came into view.

It was walking with its arms limp at its sides, like a frustrated child playing deadweight with its parent. Although the light was dim at best, he could tell the creature hadn't noticed him yet. It wasn't calling out to the rest, like a wolf over fresh carrion. It wasn't reaching out to him, fingers twisting over each other in search of his throat.

I've got something for you right here, he thought as his fingers cocked the shotgun in his hand. The hacksaw hadn't done a pretty job of shortening the barrel, but pretty was a thing of the past now. The long, carefully polished maple stock had met the same fate, now pistol-grip length and bound in tape. The mobsters of old called it a *Lupara.* The traditional kinds had a break-open mechanism, so his six-tube pump-action probably didn't fit the mold, but titles were kind of irrelevant now too.

There was already a hot shell in the barrel, a ten-gauge slug.

He had alternated between buckshot and the more lethal slugs in the tube, unsure of which would produce greater devastating effects on the infected. After his first run-in a few miles back, he wished he'd filled his pockets with slugs. The buckshot was just too damn noisy for the results.

He walked slowly, fighting to keep the sloshing of his movement concealed from the creature. It wasn't moving, instead choosing to stand like a slowly-swaying statute in the marsh. He hadn't seen that yet, but it wasn't surprising. Nothing was that surprising anymore.

Close the distance, he thought. If he shot now, the short barrel would likely send the shot wild. He'd sawn the length down for the buckshot, foolishly thinking the spray of lead pellets would serve him better than accuracy. *Maybe against the living ones, it may just work yet.* They reacted a lot better to hits to the torso, anyhow.

As he crept at his slow, calculated pace, the infected sentinel remained quiet and still, allowing him to line up the shot. There was no way he was going to get away from it. One misplaced step and it would be on his trail like a bloodhound, calling out to the rest of its feral friends.

If he was going to be revealed, he'd rather do it on his own terms.

The next camp was still a few miles away, but he had all the time in the world to escape the rest.

His finger slipped over the trigger, feeling the cold steel salute under his grasp before cooking off the round with a blast of fury.

The loud crack rang out in the night as the head of the infected exploded into a trillion glimmers of moonlight before it started. The moans rose around him from all sides, frantic splashes echoing off the trees from every direction.

He pumped the action of the shotgun, the unseen shell splashing into the water at his feet as he began to move. The smell of burnt gunpowder spiraled upwards into his nose. It was the smell of hope. The smell of redemption. Rain began to fall, trickling in the fetid marsh all around him. He thanked the powers that were for the white noise that would be his savior.

It was time to run.

He had places to see anyways, didn't he.

IX

There were sounds all around him, but none of them made sense. It was like his mind was a radio tuned just on the outside of a clear frequency. It wasn't static, but the closest thing to it he had ever heard.

There were sounds of birds chirping in the trees. A far off waterfall, tangling with screams and the sounds of blankets rustling.

A few words drifted through the haze, but they didn't make any sense on their own. *Suction. Intravenous. STAT.*

Carey fought to open his eyes, but it was if he had lead weight sitting on his eyelids.

There was a divine rush of pain, before everything went black again.

***

Time flowed like water through his fingers.

He would open his eyes and all would be dark around him. The next time he'd slide his gritty lids open, sun would dazzle his vision before he slipped into the blackness again. Dreams of the world before sometimes haunted his aching mind. Other times, he was in the horrid bedroom of his parents again, the gnashing teeth, sour milk and spoiled meat odours spilling over him until he screamed.

He tasted blood. He tasted candy. He drank imaginary beers with his friends and went shopping at the mall in his hometown. Nothing made sense, everything bent into one giant fever dream. He knew it wasn't reality, but that realization often only prompted him back into the darkness. That clinging, nagging emptiness.

***

As the shadow of time passed, his moments of clarity became more frequent.

Carey saw faces above him and only sometimes was it the visage of his late mother.

He saw Keila alone for the first while, intermingled with Morgan. They would only hover in his failing sight for a few moments of time, but he knew they were real. He couldn't quite decipher the sounds they made when their lips moved, but more often than not, it was calming. Reassuring.

Besides the visits, he lived in a world of pain whenever he opened his eyes. It came from everywhere and nowhere all at once. His blood boiled. His head ached. His stomach tied in knots before his mind would blessedly send him spiraling back into the world of the unconscious.

The faces became more frequent and more varied. A bespectacled man with a green mask covering his face. The backs of what could only be soldiers danced in his vision before he slipped under. Even Kerrigan appeared to him a time or two before stopping quite abruptly.

Though he never saw the girls together, when Kerrigan was there he was never alone. There was a woman at his side he could only determine was Keila, though his mind knew it was a trick of the light.

It had to be Morgan under the hazy blonde hair.

Carey, through the smoke of the dreams, would feel scorpions sting at his arms before relief ran like prayers through his veins. He would wake to the bespectacled man leaning over him time and time again, feeling his head, his neck. He felt plastic on his cheeks and cool air rushing into his lungs at times, while others he couldn't draw breath in the faintest.

Those were the worst times. When he would silently begin drowning in unseen water, choking and spitting, unable to yell at the apparitions of his quickly approaching demise. After eternities had passed, he would laboriously begin breathing again, coughing and hacking upwards into the heavens.

At least the heavens didn't scream.

***

It was dark when he swam back once again, though it was far from silent.

Lights were flickering all around him, the sound of a million rifles clattering around his head. He could hear explosions rattling off in the distance and barely make out white circles of light playing across his sight.

There were cries of agony, close and far. The wind howled its anguish for what seemed like hours before he placed it. Moans.

Even through his comatose state, he knew what they were. They were the rising and falling tones of the walking dead, or whatever they were. Carey would begin to nod off once more before another concussive wave of horror would hammer over him as detonations rang out in the scattered light.

After a time, the screams were no longer distant. They were all around him, too shrill and desperate to be the words of the dead. They cried out to gods, alternately praying for salvation and cursing their fates. They pleaded for mothers to save them from their misery before they all fell silent.

As he plunged into the depths of his aching mind once more, only short, staccato pops of a handgun played his lullaby.

***

"There you are," a calm, even voice called out to him through the haze.

"W-wha?" Carey mumbled, his only reply to the strange greeting.

His vision faltered as he fought to open his eyes. It felt like someone had taped high-grit sandpaper to the inner surfaces of his eyelids as he struggled to meet the world outside.

Carey's head was sore, like he'd just gotten front-row seats to an all percussion symphony on crack and forgotten his earplugs. Everything felt strange, though he couldn't place why, as he swam up through the mired depths of his unconscious mind to the shrouded world above him.

"I'm not dead," he mumbled.

"Quite the contrary," the voice agreed, soothing and reassuring. It sounded like a more compassionate version of his father's. Perhaps a kindly old uncle he'd never had the pleasure of meeting.

The light was blinding as he slowly opened his eyes, blinking away tears as they sprung to protest the stinging rays. As his conscious mind began to come around, he could feel pricks of pain in his hand and arm. It was nothing compared to the horrid burning itch erupting on the side of his neck.

"Augh!" Carey yelped, bolting upright on the cot.

His hands leapt to the source of the nagging, penetrating itch. He clawed at the spot, finding gauze and tape underneath his fingernails, the irritating purchase far beneath the folds untouched. His head swam deliriously as a dizzy spell wracked his brain.

"Whoa, hold on there m'boy," the voice continued as strong hands grasped his shoulders, easing him back downwards onto the sheets.

The scene around him finally came into focus. Lines of cots, stained hideously crimson and black, lined the tent. Intravenous tubes ran from pumps and steel trees, forcing strangely coloured liquid from a drip-bag into his system. The light was cold and harsh, the grey day outside the tent-flap only beginning to see the sunrise. The only other soul in the room was the bespectacled man, known only to him from half-visions and fever dreams. It all made sense, but none of it came together, like a coherent puzzle smashed on the floor by an insolent child.

"What... what happened?" Carey asked weakly, the burning itch subsiding a little as he fought to stay awake. Already, the calm, vacant respite of sleep was seducing him to come back to its charms.

"You've been resting for a while, but you needed it," the unshaven man in the green fatigues chuckled, leaning in to check on his dressing.

"It hurts," Carey groaned, raising a tired hand again up to his neck, feeling a dull ache radiating in every direction from underneath the sterile gauze. It spread up to his head, down his neck to his shoulders and everywhere in between like a slow poison brutally injected at the site.

"Infection tends to be like that," the doctor continued, pressing the tape at the corners of the bandage down while batting away Carey's searching hand. "Don't touch it, now. It needs to be left well enough alone."

One word, though softly spoken by the doctor, seemed to scream above the others.

"*Infection?*" Carey cried aghast, jumping his shoulders again off the drab green cot.

It's not possible, he thought alarmingly. *No one gets better from that infection. They all go crazy. How long do I have?*

It was a simple question, but one that threatened to tear him apart. His heart beat raggedly in his chest, forcing too much oxygen to his brain, overloading his senses. Everything felt electrified. He could feel every fold of gauze on his neck, every hair on his arms brushing against the wool blanket, every pulse of cool air wafting in from outside.

I was wrong. I am dead. I just haven't gotten there quite yet.

"No-no, not that infection," the doctor reassured him, a twinge of irritation present in his tone. "I wouldn't have been able to help that. I wouldn't have so many empty beds if that was the case," he sighed with a wave of his hand towards the rows of stained, vacant cots to his right.

The doctor seemed different than the last time Carey had spoken with him, about his mother. Older somehow, like he'd gone to bed at thirty and woken up pushing fifty. His eyes were bloodshot, but the good-natured twinkle still remained somewhere deep behind the thin glasses. Wrinkles seemingly carved overnight drew crows-feet at the edges. Carey could've sworn they were missing only days ago. *Days? Weeks?* How long had it been? All of a sudden, the concept of the aging process being anything but abnormal threatened once again to steal away the calming effects of the doctor's bitter prose.

"How long have I been sleeping?" Carey asked, allowing his back to remain on the hard cot, the harsh canvas tugging a little at his skin as he adjusted himself.

"Thirty, forty hours? Small-scale coma. I could have brought you back around earlier, but your system needed the chance to recover. That was one nasty bug that you got in your neck, there," he said, pointing a finger at the dressing. "That burn should have been treated immediately when you got it, boy," he continued, chiding him.

"Burn?"

Carey searched backwards in time to find the source. It was like digging a hole in a swamp — every time he dredged up a memory, mire immediately rushed in to take its place. As his mind slogged through the battle, he found nothing. As it went further back into the flight from the gas station, he found just as little.

Wait a minute.

The spent brass casing from the sniper in the cherry-picker. All at once, it was clear as Dr. Robert's too-large nose in front of his face. That one thoughtless, *stupid* mistake.

"Right," Carey muttered, feeling the sting of his foolhardy ways throb in time with the wound beneath his ear. "How bad was it?"

"Well," Dr. Roberts sighed, "the initial wound was probably nothing, but without sterilization it got a vicious little bugger of a bacteria in there, I assume. You were burning up when you came in from the battle, but I have to be honest — it was good to have someone to work on. Someone I could do *something* for besides controlling the pain," he said, his gaze becoming distant.

For a moment, he was quiet, his pale eyes studying the empty beds in the field hospital. Carey knew of what he was speaking, but somehow it was too much to take in at once. *How many had lain here?* he thought. The battle hadn't gone on long and he hadn't witnessed any soldiers down. Whatever it was, he had no desire to bring it up — it was clear the good doctor had his fill of the events to last a thousand lifetimes.

"In any case," Dr. Roberts quipped as he snapped back to his patient, "it was almost the end of you, I won't pretty it up for you. While I'm delighted to have been able to help, you must realize you'll have to be more careful. I'm losing men to the infection daily. I can't afford to start losing them to treatable conditions as well," he chided.

"I'm... I'm sorry," Carey offered. He felt three inches tall and ten years younger as he lay on the cot, tubes that had kept the bacterial infection at bay still dripping into his veins.

"Yes, well, we beat it. You're a fighter, Carey. Even still, that almost wasn't enough. We had an... incident last night," Dr. Roberts trailed off, seeming to search for the words. "I wasn't able to get back in time to give you an injection to keep you under, so there's little doubt I think you know what I'm speaking of."

The terrifying explosions, gunshots, and screams from the fever-dream came back to him in a rush. The cries of agony all around him. The deafening roar of LAV's firing their crew-served weapons. The hiss of ventilators. The short, staccato parade of what could only have been gunfire pacing along the rows of infected troops. The final eulogy of soon to rise fallen, the doctor turned into the angel of death. It was so real, so crystal, that Carey found himself at a loss for words.

'Bout time, Aaron crooned, though his tone was anything but sarcastic. He was right. It *was* about time he learned to think of

anything but his own plight. The thought of Dr. Roberts, the kindly aging practitioner dedicated to saving enlisted lives turned into the very thing he sought to combat. He didn't take lives. He was supposed to help them continue, no matter the cost.

"The battle was... bad. The one while you were out," the doctor said, filling the claustrophobic silence. "It was raining and we didn't see them on the infrared. The marksmen only made them out on the goggles and starlight scopes when they hit the hundred-yard mark, right before they hit the minefield on the west side. By then, it was almost too late. The mines didn't do much, but it slowed them down a little. After that, well... it wasn't pleasant."

Carey lay on the cot with his eyes on the canvas roof, trying his best not to let the images of his friends flash over his vision. Already, the deep, lingering suspicion of the worst kind was alighting around his chest, making his shallow breathing even more constricted as the machines filled him full of antibiotics.

"The ones... the ones I came with..." Carey half-asked, too shaky to finish the sentence.

They died while I slept. They died while I was resting peacefully, guided downwards into the otherworld on the wings of Morphine and Demerol. It was too much to bear. Too much to ask.

"Yes, they made it through," Dr. Roberts said kindly, finding his words again. "If you're referring to the ones who visited you last night. A girl came by this morning — funny, I still haven't caught her name — looking a little disheveled but not as bad as I would have figured, given the circumstances. You've got a tough little bunch, Carey."

His bunch, as if they were soldiers in his legion. Although it couldn't have been further from the truth, the mere words were better than the strongest painkillers. It was if he had lain down for a short nap after class, rather than almost lost his life to a vicious illness. Already, his legs felt lighter, the dull ache inside his quads dissipating. His head felt clearer. Most importantly, his neck itched and throbbed just a little less. Not much, but enough to make it bearable. Anything was a good reminder he was alive. Anything was good news when his only ties in the world were still breathing.

Regardless of the relief, the fact remained that there was surgical hosing running into his vital systems and walking away from that required a little more than good news.

"How much more treatment do you think I'll need, doc?" Carey asked, instantly feeling stupid for using the pet name. He was no Bugs Bunny, so hearing the mock title come out of his mouth felt all the more foreign. If he ever had to recollect the experience later, he'd be sure to blame it on the drugs.

"Treatment? Oh, not much," the doctor said with a smile. "The worst is behind you and since you can drink on your own now, the saline drip is essentially superfluous. I'll give you an antibiotic regimen you'll have to promise me to follow, but aside from that you're free to go whenever you feel up to it."

It was odd, the concern in Doctor Robert's voice. It was like Carey was his son rather than patient and the good doctor was explaining how to cross the street, emphasizing looking both ways for traffic. There was genuine compassion in his words. That, to Carey, was something more vitalizing than all the care received while he'd wasted hours chasing dragons made of smoke and battling invisible centaurs in his dreams.

"Well," Carey mused, sitting up and placing his bare feet in the dirt, "I suppose there's no time like the present. Mind unhooking me? I'm a little worried I may make a mess," he joked, feeling jubilant in spite of the bloodstained cots lining the walls. It was to be expected from a man who previously thought himself dead, only to rise again without a hunger for flesh.

"My pleasure," Doc Roberts agreed, removing the adhesive strips holding the intravenous tubes in place.

"How many?" Carey asked, keeping his tone as somber as he could manage.

"Too many," the doctor replied, quickly sliding the needle out of his hand. "The loss of life was horrific, but the saddest part is those lives meant more today than they ever had. The men panicked once the infected reached hand-to-hand range. They put themselves in harm's way, a few of them falling into the minefield as they fled, others knocked into the paths of the automatic fire from the personnel carriers."

He ground his teeth as the doctor swabbed the small hole on the back of his hand with an alcohol pad, but didn't want to interrupt his flow. What was a little sting compared to what these men had been through?

"It seems to only take one splash of infected fluid into a small scratch on the soldiers and before long he's one of them," he continued, as if 'them' and 'us' were now clearly distinguishable titles. "We don't have new recruits to help out and those men were trained for years — some, decades — on the government's bill to get to the level of skill they possessed. Soon we'll have no one left with any real combat training to man the walls. To shore up the front line or man the crew-served weapons. Only then will we see what we're truly in for."

It must be a nasty thing, being an intellectual. It seemed like the medical professional was no stranger to losing himself in his thoughts, but it did nothing to further Carey's pursuit of the man who brought him into the world. Knowledge was power and the young Cardinal knew he was seriously lacking in that department.

"Er... right," Carey offered, trying not to fall into despair himself. The words spoken by Roberts were too real, too poignant to be ignored. While the doctor spoke of his own base, Carey could hear the sentiment echoing in his search. If he didn't get moving soon, he wasn't going to get moving at all. He was no soldier, but before long he may be the closest thing.

"The camps to the north may do better, farther away from the cities, but the reports on the radios haven't been particularly encouraging either," the doctor continued, placing a small cotton ball under a piece of tape to stop the slight bleeding. It made Carey like a child getting his boosters, deliriously waiting for a lollipop before being sent on his way. The news of other camps broke down that charade in a hurry.

"There's more?" Carey asked, forcing down the excitement in his voice. The last thing he wanted to do was sound enthusiastic about leaving before he got a better read on the situation. Jaded opinion was often worse than no opinion at all.

"Oh, yes," Dr. Roberts answered, a measure of cheer rejoining his tone. He slapped Carey on the shoulder as he sat back down on a cot, his work complete. "Two, I believe. I'm not the fountain of knowledge on the subject, but the radio operator would likely be your best bet if you're interested. There's always work to be done and the amount of men your age not currently tied up in guard duty is dwindling," he continued, seeming to mirror Carey's previous concerns.

"Thank you," Carey said, only half hearing the words. His mind was a thousand miles away. A thousand miles north.

"Your clothes are on the bed and I'll give you my leave to get dressed. I've seen more of you than I've ever wanted, m'boy," he chuckled.

The crack brought a twinge of hope back into Carey's spirit. If the doctor could laugh, he could laugh.

As Dr. Roberts walked out of the tent, Carey found his shaking feet under him. His legs quivered and protested, stiff and sore as he rose to stand, but they bore his weight just the same. His ankle was still a little rusty from the incident at the overpass a few days prior, but for a guy brought back from the grave, he felt like a million simoleons.

He stretched his arms, turning his shoulders in broad circles as he walked towards his clothes, clad in nothing but his boxers. He smiled to find them folded neatly and carefully like his mother used to. It stung a little, the memory rising unbidden in his mind, but it was a good hurt. The hurt that let him know he still cared. The hurt that reminded him no matter what may get in the way, he would never forget.

He pulled his slightly-bloodstained tee over his head and was amazed to find the developing stench of sour sweat gone from the armpits. Whatever short resources they may have at Base Alexander, the good doctor must've put in a requisition for some laundry. Probably even wrote them a script for their trouble. *Prescription — clean clothes.*

As he shrugged the cheap v-neck over his shoulders, he was surprised to see a pair of army fatigue pants waiting, folded on top of his jeans. The old denim had clearly not received the same soap treatment, but he couldn't give a shit. They had chafed his legs while he ran, constricted his movement when he'd tried to maneuver and generally been lacking in the pocket department.

The new — at least to him — drab olive green pants were exactly what he'd silently wished for the whole journey to the camp. Double-stitched knees, button waist, and plenty of pockets for all his treasures.

Fruity thing to call a gun and some bubblegum, kid.

Aaron, thank you.

As he slid them on, he was delighted to find they fit him perfectly. As he buttoned the waist and drew up his fly, he couldn't help but notice a small tear carefully mended near the left thigh.

It sent a chill down his spine, but it would be the last time he'd look at it, he swore it. To imagine someone far less fortunate than he had taken the final leap off the mortal coil in these very slacks while he slumbered was a little too much to be comfortable.

"All clear, sir," Carey called out, feeling very military professional in his new duds as he laced his boots.

"Not taking these?" Doctor Roberts said with a wave of his hand towards the cot as he entered the tent once more.

"My hat and sweater? Yeah," Carey answered, a little put off by the comment. While he appreciated the sentiment of the fresh new pants, he didn't feel too keen about giving his trucker hat and hoodie to the surplus stock.

"No-no," the doctor continued, shaking his head as he bent down near the desk. "These." He held out a large black vest and matching helmet.

"Wh-what?" Carey asked, confused and slightly wary.

The vest was obviously of the ballistic variety employed by the military — he had seen the other soldiers wearing them about their daily duties, along with the helmets. They looked a little different than the ones he saw on police officers. Bulkier. More straps. More webbing.

He wasn't sure what Doc Roberts meant, as he'd certainly never owned such implements, as much as he had craved for such resources when he left St. Albins. If taking them made him a soldier, complete with the responsibilities it entailed, he wasn't taking that deal for the world.

"Not being used anymore," Dr. Roberts said with a wan smile, obviously fighting through the bitter taste in his mouth. "While I'm not sure what value they may be to you, Captain Meyers instructed me to issue them to you. Take it or leave it, but be aware the Captain isn't likely to be making such an offer again anytime soon." He tossed the equipment onto the nearest cot. "I made sure to clean them up and sterilize them the best I could, so they *should* be safe to wear if you so choose."

Carey mulled it over for a moment as he tied his boots tightly, relieved to see the cuffs of the pants fit over the shafts of the leather. He may not be attending a fashion show anytime soon, but looking like a wiener in front of Morgan, Kerrigan and Keila wasn't high on his list of things to do.

"The vest, sure," Carey agreed after a moment, standing to pick the heavy black vest up off the bedding.

It could be of some use to him, no matter how slight. He didn't intend on getting shot, but if it could stop a bullet, it could certainly stop a set of teeth. Any protection he could get from *that* threat was worth the added weight.

"And the helmet?" Dr. Roberts asked, rummaging around in a drawer before emerging with a bottle of pills.

"No, but thank you," Carey declined sheepishly. "My hat will do just fine. I have trouble being observant as it is, let alone with that thing blocking out my peripheral vision."

"Suit yourself, but I assure you it was designed for both functionality and protection."

Carey dismissed the idea with a small shake of his head as he bent to retrieve his hat before sliding the vest over his shoulders. It was heavy on his frame, but in a safe, reassuring way. It was hopefully built to last, more than could be said of what he saw in the world he now called home.

"Er... other way around," Dr. Roberts said with a laugh, pointing at Carey's newfound body armour.

"Right," Carey said, blushing. He raised the vest back over his head to place the front facing his chest. *Stupid.*

"Here are your meds," Doc Roberts said, still chuckling as he tossed the bottle into Carey's waiting hands. "Two, twice daily. I'd say with food, but it's a bit of a formality."

"Gracias," Carey replied, shoving the bottle into one of his magnificent new pockets before pulling on his trucker hat.

"If you would like some pain killers, I'd be more than happy to send some your way. There aren't many your age who turn down such a thing either, so what do you say? Little Oxycotin to take off the edge?"

"No," Carey snipped abruptly. His mind was a million miles away as he checked the pockets of his hoodie, still draped on the cot. *It's missing.* "I... I think something got misplaced," Carey stammered.

Dr. Roberts peered down his nose at Carey, a small smile again alighting around the corners of his mouth.

"Ah, that," he remarked, turning back to a trunk against the wall, bound shut with a heavy steel lock.

"Oh, thank god," Carey commented a wash of relief pouring through him. To think of that last remainder of his mother buried along with a pile of slaughtered infected was too much to consider.

He emerged with a slightly grimy-looking extendable baton and the Taurus revolver, the single bullet sitting neatly in his palm beside it. *What's with these people and pointing out I only have one bullet! I get it, already!* he thought, irritation rising in his chest.

While it came as a slight consolation to see his well-travelled companions hadn't been tossed aside in the shuffle, the prize he sought was still firmly out of view.

"A ring," he said, hollowly, taking his arsenal and placing it on the bed. "A gold ring."

Recognition poured over the doctor's face before he turned back to the trunk.

"That was part of the records and you're lucky I got it back in there before the Captain noticed," Dr. Roberts answered quietly. "It'll be safe there, Carey. You'll be able to get it when this is all over, but for now you have to leave it," he finished, turning back to face Carey with something in his hands.

"That's not mine, either," Carey said dejectedly, miserable at the thought of leaving his mother's ring in a camp full of strangers, but seeing no alternative.

"It is now, if you want it," the doctor said, still holding out the pistol and holster in his hands towards Carey. "Last bit of goodwill from Captain Meyers. He wants everyone armed who can be armed, given the recent decrease in active-duty troops."

Carey examined the pistol for a second before taking it without further hesitation.

"SIG Sauer P220 Combat semi-auto, chambered in .45 ACP. Eight in the mag, one in the tube when fully loaded," Dr. Robert's rattled off, sounding more like a gunnery sergeant than a medical professional. "Safety on the right side and it has a crisp trigger, so pull quickly; magazine release on the left side behind the trigger on the grip."

Carey pressed the small button and the clip indeed dropped out into his waiting hand from the grip. Glimmering brass bullets winked back at him. *Hmm,* Carey thought, the faintest trace of boyhood amazement stirring in his soul. The rifle hadn't been his. *This* was.

"Ammo, if I need it?" Carey asked.

Awestruck, he forgot to thank the good doctor for his charity as he strapped the holster to his right thigh, tightening the straps snugly before jamming the pistol inside.

"Available just about anywhere and everywhere. There's crates of the stuff all over the camp, more than food and water put together."

"How about for this one?" Carey asked, waving at the Taurus Model 85 sitting on the bed, looking very lonely with its one shiny brass friend so far away from its chambers.

The doctor plucked the bullet from Carey's palm and turned it over for a moment before shaking his head.

"Thirty-eight cal isn't a military favourite, so I'm afraid you're going to be out of luck. It doesn't pack much punch beyond a hundred yards, which the higher-ups have deemed too close for comfort in our present scenario," he said, adjusting his glasses on his nose before handing it back to Carey's waiting hand. "Besides," he continued, "it would be generous to assume you could even hit a tree outside of fifty yards with that little belly-gun, let alone a bobbing brain-case while the pressure is on."

Dr. Robert's analysis of his weapon may have been spot on, but it didn't stop him from feeling a twang of disappointment. The Taurus tranformed from an omen of his impending death into something similar to a luck talisman, much like a severed rabbit's foot. To hear it wasn't good for much in the present day besides the original reason for which he purchased it wasn't welcome news. He breathed a small sigh as he popped the round into the exposed chamber before slapping the spinerette back into the housing.

On his shoulder lay a large pocket, likely home to a radio handset for long range communication. Since tactical worth was still dear to the Green Machine, he likely wouldn't be graced with one anytime soon. The revolver made the Velcro pocket its homely abode. *Yeah, until I need to splatter my grey matter all over the place. Great.*

Reluctantly accepting the fact, he drew on his hoodie before jamming his other belongings in assorted niches and crannies lining the thick black Kevlar. His sweater fit comfortably over the vest, but with the warm day beginning to steam towards twenty degrees outside, he doubted it would last long.

"Are you quite sure about the painkillers?" the doctor asked, obviously concerned about the way he winced as the fabric grazed his dressing.

"Quite," Carey remarked, trying his best to keep on a steely visage. *Glenfiddich may do the trick, though*, he thought.

The image of Morgan — the original leggy bitch — flashed across his mind, followed by Keila hammering rounds out into the night. He winced again, this time completely unrelated to the brand on his throat.

Looks like you have some 'splainin' to do, mano, Aaron mocked as Carey thought back to his previous encounters. The battle hadn't been the place to get into shades of grey, but he doubted Keila had forgotten about the little interlude she'd walked right smack dab in the middle of.

Carey walked towards the door and offered his hand. It was the unspoken thank you he simply couldn't put into words. How did you thank someone for saving your life? How did you offer appreciation to one who pulled you back from the depths?

Dr. Roberts only met his eye and nodded, grasping his hand firmly in his own. The world had to maintain some civility, after all.

The dazzling day forced him to pull down his black trucker hat to keep the daggers out of his eyes. While Dr. Roberts had said that the loss of life had been dramatic, as his vision adjusted to the light it staggered him to see such a profound difference in the camp.

Many of the makeshift tents lining the edges of trucks and shipping containers were gone, the canvas and tarps neatly folded and laid down beside bedrolls in their place. The usual white noise of chatter and gunfire was gone, replaced with only the occasional blast echoing out from the walls. The soldiers who had strode in number back and forth like marching ants between crates of ammunition and the cherry-pickers were no longer. Only a few soldiers tallied here and there, cleaning weapons and making repairs to chinks in their body-armour with pilfered sewing kits. *They died while I slept*, he thought. *They died without me*.

To think that all three of his small bands number had ridden through the storm unharmed was ludicrous, given the circumstances, but the doctor had said it was so. Nagging doubt pressed on his temples. *What if they just never made it to the tent? What if they were pushed with the LAV's into pits with the rest of the corpses? What if they're still wandering out there, begging for it all to end but unable to scream?*

He shook his head hard to clear the thought, but a small part held valiantly on, refusing to be ignored.

The mess tent was his only destination, the only place he knew where they could be. His legs were weak and wobbly, his stomach growling with undeniable hunger. With the handgun strapped to his leg, he felt more like Dirty Harry than ever, but it wasn't a triumphant persona. It was more like walking the desert without anyone to back him up, left completely alone. He'd never seen the movies but if there were any parallels to be drawn, his mind was working overtime to make the connections.

Just don't blow your leg off, Aaron chuckled, raising a similar small laugh from Carey as he navigated the tent city. Drawing the SIG from its holster, he double-checked to make sure the safety was indeed still firmly on.

Finding the pistol hadn't turned against him, he placed it back in the holster, praying that his next misadventure with firearms would be more effective than his last. Even the thought of the C7 bucking wildly in his arms made a slight blush rise in his face as the few soldiers around him field-stripped their own weapons, taking care to oil every piece of exposed steel.

He yearned for such knowledge, but the idea of formally joining their ranks to protect the meek and innocent wasn't going to happen. The weak protecting the weak was almost worse than having no protection at all. He didn't deserve to stand on the frontlines amongst them. The pistol weighed heavy and reassuring in his hand, but knowledge or not, an assault rifle strapped across his shoulders would've been far more calming.

The mess hall came firmly into view, still standing resolute in the April sunshine on its steel poles. The canvas looked no worse for wear which was also reassuring. The thought of infected having breached the perimeter for even a moment while he recovered in the medical centre was poisonous to his morale, even in the calming glow of the early morning sun.

Guards stood sentry by the provisions truck as usual, but their faces no longer held steely gazes. One even nodded at Carey as he passed towards the mess. He returned it nonchalantly, but didn't know what to think of it. Were they acknowledging him now because he'd been proven a warrior or just because they had fewer brothers in arms left to talk to?

The vest was tight around his shoulders as he closed the final steps. It constricted his chest, forcing him to consider readjusting the straps as he paused to catch his breath. *Is it the vest? Or are you just afraid to face facts, bud? Don't feel like dredging up demons this early in the day, do you? Swearing on a dead man's life to protect someone may do that*, Aaron observed. Carey imagined him standing behind a lectern, adjusting out-of-place spectacles on his ghostly nose. *I'm going, I'm going.*

Carey walked through the open doors of the mess, the lack of bodies at the tables again causing an uncomfortable spasm in his stomach. The benches were no longer teeming with fatigued men in arms. Quite the contrary, he witnessed as he took in the tent looking for his friends. *Please just let more be out on rotation,* he thought. *Anything but cooling six feet under, piled on one another.*

Finding his *compadres* fully upright and still breathing was the single most beautiful sight he'd ever witnessed in his short twenty-two years, a second small blow followed the first.

Keila, Kerrigan and Morgan sat together at a repurposed picnic bench, but something about their seating arrangement sent a grim message beneath their animated chatter. Kerrigan and Morgan sat on opposite sides of the table. That part wasn't all that surprising, given that Morgan had some less than kind things to say about the enormous blonde bastard. Keila, however, sat directly beside him, her shoulder pressed against his, painfully visible even in the relative gloom of the tent. *She's not supposed to be there,* he thought.

A simple equation. One plus one equaled two. Carey plus Keila, plus a picnic bench equaled shared seating. Something minor, trivial, but it shot sour bile up the back of his throat.

Did Morgan tell her something? he wondered, praying it wasn't the case.

Some part of him wished it had been a matter of chance; some random decision without any thought behind it that led to the odd arrangement. Reading into things had often gotten him in trouble over the years, but he'd learned from years as a bouncer that often the most innocent gestures could contain blades and poison.

"Carey!" Morgan cried as she spotted him standing near the open door.

She leapt to her feet, her face opening up in pure jubilance. Her eyes were wide, her black hair tossing as he rushed towards him, wrapping her arms around his shocked frame. Her grasp was stronger than he anticipated, pinning his arms at his sides under her passionate bear hug. He squeaked out a sound, aiming for something friendly but emerging mouse-like and frail.

After a moment, she pushed him back and held his elbows at length, looking him up and down in his new clothes. Immediately, Carey regretted playing dress-up before reuniting with his friends. He felt like the only one in costume at a feigned Halloween party, where he was to be the source of everyone else's entertainment.

"New duds," Morgan observed as she linked her arm in his, guiding him towards the table.

There was no condescending tone in her voice. It was completely out of character for the sultry Barbie doll from Hell he had previously known, but somehow it was reassuring. *At least someone is happy to see me.*

Keila and Kerrigan had half-risen to their feet. Keila had a look of bemused interest all over her face, though if it were made of paint it would have been full of cracks. It was too forced to be real; her eyes gave it away. Those *goddamn* aqua-marines, so much less vivid than Morgan's emerald, so much more telling than her brother's.

Her brother, Carey thought, feeling another pang of loss as he took a seat at the table beside Morgan.

"So, I guess you lived," Kerrigan observed keenly.

The smug look on his face would have been fitting for a professor unleashing the secrets of the universe on society, had his statement not been so mind-numbingly stupid.

"Yeah," Carey said with a cough, reeling at the cold shoulder he was receiving from Keila.

No matter how large and intimidating the blonde idiot next to her might have been, Carey took no small pleasure noticing that he wore no vest or holster. Just that same damn expensive t-shirt with the bloody sequins strategically sewn on.

Keila sat silently beside him, barely touching but so much more than distant. She didn't weep at Carey's feet, thanking the heavens above that he had indeed pulled through. She didn't shower him in kisses, making up for each and every one she missed giving him while he recovered in slumber.

She just looked at him doe-eyed while Morgan chattered excitedly about the marvels of modern medicine, taking no care to avoid calling Carey stupid, inconsiderate and worrisome as she playfully punched his shoulder. Each light tap on his arm made his resolve a little stronger. *We'll make this right*, he thought. *We'll find them.* It would set the world back in order. It would bring light back to that which was dark. *I fuckin' hope, anyway*, he thought.

"Nice vest," Keila finally said when Morgan piped down, a touch of sarcasm present in her tone.

"I hope it helps," Carey replied quietly, rubbing his neck with his hand, again feeling more out of place than he ever had in his entire life. *Third wheel? I think we're up to about seventh or eighth now.*

"I passed up on that offer," Kerrigan observed, looking down his nose at Carey's Kevlar. "I took the gun, but I won't be needing that prissy shit. Just gotta knock 'em down before they get close, after all."

Keila burst out laughing at the almost-joke, animatedly patting his tanned brawny arm and wiping feigned tears from her eyes. Carey almost joined in. He stopped dead when he realized she wasn't being patronizing.

She actually likes him, he thought, quite taken aback at the grim realization. *She's throwing herself at him like paint to a canvas. It's bloody textbook.*

Kerrigan let out a hearty guffaw before setting his fork back to work on his MRE, shoveling the cold rice past his too-perfect teeth. *What a warm reception.*

Keila's hand ceased its incessant patting, coming to rest on the bear-man's thick forearm and there it remained. It sat on his tanned skin like a dead fish, dirty fingernails on smooth flesh. It was a white flag of surrender. *Give it up and move on*, it screamed. *I don't need you anymore.*

He looked up from the table to see Keila gazing down her nose at him as well, eyes half-lidded and cold. *Well I guess that seals that.* Carey erked a little closer on the bench to Morgan. Her leather-clad thigh brushed against his new fatigues, but she didn't move it. *You wanna play? We'll play.*

"You gonna eat, or just play mime?" Morgan quipped, snapping him out of his miasma.

She had a point. His stomach growled and lurched beneath the vest, a bottomless pit in the centre of his gut. *Touché.*

"Yeah," he remarked, blessing the opportunity to walk away for even a moment.

He took his MRE from the truck under the soldier's watchful eye. Upon asking for a heat-pack, he got nothing but a laugh in return. Camp fuel and kerosene were being reserved for when the petrol truck ran dry — a situation that was coming closer to fruition by the hour.

"The nighttime assaults have been getting worse," the taller soldier explained, quite unapologetically. "We've been burning more and more gas just to keep the search lamps lit not only for the marksmen, but for the combat engineers and their minefields."

"*Minefields,*" the shorter exclaimed, his Northern Ontario drawl drawing it out. "They don't *need* legs. It just makes them harder to hit when they're on the ground."

"We've been getting hit at all hours, but we can't keep them at a distance once it gets dark like we can in the day. The lights just aren't strong enough and we keep getting overwhelmed," he continued, ignoring the stockier soldier and his unhelpful observations.

"Never can come on our schedule, can they?" the northerner continued, his shrill voice grating on Carey's patience. "I still think they're like vampires. They come out in the night, don't they? Soon as we can go for a supply run I'm tryin' out the garlic, no matter what the Cap' thinks!"

Carey considered correcting the man, but found he lacked the testicular fortitude. The superstitious soldier still had a rifle, after all.

He had a cold meal, and that was that.

Carey took his seat back beside Morgan, again sliding a little closer than chance would casually allow. The cold meal-ready-to-eat would have been far from enjoyable — or even palatable — in his previous life, but as a man roused from the dead he dug into its cold confines as if it were a Thanksgiving cornucopia.

"It was scary," Morgan confided as the mellow conversation turned back from the mundane to the previous battle. "They don't move like a shoal of fish or a flock of birds," she observed, twirling a rogue noodle around her fork. "They don't move as *one*, they just... *move*. They fall over each other until they pile up, but then more just kept coming over the top."

"Kill't probably around a hundred on my own," Kerrigan bragged, holding an invisible rifle up to his eyes and miming the shots. "They all fall the same when you knock'em between the eyes."

"Sure you did," Morgan mocked, placing her utensil back on the table and lacing her fingers. "How about those ten you got with your fists?"

"Oh ha-ha," he shot back. "Least I wasn't snoozin' in the nursery while everyone else was out doing the *real* work," he said, slicing as if with a knife.

The invisible blade cut Carey to the bone. In his younger years, the spark would have set his rage aflame, sending him into a burning anger singeing everything around him without any regard to the victims. This time, it merely sunk him lower. He *had* slept. And it wasn't a heroic action that landed him there. He'd been stupid and paid the price. Well, others had paid it for him, anyway. His guilt would be his own cross to drag. Keila's lips pursed, but she far from raised her voice against her new *paramour*.

"Shut *up*," Morgan hissed, slamming her fists down on the table.

The already-quiet tent fell dead silent. Kerrigan's eyes leapt open, his lips peeling away from his teeth in a sneer.

"You don't know how he feels, you asshole," she continued, fists quivering on the picnic bench. "You don't know what's going through his head, so shut your damn *mouth*."

Kerrigan's initial shock quickly dissipated into apparent general distaste, but he didn't have any malice left to spread. He merely pushed his empty MRE tray away from his place and folded his broad arms across his chest, seemingly resolved to silence.

What the hell was that? Carey thought in bemused curiosity, still stinging from the attack on his character. He didn't know whether to be grateful that the gorgeous woman beside him was standing up for him, or furious that she was fielding his questions. *I'll take "What Is Some Damn Confusing Shit" for five hundred, Alex.*

Carey glanced across the table at Keila, expecting to see her sitting stock still, eyes wide with surprise, but found the opposite.

Her bottom jaw trembled as she examined her feet under the picnic bench, stare resolutely held to the dirt to avoid his eye.

So, sort her out, Aaron advised quietly. *Take her outside and spill your friggin' guts. It's not like it can make it any worse.*

I'll just tell her tonight when we go to bed, he replied silently, dropping his own gaze to the mangled husk of his meal. *When we go to bed.* That's when it would all come out, everything laid in the open for her to see. He didn't know how she would react in the quiet confines of the blue tarpaulin tent, but at least they would be alone. Any sort of privacy would be better than the strange triangles forming in the group, sitting silently in the mess tent.

At length, small, trivial conversation started up again between the four. It conscientiously steered away from any talk of Carey's absence and even further away from the previous night's siege. That dead horse had been flogged into oblivion with one small comment. Kerrigan talked about his desire to get into one of the cherry pickers and try his hand with a rifle. Morgan spoke of how much she wished she had brought a change of clothes — *those military duds are just so enormous!* Keila only giggled quietly at the exchanges, piping in a word here or there to let them know she hadn't fallen asleep. She wouldn't meet his eye, but Carey wasn't all that fixated at finding it anymore. That issue had been laid to rest until they laid themselves to rest the same way.

The foursome eventually rose to their feet, discarding the remnants of their begotten daily bread into the mostly-empty bin in the corner before stepping back out into the sunshine. The glorious rays registered on Carey like the leaves of a plant, revitalizing him with strength and energy as if he had solar cells stitched into his skin.

Standing in the warm spring breeze, Carey relayed the information gleaned from Dr. Roberts about the other camps and the radio operator he sought to speak with. It would only be a quick jaunt to the other side of the camp if the doctor's directions proved reliable, but hopefully it would be the most productive fifty-metre trip he'd make in his entire life.

They all listened attentively — even Kerrigan pulled his head out of his ass long enough to genuinely find interest in the recent news. Carey finished, waiting in silence for Keila to offer her company. It would have been a perfect time to get away for a bit without the Gruesome Twosome, but she only zipped up her sweater and looked towards the gate at his unspoken prompting. *Guess not.*

"I'll come," Morgan quipped enthusiastically, already taking a step away from the small circle.

Carey turned it over for a moment before nodding his approval. Part of him wanted to grab her by the shoulders, screaming that she'd done quite enough for the time being. In the end, the desire to have any companionship after his stint in the dark won out, quieting the blinding rage threatening to spill from his lips. His pulse slowed as he pasted a smile on his face, faker than a Mona Lisa print, but it would do.

"We already promised to help the soldiers clear bodies from the field," Keila remarked with a wave of her hand towards Kerrigan. "It's really the least we can do, after all they've done for us. We should really try to contribute any way we can," she concluded, her immature voice rattling with a condescending flair.

"Hopefully there'll still be a few left crawling to put down," Kerrigan said with a roar of laughter, a pistol identical to Carey's appearing in his hand seemingly from nowhere.

He racked back the slide with a loud metallic series of clicks. It would usually slide a bullet into the empty tube by way of the magazine. The chamber must have already been loaded, as an unfired round spiraled out of the ejector, landing in the dirt at his feet. Carey pitied the handgun, the owner even more.

"Plenty more where that came from," Kerrigan said, laughing again, kicking the round with his shoe, sending the bullet skittering out of sight beneath a crate.

Carey felt the trademark heat rising in his face. His lungs wanted to boom with fury, cursing the stupidity of the man involuntarily thrust upon him as a compatriot. The anger abated as he watched him walk away with Keila towards the gate, stuffing the pistol into the rear waistband of his jeans like a street tough. Hopefully, he would sit down too hard in the near future and find himself one cheek short of an ass.

Not all that romantic maybe, but the thought was enough to keep his temper down as he walked off towards the radio operator's last known whereabouts.

Stupidity always had a way of working itself out.

X

The radio operator proved to be an easy find. He perched in the highest cherry-picker beside a marksman merrily plugging round after round into the would-be glorious day outside. Would be, had the taking of life — infected or not — become so damn common it was beginning to scare him.

He remembered mere days ago — days that felt like months — how he had felt as he bludgeoned a man's hand to pieces with his baton. The horror of the skin peeling from the knuckles. He had been terrified of the lumbering grey dogs pressing in on all sides, but later when he rested, he had wondered about that man seat-buckled in that automobile hell. He had thought about his family, his history. He had still been a person to some degree, despite his homicidal tendencies. Serial killers still had human rights. Child murderers still got three squares a day in prison.

At that time, he supposed the infected weren't all that different in his eyes. They were lost souls, possessed by a disease, wandering helplessly to their urges brought on by a virulent devil. They were one far beyond their power to control.

Now, they represented something larger. The outside world had always been a dangerous place to tread alone, but never had it felt so claustrophobically harmful. The camp was already becoming a six-by-six cell, complete with steel caging him in on all sides. The violence no longer made his skin crawl or his stomach clench. With each loud *crack* from the cherry picker, another one was falling. Another infected. Another grey dog. Another goddamn hindrance in his journey to find his father.

He wondered how he could explain it to Morgan as they drew nearer to the edge of the camp. He could almost picture her reaction when the time would finally come to leave the confines of the base and seek out on his only remaining purpose. *To find my father.*

Why? she would ask. She undoubtedly had parents too. Family somewhere, at least remained, or at least could have, yet she hadn't once brought up a fool's errand to find loved ones.

Because I have to. It was his only response and even in his head it sounded stupid and juvenile.

He wasn't a hero in a film, cast to portray the everyman's struggle against the world. He was a twenty-one year old kid, scared to hell that the only connection he had to his previous life had vanished as quietly and insignificantly off the face of the earth as his mother had.

But why?

It was a nagging question that had tugged at the corners of his mind like an insolent child since he first read the email in St. Albins in his rented half-a-house. *But why?*

So he could reconcile his fate, after neglecting the ones who raised him for so long? It had just seemed right, but he hadn't had to explain it to anyone then. Convincing himself had required no effort — even Aaron hadn't been able to hold him back then.

But you didn't think anyone would die for it.

The realization dawned on him and his feet filled with lead. He hadn't intended to have anyone to rely on, but he also hadn't considered anyone would have had to rely on *him*. Already, three lives had come to a screeching halt because of his actions. Four, if his worst fears about his father were ever confirmed.

Do you really want to put more on the line with this one?

The idea of bringing them with him suddenly seemed something even worse than a bad idea. It sounded like outright murder.

"You coming?" Morgan called from a few metres ahead.

His feet had stopped their usual routine duties as the internal struggle threatened to tear him apart. *Shit.*

So are you? Aaron questioned him, referring to something far darker than catching up with his female accomplice.

"Yeah, yeah," Carey shrugged it off, jogging slightly to reach her side.

The sniper was blasting round after round into the afternoon warmth, sending glittering brass cases careening down to earth in lazy arcs. Carey's hand involuntarily shot to the patched wound on his neck, watching wisps of smoke curl up from one that rolled near his boot. *Not making that mistake twice.* Morgan was hypnotized, watching them spin through the air until they landed in the dirt with a metallic tinkle.

Carey carefully walked around to the left side of the boom crane, away from the raining shells and looked up to the radioman. He was busy fidgeting with something in his hands — *probably a radio, you genius,* Aaron chided — and took no notice of the pair beneath him.

"Hey!" Carey called, only to be drowned out by a .50 calibre bullet being sent to its death. That gun was friggin' loud — more an artillery barrage than a varmint rifle.

"*Hey!*" Carey tried again a little louder after a pause. Once again, the marksman chose that exact moment to end a life. *Fucking Christ.*

"HEY, UP THERE!" Carey bellowed in anticipation of a bullet that didn't come.

His voice raw and his face turning red, both men in the picker jumped a little before casting puzzled glares down in his direction. Morgan laughed and gave him a small shot in the ribs. He couldn't help remembering Keila roaring with glee and slapping Kerrigan's arm the same way. That thought quickly transformed into Morgan on top of him in the tent, wearing nothing but a motorcycle jacket and a smile. *Oops. That's enough sin for one week.* He just rubbed his neck some more, praying it would drain the blood away from his cheeks faster as the crane descended once more to earth.

In a heartbeat, he was eye level with yet another rough-looking man toting a spool of wire and an oversized radio handset. The marksman dropped the clip from the rifle, gave a small smirk to his compatriot and lumbered off towards the porta-potty nearby.

"You mind if I ask you a couple questions?" Carey asked, feeling like a lackluster reporter rather than a man on a mission. Some transformations required time. Unfortunately, time was something in rather short supply.

"*What?*" the soldier boomed, leaning towards Carey until his cigarette breath was deep in his nostrils. Shaking his head, the soldier dug into his ears with his fingers, plucking out small yellow earplugs from deep within.

"You're trying to talk on a radio with those?" Carey commented, biting his lip to stifle a giggle. *How stupid!* The point of the picker was to get better reception or something wasn't it? What the hell was the point if you couldn't *hear* it! Carey fought hard to keep the outburst thoroughly contained, his diaphragm working in and out in rapid heaves.

"Not talk," the soldier chided, obviously finding Carey's prod to be a personal affront rather than a humourous observation. "Morse code."

Carey burst out in full laughter, unable to contain it anymore. The military was worried about the *zombies* decrypting and intercepting their communications? He had heard some things in his day, but this was just ridiculous. The irony drove the wind from his lungs in howling tunes, the cackling of a deranged silent film villain.

The infantryman and Morgan exchanged bemused glances and shrugged their shoulders, but waited for the fit to pass all the same. Besides, it wasn't like they hadn't seen stranger in the previous days.

When Carey settled enough to share the cause of his minor breakdown into hysterics, the soldier's amusement changed to frustration.

"Morse code can be heard farther, you fucking idiot," he grumbled under his breath, rubbing his temples with his fingertips. "Listening to static is a waste of time, this is all arranged. You can interpret little beeps through the crackle a hell of a lot better than words, thank you very much 'ya smartass. Do you really think I don't have better things to do with my time?"

The razor sharp retort made Carey shrink to a monumental three inches tall. His abs and sides were sore from laughter, but the grin was wiped clean off his face. He'd made some silly assumptions in his time, but this about took the worm-filled cake.

Morgan took the opportunity to burst into hysterics herself. She slapped the back of his vest and much like Keila's display with Kerrigan, he felt it. This wasn't about to just disappear. He considered snapping at her, screaming at her to cut the shit, but he'd had enough outbursts for one day in the wasteland.

"S-sorry," Carey mumbled sheepishly, feeling dumber than ever.

"So, what did you want?" the radioman asked, reminding Carey of his purpose and bringing him back from the wallow in self-loathing.

"Camp to the north, what do you know about it?" he asked, trying to sound as informed and direct as possible to counter his horrible first impression.

"Camps, you mean," the soldier replied, a small smirk alighting to the edges of his mouth. He was clearly glad to still have the upper hand over this dumbass suburban white kid. "Two that we've found anyway. There are a few small pockets of entrenched resistance here and there, but only two worth a damn after the last few waves of infected. Camp Robinson, currently in some dire straits and Forward Base Jackal — y'know, for the special operations regiment that set it up. Buncha former C-SOR guys, all formerly JTF-2... that's Joint Task Force 2," he elaborated with raised eyebrows at Carey's obvious confusion. "The Jackals, they call 'em. They always find a way — it's their fucking motto after all. Those guys always get the coolest names, better than Queen's Own Rifles," he mocked with a slap to his shoulder crest. "Robinson's set up a little larger, but I know the Jackals can handle themselves. Been running interference operations with the hordes ever since that raid last night. Really helping to keep 'em off our asses."

"Oh," Carey said, taking a moment to absorb it all before spitting out the question sitting on his tongue like a hot ember. "Have any survivors shown up at either in the last few days?"

He tried to play it off, but the desperation in his voice must have leaked through by the way the operator narrowed his eyes. It was like his very intentions were being examined by x-rays.

"Who are you looking for?" he asked, seeing straight through with laser-guided precision.

"My dad," Carey answered, quietly, trying to keep as much emotion out of his voice. He didn't need to turn this into a pity-fest.

"We're not relaying civilian presences except for high-value assets," he answered after studying Carey for a moment with his hazel eyes. "Trying to keep the rest of the survivors where it's safe, so they don't get slaughtered trying to find each other. We lost too many in the first days that way," he continued, quite pointedly emphasizing the hazard.

"I understand, but—"

"But nothing," the soldier cut him off, though his voice was gentle. "We had six year-old kids sneaking under the fences in the middle of the night because we said mommy could possibly be alive somewhere else. In that case, mom disappeared in the forest trying to find the daughter, now they're both as good as dead. Hope is good, but it will destroy you if you let it do the thinking for you."

"Well could you just ask over the radio?" Carey asked, trying not to plead. The next step would be groveling and he hoped it wouldn't come to that. "Just one quick question — just tell me how and I'll knock off the beeps myself. I just need some closure," he sighed, true intentions bared.

"I wish I could," the soldier replied. He splayed his palms in the air, letting his radio dangle by the strap on his webbing. "Batteries suck up a lot of juice and the priority today is finding some more gas for that helicopter. Bugged out a couple of days ago, full of all the supplies and specialists we could spare for Camp Robinson. Camp Alexander is the best fitted around, in no short measure of our training," he said with a waggle of the radio, as if he had done it all single-handedly over the airwaves.

Carey felt his frustration abate, the true nature of his reality once again sinking in. He didn't want to, but it was the nature of his circumstance. And everyone in this circumstance was far more valuable than they had been.

"Did they bring medicine?" Morgan asked, seemingly out of nowhere. "Or are there still stockpiles here?"

Carey had expected a courtesy query about her family — like anyone would wonder, but the question took him completely by surprise. She may have had a little first-aid training he didn't know about, but she was no nurse and he was no doctor. Though Carey looked at her, for a split second he thought he saw something else in her eyes. Before he could place it, it was gone, like the afterimages remaining from the flash of a camera. One moment they danced in your vision, the next they unapologetically vanished without saying goodbye.

"We're outfitted for the time being," the operator replied evenly, apparently also picking up on the strange nature of her inquiry. Instead of asking why, he merely stared at her and let the silence do the talking.

"I'm on some meds... I just wanted to make sure I would be alright," she answered cryptically, staring at her boots.

"Well, talk to the medical corpsman. He's got a few of everything, so I'm told," the soldier replied with a wave of his hand, dismissing the topic from the urgent corners of the conversation.

Carey lingered for a moment, taking a second to ponder her words before brushing it aside himself. *Meds?* He hadn't seen her take anything.

Oh, you have her medical history? Maybe she's embarrassed — if it's epilepsy, she just doesn't want to seize and piss herself in front of you. Get your head out of your ass, Aaron observed coolly.

It had been an underlying thought, but Aaron's poignancy disturbed him at times. He wasn't about to scratch at his ears, screaming *GET OUT OF MY HEAD* just yet, but he hoped it wouldn't come to that.

He was right. It wasn't worth dwelling on and it could be dealt with at a later date. This was his opportunity to gather information, not gather dust. As if on cue, a small light bulb illuminated his mind. Not a blinding stroke of brilliance, but the Cardinal wit began to churn.

"So Robinson's doing worse than Forward Base Jackal?" Carey remarked.

"Yep," he said, pulling his canteen and drawing a long swig. "That's why we sent the airlift. The spec-op's kids are the best of the best, taught early on to make do with what they have and repurpose to account for what they don't. Y'know, how to make an IV from a marinade injector and a water bottle and all that MacGuvyer shit. Jackals are too busy keeping the heat off us to account for many refugees though, so Robinson's bearing the load. They don't get assaulted as much with Jackal nearby, but they're burning through supplies alarmingly fast."

That has to be where he is, then Carey thought, picturing his father sharing a bunk with an entire family. *He deserves better than that for his sacrifices.*

"How far is Camp Robinson from here?" Carey asked, steeling his voice with all the will he had. "The remnants of the Canadian Forces saved us and I feel we have a heavy debt to repay. If the chopper's there, I can probably help. I was in school for aeronautical mechanics before this shit went down," he lied through his teeth, trying to mirror the soldier's speech for all he was worth to better sell the feint. "It's the least I can do, keeping that bird up and whirlin'."

Morgan shifted at his side, but stayed blissfully silent. She saw through it without a doubt, but he prayed the radio operator could be played easier than a rough and tumble leather princess from hell. A good part of him just hoped 'aeronautical mechanics' actually existed, being a title possibly regurgitated from some Discovery special rather than a creation of his desperation.

The soldier keenly observed Carey for a moment before clapping him on the shoulder with a short laugh.

"That's a far better idea than setting off after a poppa that isn't there," he chuckled callously, though his eyes sparkled like opals.

Carey ground his teeth, again at odds with his anger. *Temper, temper son. Better keep it in check.* It felt like anything could set him off these days. His previous eternal patience built up through years perfecting the craft of bar security had begun to erode, crackling through to the black abyss of unbridled rage brooding underneath in silence.

"That wouldn't actually be a half bad idea," the radioman remarked, clearing his throat. "Lost our last tradesman a few nights ago, that asshole. Ran clear into the minefield when an infected lady caught him by surprise. Blew his legs clear off, didn't last long either."

As the soldier unfolded a map from his chest pocket, Morgan and Carey exchanged a small glance. It was the first they had in some time, but the unspoken feeling conveyed was mutual. Relief, tinged with dread. Carey had sold it, but what exactly had he sold them into?

"Robinson's up here, to the northwest," he pointed with a thick gloved finger, "and Jackal's over here to the east of it." The three spots on the map of the region were no more than a few inches apart, but Carey had a feeling the trek might seem longer than that. A little ink dot on an impersonal map. Is that what his future had come to? He traced a line across the page with his eyes, but beside a clump of green bisected by a series of grey lines, the map revealed nothing.

"You can take this," the soldier furthered, extending the map. "This is a freebie too," he said, passing over a pristine explorer's compass, looking very much unused with the exception of small notches running along the edge. Carey recognized them from when he used to open pop-top bottles with his lighter when a proper opener was out of reach. *Classy.*

"You'll have to get permission from the Cap before you go, but I'll soften him up for you. It's not every day we get someone with aeronautical expertise — you could be the only one we have besides the pilot now."

The thought of the verti-bird crashing into the new wastes because of his inexperienced mockery of a flight-check was daunting, but that could be dealt with when he got there. He needed a hall pass and this particular teacher wasn't handing them out to just anyone.

"What about a GPS?" Carey asked, staring at the alien map and compass in his hands.

He couldn't journeyman his way out of a hallway with one exit, let alone carve triumphantly across the godless plains with grey dogs nipping at his heels at every corner.

"Yeah, right," the soldier said, laughing in his face. "I haven't used those things since basic and that map to me isn't worth the paper it's printed on. If we go out on patrol and I have the misfortune of getting separated from the herd, this is my only lifeline," he said, gently patting the small tan unit on his webbing by his hip.

Wonder how good that things going to be when the satellites start falling out of the sky, you jackass. Carey prayed it wouldn't go on that long, but with each minute spent in this living nightmare, his expectancy of normalcy decreased tenfold. It was as if his hope to get lost in a corporate cubicle maze for the rest of his life erking by and doing just enough not to get fired — was disappearing like hoarfrost with the sun. In all likelihood, the generators would fail long before the units the GPS relied on to triangulate location dropped from space, but it was a rewarding statement nonetheless.

"I'm not bad with the old ways," Morgan piped up, snatching the map and compass from his loose-held fingers. "We did a little orienteering in the Girl Scouts, so it shouldn't be that hard."

Both men exchanged a glance of their own that said it all. *Girl Scouts? That must have been one short stint.*

"Thanks for the help, Sgt. Saint," Morgan crooned in false lust at the soldier as they walked away, as if she'd read their thoughts.

The soldier gave a small laugh and a wave and Carey couldn't help but join in. Forward motion — any kind of forward motion — was better than growing stagnant within the steel walls.

As they walked back to the centre of the camp, hands in pockets in silence, Morgan looped her arm through his once more. So many months ago, it would have been his dream to have such a woman to parade willingly at his side. She was pretty cool and all kinds of confident — traits very much fleeting in the women he typically encountered in his former life.

Now, the small gesture threatened to detonate him like a bomb. His arm went rigid, muscles and tendons tensing at once underneath the skin.

Let it go, his own mind crooned at him, banishing his uptight demeanor with a rush of much-needed endorphins. *Just let it go*. It was so simple. The two prancing back together arm in arm like munchkins along the yellow brick road may raise some eyebrows from those who knew them, but it was harmless. Completely innocent. He had no blood on his hands. None he could see anymore, anyway.

Back near the centre of the camp, Kerrigan and Keila leaned on shovels, the pair drenched in sweat and panting. The steel trowel blades were stained dark with clotted, oily blood. Carey had a feeling they'd probably had more of a workout than intended. Those bastards didn't always stop once knocked down, as that crazy old bitch in the alleyway chewing on Barbra's arm had shown. They guzzled water from bottles without labels, hungrily lapping up the cool droplets as they approached between gasps of air. Soldiers around them gave a few chuckles and pats on the back to the pair as they walked by, combat vests draped open over their shoulders to better cool themselves down.

Keila was covered in sooty dirt from head to toe, smearing a dark brown smudge across her forehead as she wiped the sweat off with her forearm. Her shirt, formerly turquoise, was splattered with dark spots, making her look like a rather fashionable Dalmatian after a long day out. Her hair, frazzled from humidity, hung in crazy arcs from her scalp, falling everywhere but directly in her face.

It took a second before he placed it, but as soon as it hit, he couldn't make it go away. She looked downright *beautiful*. The perspiration careening off her in droves from a hard run of work instilled her appearance with competence, no longer a small girl to be protected. The shovel supporting her weight was almost as tall as she was, but it didn't diminish her stature.

Kerrigan, on the other hand, all tank top and jeans, looked more like a Ken doll after a few too many regimens on the sauce than ever before. Sinewy cords stood out in his muscles beneath the perfectly false-tanned flesh. As the moisture ran down his biceps, Carey half expected it to drip in amber droplets from all the self-bronzer. He couldn't help but notice the handgun had migrated from its former home in the rear of his jeans, now tucked in the front behind his belt buckle.

Carey bit down on his lip to keep the bitter remark from leaping off his tongue and approached the two with a smile on his face, slightly shaking off Morgan's half-embrace as he drew close.

"Hard day?" Morgan chirped at Kerrigan, his heavy frame still breathing laboriously over the shovel.

His eyes, bloodshot and exhausted, played over her before he shook his head, seemingly unable to find the wind for an equally snappy reproach.

"They weren't all still," Keila said, panting, rolling her shoulders in wide arcs. "It wasn't pretty, but it had to be done."

"Ah," Carey commented, the image of the sixteen year-old girl slashing craniums in half with the entrenching tool burning in his mind. "Well, you may not have to do that again for a while."

Her eyes sparkled for a moment before something wiped the gleam from her stare. Something murky, something insidious. Her flash of intrigue vanished as soon as it appeared.

"Why, you actually going to give it a shot?" she quipped, acid tongue flashing.

"We're leaving, if you're coming," he replied evenly, blaming her rebellious tone on her young age. Praying he was correct.

"Where?" Kerrigan gasped, tilting back the bottle to get the last of the water from where it pooled in the bottom.

"Camp Robinson, to the north. They've got a chopper and it's likely where my d-"

A deafening crack rang out beside his right ear. His hand leapt to his holster for his sidearm; thoughts of the future banished in an instant.

"Almost," Morgan mocked quietly, her silver-sheened Liberator pistol trained on the ground.

An infected, mouth bound with a gag an unmistakable surgeon's-scrubs green, lay half under the nearest perimeter LAVIII. A single small hole was leaking black fluid from its head, its fingers still quivering from attempting to reach the foursome. Its hair had been shorn to standard military length, revealing the neat circle just above the right temple driven through by the nine millimeter round.

"Looks like you missed one," Morgan hissed at Kerrigan, though Keila was the first to look away.

Carey shook his hand free of the butt of his handgun, his fingers sore from the sudden firm grasp.

"Where my dad probably went," Carey exhaled, taking the stress away with it like the fragrant smoke of a cigar.

"The army guys think it's suicide, leaving here," Keila said quietly, looking shameful for her failed cleanup operation. "They don't even like leaving the fences."

"Well I don't," Carey fired back, a little too quickly. It felt lacking, but he had nothing else to say. "Are you coming or are you going to carve out a life here? I won't hold it against you either way," he addressed his former friends, all now held in the haze of the decision.

"I already told you, I'm coming," Morgan replied, pushing the round from her insurgent pistol with the small dowel. "I don't care if you try to stop me."

Keila's eyes traced the spent casing falling to the ground before meeting his gaze. Her head nodded only once and then only slightly, but it gave him the nerve he needed. They may have been drifting, but he needed her support. They had come here together — leaving alone would be deadwood.

"Well, I ain't hanging out here all by my lonesome," Kerrigan barked, apparently finding his voice once more. "I don't get along with these soldier pukes. Too caught up in the old ways and we gotta make our own now."

Carey, seemingly for the hundredth time that day, held back the urge to laugh. He sounded like a sergeant in a bad sixties army movie, preparing his men to go out into the post-apocalyptic landscape and create the new world in their image. It wasn't the worst thing, bringing Kerrigan along. Every expedition needed a pack mule.

"Fine," Carey breathed, rubbing the sore patch on his neck. The tape was pulling on the fine hairs of his throat, binding the skin too tight.

So take it off and let that good ol' fashioned infected brew splash in there a bit, chum, Aaron mocked, resolving his decision to keep the dressing on.

Beside him, Morgan calmly loaded another round into the chamber of her little sidearm, working the firing pin back into position before holding it in place with a tiny, delicate plastic clip. It was almost laughable, to think the weapons mass produced by the CIA were even in working order, but Carey knew as much about guns as he did solar sunspot activity. Another question for another day. He made a mental note he'd want her on his six o'clock for the entire journey.

Sure, you just don't want her on your own personal hour hand? Aaron cried jubilantly within his skull. Carey almost shook his head, before realizing the others couldn't hear it. *So what, they'll load you on the crazy train? Think we're all past that point, compadré.*

"If Neil's there, my dad might be too," Keila said, barely loud enough to hear. "I can't get him out of my head."

"I can't get wasting these sick motherfuckers out of my head either, so I'll lead the way," Kerrigan bellowed, patting the butt of his gun, all too close to his junk.

Carey prayed it would discharge, but unfortunately, the big ape had apparently learned to use the safety. *Too bad.*

The resolute determination felt within the group dissolved into shocked silence when Carey told them to clean up and go pack. He claimed they'd burnt enough daylight and needed to get moving, but really he just wasn't sure how much more chain link he could take.

"It's too soon," Keila mouthed, near silent.

"We don't even have supplies," Morgan opined.

"We don't have any fucking rifles," Kerrigan rounded out the chorus.

"Well I'll go ask for packs and some gear, but we need to get this show on the boat. What, do you think there's going to be some changing of the guard? Some raising and lowering of flags before the gates open and send us out into the world?" he growled, temper rising. "This is all we have, this is all we fucking *got*. The more minutes we spend talking about it, the closer we are to another attack. We have to go." He quieted down, splaying his fingers in the air as if he could draw in their sympathy with his hands.

"In the morning," Morgan stated. It wasn't a question. "Let's get our shit together, yes, but we need to get some rest. These guys are about to bloody keel over and you're not looking so hot yourself."

Carey wouldn't admit it, but the creeping lull of sleep was calling to him harder than ever before. His head felt dizzy, his legs weak from the coma. His joints felt like corrosion and sand had worked themselves in every nook of his bones, grating as he walked.

"We need to go," he said, the conviction draining from his voice.

Morgan unfurled the map from her chest pocket, holding the tiny dots in his vision.

"This is going to be a full day's travel, if we're quick and don't get hung up. I don't like the thought of sleeping out there," she said sincerely, patting his shoulder with her still-manicured hand.

"Fine," he repeated, nodding his head solemnly. "In the morning, but then that's it. No 'one more days.' No 'just a few more minutes.' As soon as light breaks, I want to be past that fence and halfway to hell."

They all nodded back to him in turn as his steely blue gaze played over them, the ferocity in his stare only a façade.

***

The mess hall was mostly empty that night. Only a few soldiers clutching crooked cigarettes sat in the back corner, smoking and muttering softly under their breaths in conspiratorial whispers.

Carey listlessly played his spoon amongst the dregs of his stew. While there had been some kind of protein in it, the source was unidentifiable. Hell, anything was better than the MRE's, but he had a sinking feeling either rat or squirrel was the key ingredient in the soup de jour.

Morgan once again sat on his left, the paired Keila and Kerrigan sitting across the bench. They occasionally traded glances, but the conversation was light and meaningless. Everyone had their mind somewhere else, none of it on things they wished to discuss. If they had been planning a party instead of a possible trip down nightmare lane, they would have been eagerly exchanging ideas, animatedly forecasting the future.

Instead, they slurped the tasteless stew in silence from steel bowls with relish, all wondering when or if they'd experience hot food again. At least, not the kind they had to chase down once the infection ran through them.

Carey glared across the table when Kerrigan's arm slipped around Keila's waist. *K-squared. K-Fed and K-Frizz. Assholes.* He couldn't hide what was really going on from himself any longer. He had tried to shroud it in half-truths, covering it with the guise of unfounded speculation, but here it was. Staring him in the face. It wasn't worth rationalizing and it wasn't worth burying with guilt. He hadn't done anything wrong, despite what she must think.

Before long, even the quiet, empty conversation was drawing to a close. The soldiers had long up and left their quiet meeting in the corner, off to guard duty or bunks. The chatter quieted, broken only by the odd crack of a rifle from somewhere up above as the searchlights cast shadows on the canvas. There was nowhere left to go but the dreaded — bed.

"I've gotta use the facilities," Carey lied as he rose to his feet, unable to take the forced smiles and chuckles any longer.

"Oh, okay," Keila said with a disjointed air as he snatched up his bowl and spoon, though she made no move to leave.

Figures, Carey thought, amazed she didn't take his lead. *What do I have to do, grab you by the shoulders and shake the stupid out?*

Tossing his utensils in the soapy bucket, he strode from the tent without looking back. Though a lingering gnawing held firm in his gut, using the can was last on the agenda for the night. Avoiding the awkward parting of ways when they left the mess tent and made for beds was more on the roster.

Carey strode the short distance to the tent, peeling back the familiar blue flap and admitting himself into its empty embrace. What had felt like a home carved out of the side of an impenetrable mountain now just felt like a goddamn blue tarpaulin. *Fuck.*

He plunked down on the bedroll, messing the neatly-made corners with his boots. He bent down, reaching for the laces, wanting nothing more than to kick off their too-tight chafing and relax before stopping himself. Running from St. Albins in clothes better suited for a skateboarder was one thing. Being caught in the night fighting for his life in his boxers and socks would be quite another.

Shaking his head in frustration, he lay back on the camp padding. His vest dug into him in all the wrong places, putting uncomfortable pressure on his hips and into his armpits. He shifted from left to right, but every position was worse than the last. His hair fell in his eyes when he laid on his back, his boots digging into his ankles when on his side. His belt was too tight, his blankets scratching his face.

Restless? Aaron chimed in, evaluating his condition from afar.

"No." Carey said aloud. "Terrified."

If saying it made it real, it all came crashing down like a lead weight on his face. The lumbering almost-dead outside the fences pressed in on his abode in his imagination, tearing at the petty tarp to get the prize inside. His father was stuck under a boulder, countless grey dogs closing in on him, arms raised and jaws wide.

More realistically, he didn't know who was going to pull back the tarp. He didn't know who was going to make his acquaintance all over again. *It could be fucking Chuck Norris for all I know,* garnering a half-hearted chuckle from his throat. Stranger things had happened.

Fuck, he thought, the solemn apathy creeping into the edges of his mind. *Get your head on straight.* There was a time and place for senseless drama and fighting for your life wasn't helped with outside matters of the flesh.

Carey shifted onto his back and closed his eyes, praying that the next time he opened them it would be light outside. He didn't want to sleep for the sake of rest, only to make the time pass faster. He wanted to assemble his meager supply cache, mount it in a pack and steal off like a runaway, but knew he'd never bring himself to do it.

Eventually, he drifted into a light doze, the staccato bark of rifle fire his only lullaby.

***

A rasp. A scratch.

The drag of broken feet across uneven ground.

Breath, or something far worse, panting.

Carey's eyes leapt open at once as the tent flap rustled. Panic, sour and acidic, flooded his mouth, banishing the fever-dreams from his mind.

He fumbled with the Velcro safety-strap covering the butt of his pistol in the holster, cursing the designers. As the flap began to peel away, his fingers slipped and slid over the holster, fighting to gain purchase on the constraining band of fabric.

The silhouette of legs appeared under the withdrawing flap, knees bent in and feet unsteady. They took a small step towards him, then another. Carey finally ripped away the strap, drawing his handgun and leveling it on the creature trying to find its way in. His finger looped over the trigger, so much smaller and dainty than that of the Taurus. One tiny flex of his hand and the beast would move no more.

Give me a head, he begged, the seconds drawn out in slow motion to encompass years. *Give me a fucking target.*

His hands shook, sending the barrel of the SIG Sauer P220 wildly jerking from left to right. His mind raced, evaluating his plan of action. Would infected blood rain down on him like a crimson geyser, dooming him to the same fate? How many shots did he have before he missed?

The gun quivered as he clenched his jaw.

The infected took another half-step forward into the tent, a small gasp emerging from the creature's unseen lips before falling on top of him.

"*Fuck!*" he screamed, pulling the trigger with all his might as the zombie careened towards him, still wrapped in the blue funeral shroud of the tent.

Tick, tick.

"How about you turn on a fucking light?" a female voice cried out in dismay as he slid on his ass towards the back wall, gun still leveled on the writing form.

Breath hitched in his throat, he pulled the small flashlight from his pocket, bathing the scene in the white light of the LEDs.

Morgan stared back at him, half wrapped in what served as his doors, green eyes blazing.

"'Bout time, asshole. Nearly killed myself out here."

"Jesus," Carey breathed, tingles shooting up and down his frame. "I almost bloody shot you!"

"No you didn't," Morgan mocked, untangling herself from the tarp. "I can see the safety's on, you dumbass."

Carey's eyes flitted over the gun. A flood of shame pushed aside by relief washed over him to see the small red box staring him indignantly in the face on the left side of the action. And here he was thinking he'd gone deaf.

"*Fuck*," Carey hissed, dropping the toothless semi-automatic back onto the bed, the defanged cobra shining listlessly in the glow of the flashlight.

"You're telling me. Thank god you're incompetent."

Carey took the abuse, far more thankful he didn't pump his only remaining friend full of lead, rather than being truly concerned about his lack of prowess with firearms.

"Well, be as you are," he replied, rolling his shoulders now stiff from the sudden terror.

It was full dark outside. Only the faint glow of the searchlights facing outwards illuminated the camp past the half-removed door. It had barely been sunset when he'd made to go to sleep. It told him two things. One, he had managed to pass out, somehow achieving the impossible. Two, some time had passed and Keila still hadn't shown up. *Hmm.*

"What, your tent full?" he asked, the implication in his voice apparently quite lost on Morgan.

"Nah," she replied, reattaching the bungee cords gone rogue to the tent flap from her accidental assault. "Stuck around and played some cards with some soldiers coming off the fence for a while. They wanted strip poker, but you know me. They just had to settle for Crazy Eights." She laughed, eyes twinkling in the wash of the tiny flashlight.

"How did Kerrigan and Keila do?" he prodded, trying to keep his true intentions beneath the radar.

"They didn't. Sauntered off into the night right after you did. Guess I'm the only one still rockin' the nightlife around here."

"Oh," he said, feeling downtrodden and weak.

"Don't be so angsty, bud," she chided him. "They weren't in my bed. No body heat means a cold night and I wasn't about to settle for that. Figured I'd come where the furnace lay," she remarked quite unabashedly to Carey's surprise. *Don't underestimate her intelligence,* he reminded himself. He'd gotten in more trouble for doing less.

Carey debated for a moment before admitting her to his fold, but it was a short, bloodless battle for his conscience.

"M'lady," he grumbled, pulling back the blankets.

"Too kind," she replied, leaving her boots on as she slid in. At least he wasn't the only one breaking down the norms. *Take that, society!*

Morgan lay beside him, pressed against his hip, but the Stupendous Vanishing Pants hadn't worked their magic yet. *Whew*, he thought, wondering what his mind would let him get away with if the opportunity presented itself.

"So, you fix helicopters?" she asked, a small grin on her face as she turned towards him, laying her head on his arm.

"Just on the off-season from being a world-class bullshitter," he laughed, glad for the opportunity for real human emotion. "I don't give a fuck about that whirly-bird and I can't believe he even bought it," he admitted, still slightly amazed his awful lie had worked.

"People believe anything when they have nothing left to lean on," she mused, sounding nothing like the ex-stripper he knew she was. Wise, almost, had her leather outfit not been so damn apparent. It really didn't lend itself to the pleasures of the intellectual realm.

"Yeah, well the last time I had a run-in with a helicopter, I was looking down the business end of a missle," he revealed, feeling strange to talk about his journey. The fresh memory still felt too raw to properly discuss. The last person he had told was his father.

"Oh," she whispered, biting her lip.

"Hell, karma I guess. Crashed a remote-control 'copter all liquored up in second year, suppose I had it coming," he joked, finding the pistol on the bedding and blindly shoving it back into his holster. *No idiot straps this time.*

She laughed, just enough to let him know it wasn't fake. Just enough to let him know she was listening. Enough to let him know she cared.

"If we end up seeing the helicopter, you can give it a kick. I won't blame you."

"Now you're being too kind," he fired back, feeling more at ease by the second than he had since leaving New Braniff.

It was like he was back in the basement all over again, before the infected poured in like a deluge. The straps of his ballistic vest no longer cut into his sides, his boots no longer dug at his calves.

Morgan turned up the collar of her motorcycle jacket and settled into his chest, her frame relaxing against his. Her breathing drowned out the gunfire, though it didn't make sense.

Breathing was all he knew.

Breathing was all he had left.

XI

The stench of rancid potpourri pressed in on his nostrils. Spoiled milk. Putrid meat.

It poured over him, bathing him in the nauseating stink until he could feel it on his skin, slimy on the surface. His face was slick with it, his arms dripping.

The carpet was damp with clotting blood, welling up around where his feet pressed in on the floor. The same lifeless taupe walls surrounded him, the same pale pink curtains hanging listlessly from a tarnished rod. The same painting hung on the wall, a crow flying upside down in its swamp ash frame, boxing in the scene like a coffin.

He was back in his parent's bedroom. The spectral place he found himself in anytime he closed his eyes for more than a few seconds. Anytime he let his guard down for even a moment.

Where his parents had lain together, dying with rasped breaths under the floral bed spread, was now over laden with bodies. Snapping and screaming, he counted their faces in turn. The matted, bloody hair. The ravenous jaws, clacking together like steel traps. The hands, reaching out for him with broken, gnarled fingers. Six pairs of feet jostling and rattling on the mattress, seizing upwards before crashing back down.

Morgan. Keila. Bennett. Roman. Neil. Rosslyn.

Their lifeless, crimson-streaked eyes, devoid of their true colour, stared at him accusingly. Hungrily. Their limbs tangled, smearing blood and pus on the walls, the headboard, the duvet. They bit at each other's flesh, tearing skin from the muscle before delving down to bone. They ripped at their own, feeling nothing as they swallowed mouthful after mouthful. Ichor, black as a pedophile's sins, poured in rivers until the bed was soaked a horrid scarlet.

His hands shook at his sides, his eyes fixated on the scene. His teeth grew beneath his lips until they pierced his gums. Carey cried out, dropping to his knees in agony as the incisors pierced through his cheeks, blood as hot as magma burning his face as it streamed down his neck.

His eyes alit once more to the painting, his vision swimming. The bird was gone, replaced by a portrait of Kerrigan. His skin, no longer that of a bronzed statue, was white and ashy. His veins stood out in black, painted like branches on his forehead where they ruptured. His fingers were locked on his jaw, his lower mandible ripped from his skull by his own hands.

Carey stared into the black abyss of his gaping throat, barely making out the thousands of lives painted within.

He screamed, only to see crimson pour from his lips onto the carpet.

They were all one in their lifeblood.

They were all the same.

With the last of his strength, he flung himself back against the door, sending it rocking on its hinges as it banged out into the hall.

Aaron stood in the doorway, skin grey and mottled. His eyes, two gaping portals to nowhere, hung empty in their sockets.

Before he lunged, Carey swore he saw him smile.

***

Carey awoke with a start, the silent scream still hot in his throat.

For a moment, the mass on his chest was Aaron, still heaving rancid breath on his neck before the teeth ripped open his jugular. Slowly looking down, he felt his fingers ache, cramped on something hard and cold.

His handgun, obsidian black and unapologetic, pressed lightly against Morgan's head on his chest.

"*Fuck,*" Carey hissed, loosening his grip on the pistol. Turning it over slowly so as not to wake her, his stomach dropped to see the safety firmly off.

Horrified, the sidearm slowly slid into his holster. The click of the safety engaging rang out like a funeral march. He strapped the Velcro across it once more. While it was designed for weapon retention, he needed to take every precaution against his subconscious.

Carey's head lay back against the pillow, Morgan feeling warm and safe in his arms. She'd never know. He wouldn't tell a soul.

More and more, he wondered who the true opponent was.

The grey dogs?

Or himself.

XII

He hunched in a ditch, the firelight in the camp only a short distance away.

If they had sentries posted, they were either doing a shitty job, or he had adapted to his new duties better than he ever imagined.

The trek through the swamp had been worth it, the beginnings of his salvation only a mere hundred yards or so away. He debated walking straight into the camp, but hesitated. You put someone's back against the wall with a rifle and before long, anything looks like an enemy.

So don't move like them, he thought. *Be human.*

It was easy to tell the infected apart from the living, even from far away. You didn't have to hear the moan rising in their throat to know they were sick. You didn't have to see their bloodshot, lifeless eyes to know they had succumbed to the plague. They just didn't *move* right. They jerked and swayed like a sailor on shore leave, their arms never quite getting the right signals from their poor, diseased minds. If they had minds anymore.

There was something disconnected about the way they walked, something that ran deeper than putting one foot in front of the other. If you caught their attention, they switched on. Their hands shot straight out in front, the rest of their frames coming around to face you. They didn't move fast, but every uncoordinated step was taken with purpose. Catching you and making you one of them.

In the swamp, he'd seen the ones who hadn't heard him coming. They stood stock still, like a robot in hibernation. Their arms swayed at their sides, rocking slightly to keep them upright when their balance faltered. More interestingly, they often faced the wind. He didn't know what it meant, but it wasn't a positive sign. They were doing something more than just *being*, but he couldn't put a finger on it.

Like when they took a victim down. Sometimes they ate and devoured the flesh until little more than a writhing, eviscerated corpse remained, reanimated but immobile. Other times, after inflicting only a single bite, they turned their attention to other healthy potential meals, though they could have feasted on their original target for hours undisturbed.

He hadn't put together what it meant, but the more time he spent outside of the remnants of civilization, still fighting for survival, the shorter he felt his own survival would be.

Survival.

Nothing more, nothing less. He didn't yearn for company, didn't miss the ambivalent conversations. He needed food. Shelter. Water. Ammunition. Resources he couldn't gather on his own with this many feral hunters shambling about.

Watching the figures pass by the firelight, his thoughts fled back to the swamp once more.

There was a girl, no older than five wading through the mire as he rounded a fallen tree. Her voice was shrill, even through the empty moan rising from her throat. Her hair was brilliant blonde, though stained and blackened with the poison stew of the wetland. She had been half-crouched by the dead log, rising to her feet and grasping upwards at him with outstretched arms as he drew close. Her tiny legs fought to seek traction in the soft mud, the muck sliding and giving way beneath her, those miniature fingers like those of a doll desperately longing for his embrace.

For a split second, he almost stooped to pick her up. That's what you did to comfort a child. You removed them from the very ground they stood on, swaddling them in your strong, capable arms to let them know that nothing could hurt them.

What did you do for a child whose mind was now that of a virus? The girl didn't clutch at a teddy bear, crying for a father who wouldn't come. Her baby-teeth gnashed at him, viciously snapping and hissing like a wounded dog.

He leveled the *lupara* on her forehead, finger clutched deep in the trigger-well. She reminded him of a girl much her age he had known long ago, but carving through the fog of memory was getting harder by the hour. Since the blow in the basement that left his head a poor, aching mess, reflex and instinct were taking control at an alarming pace, leaving his rational mind coiled in the fetal position in the dark corners of his skull.

Was it his daughter, seeking to feast on the soft flesh of his thighs, wallowing in the filth before him? Did he have a daughter? The gun still trained between her eyes at five paces, he ran a hand through his close-cropped silver hair, feeling the hideous crack in his scalp just below the crown. Lightning bugs danced in his vision as his fingers touched the wound, a sharp gasp ringing from his mouth. *It won't be much longer now.*

Dropping the barrel slightly, he approached her, all too aware of the empty howls beginning to draw nearer from all sides. Placing the muzzle in her snapping mouth, he'd breathed deeply. Her teeth rang and clacked off the steel, but she made no effort to get away.

Without another moment's deliberation, he'd sharply drawn back on the trigger, painting the fallen poplar with a million would-be dreams, lost to the world forever.

The only remorse he held was the wasted bullet.

A small bark of far-off laughter in the camp brought him back to his surroundings, the warm blood from his head flowing once more down his neck. It made his collar sticky, the back of his shirt damp. Uncomfortable. His bones ached, but he paid them no heed.

If he approached the entrenched soldiers' last bastion too casually, they'd slaughter him like a pig. They probably wouldn't even bat an eye to find out he'd been among the living, before their bullets tore through his skin.

Then again, he had something the infected didn't.

It still had six shells in the tube and a pocketful remaining in his jacket.

Jumping to his feet, he sprinted at the camp, his eyes no longer truly seeing the scene before him. *At least they won't carve me down like fall wheat.*

He screamed as he charged the hastily-erected fencing, his shotgun barking hatred and death at the campfire.

"HEY COCKSUCKERS, GET A LOAD OF THIS!"

XIII

"Good thing we don't have far to go," Morgan mused, staring at the over-laden packs.

"Anywhere is too far," Carey admitted, the sun's faint rays filtering through the open tent flap.

The rucksacks sat like sleeping sentries on the ground, the bedrolls snugly bound on top. Though on a normal day they'd seem an easy haul, to Carey they looked like coal-filled boxcars, more suited for drag by a train than on his aching shoulders. The vest he wore felt heavier by the second, more like a straightjacket keeping the last of his sanity firmly inside.

The packs were full to the brim. Canteens. Purification tablets. Spare socks. The less-appealing MRE's and dehydrated food the captain had been happy to part with. Emergency blankets. Signal whistles. A hundred rounds of ammo each. A single grenade in the side pocket he hoped he'd never have to use. Flares. Survival knives. First aid supplies. The last of his antibiotics. A host of other odds and ends thrown in by enthusiastic soldiers, all more than willing to help the fabled "mechanic" who held the hope of returning their sacred whirlybird to them. The last vestige of a better world, Carey couldn't blame them, forcing small droplets of guilt to pool in his stomach.

Lastly, handed in four small vials, yellow caplets. They smelled of almonds and promised sweet release. Dr. Roberts insisted they take them along, but cautioned at their use. No matter how bad things got, cyanide poisoning was permanent. A good way to throw the cards from the table if the deck became too stacked with opposition.

Carey made sure the vials lay at the bottom of his pack, wrapped in an old pair of military-issue underwear. One capsule each was four too many in his opinion. Though he considered himself something far from the wisest man left in the world, he trusted his own judgment above the others. Carrying a corpse to Robinson wasn't in his plan.

Testing the weight of the pack, he smiled a little, reminiscing on his last experience in St. Albins planning for a journey. There was a decided lack of scotch in the bag, but he could think of worse things to do without. His hands didn't shake, the dreaded delirium tremens far from his concern. Alcoholic was a title he'd only begun to bear, thankfully.

They donned the packs and strode in silence in the cool April morning to the centre of the camp. Kerrigan and Keila stood by the flagpole, rubbing their hands together for warmth, their breath blowing ghostly clouds into the day.

Nodding at them, the silence remained unbroken. The pair similarly mounted their burdens squarely on their shoulders and set off towards the gate, the caravan finally in motion.

Only the night watch stood sentry at the fence, but Carey preferred it that way. No trumpets rang as they strode through the break in the line. No triumphant cheers to support the expedition. No melodramatic speeches of the integrity of the human spirit.

Captain Quincent Meyer stood solemnly outside the gate, shaking their hands in turn as they left the confines of his protection. His horribly scarred face showed no emotion, no elation. A firm grasp of Carey's fingers was all that needed to be said and they made off without another word.

He'd taken Carey's request the previous night exceptionally well, blessing them with all the supplies he could muster from the rapidly-depleting stores. Though he wouldn't part with the rifles, he issued another pair of SIG Sauer P220's for Morgan and Keila. It wasn't the best outfitting he could have provided them with, but any protection from the staggering husks beyond the fence was better than none, though he wished an eight-wheeled Light Armoured Vehicle had been offered up.

The whole conversation that morning hadn't been an interrogation, but Carey knew the Captain saw through his lies. If he had truly believed him, Carey had a feeling the whole squadron would have mobilized along with him to secure an asset like the helicopter. The Captain had merely signed off on the requisition papers for his gear with a skeptical eye and asked no further. He knew the last commander of the fighting force wasn't about to lose any more of his gear than he had to on a suicide mission.

The short stretch of green former pastureland ended abruptly at a forest a few hundred metres away. Carey was just *overjoyed* to learn from Morgan's apparent expert map-reading that the only viable option was directly through the underbrush. *Fantastic.*

Only a few minutes outside of the camp, a few infected presented themselves on the rise of the shallow hill. They were far off, apparently very much unaware of their position by the way they lumbered back and forth like dazed bees around a hive.

"I got 'em," Kerrigan growled, drawing his pistol like a bad western movie actor, lining up the barrel on the distant targets.

"Hold on!" Carey hissed, slapping down the sidearm, spurning an indignant glare from the older man.

"What?" he quipped, resisting Carey's hold on the handgun.

"You wanna just let out a warning call for them?" he snapped, amazed to experience such wanton disregard so soon. "First off, you'll miss. Second, we'll get swarmed. If the snipers aren't getting them, then you sure as hell shouldn't be trying."

Kerrigan held his gaze with fire in his eyes, but reholstered the weapon before proceeding. Carey only prayed the sharpshooters indeed agreed with his sentiments. *At least he listened,* Carey thought. *Don't expect that to go on for long,* Aaron corrected.

"Guys, we have to make a left if we want to see anything but Toronto in our near future," Morgan mocked from behind, the map unfurled and crinkling in the breeze.

"Right," Carey said, face growing red as Kerrigan guffawed under his breath.

The small talk quickly vanished as they picked their way over the uneven, rocky ground. The cows formerly inhabiting the field had carved deep channels in the earth with their daily comings and goings. The trenches constantly snagged their feet, forcing every step to be carefully calculated to avoid going ass over boots with the heavy packs leading the way.

A few solitary wanderers occasionally appeared over the ridges, though they were easily dodged. Carey would hiss at the group to get down, moving only when the infected had turned away. It grew maddening, the constant interruptions in their travel, the remaining hundred metres to the tree line feeling as far as Red China from their feet.

They were only fifty yards from the forest when Kerrigan screamed.

Braying out like a sow caught in barbed wire, Kerrigan let out a cry, cooking round after round off into the grass at his feet. Carey sprinted towards him, drawing his sidearm as he went, prepared to either secure or end the blonde bodybuilder with a single bullet if he saw a bite.

Kerrigan was only half in sight, the short brush hiding him as he hunched over his attacker, his shoulders bucking and hitching. His handgun leapt as it spewed lead and fire from the muzzle at the ground, perforating his unseen enemy.

Carey whipped around before doubling-over, running in a crouch to backtrack the short ten yards to his position, not missing the few grey dogs coming their way from the left.

Carey closed the distance, the infected coming into view beneath Kerrigan's powerful legs, pinned beneath his knees. The creature was a young man, his olive fatigues signaling his former military occupation, his skin purple and bloated.

The flies, startled off with the gunfire, calmly went back about their business flitting in and out of his open, maggot-filled mouth. They congregated in the grayish folds of his exposed brain where something had taken off the top of his skull. Bloodless puckers appeared on his chest where the recent bullets tore through his ribs. Kerrigan stood wild-eyed and panting, still pulling the trigger though the clip was empty.

"Are you alright?" Keila called, sprinting to where Kerrigan hunched over the body, the concern in her voice bordering on hysteria.

"It's just a fucking *corpse!*" Carey cursed, the supposed infected beneath Kerrigan's knees long-cooled and rotting. "He's fine, the bloody idiot!"

"He grabbed me," Kerrigan breathed sheepishly, drawing a fresh magazine from his pocket as he discarded the empty. "Motherfucker almost had me."

"Had you? *Had you?*" Morgan screamed in his face, spittle flying from her lips. "This asshole hasn't had anything but a bad day for a week!"

"Don't talk to him like that!" Keila snapped at the pair, fawning over Kerrigan as she helped him back to his feet. The howls of the approaching infected growing louder.

"Too late now," Carey observed, training his head back towards the four infected to their left.

They were hideous in their irony, the afflicted.

A pair of disfigured middle-aged gentlemen accompanied by a rather regal-looking pair of ladies bathed in blood raised their hands twenty yards away, clumsily shuffling over the pasture towards them. They were dressed for the old time theatre, taking in a dose of the lethal virus instead of the engaging opera they'd likely set out to see.

Carey's hand felt clammy on this pistol, shaking with a mixture of rage and adrenaline, overlaid by fear. *Take your time,* Aaron crooned, any semblance of sarcasm vacant from his tone. *Just slow down and take your fucking time.*

"Wait," Carey echoed the thoughts allowed aloud as Morgan raised her own black semi-automatic, so much more imposing in her hands than the silver Liberator ever had been.

He could feel his boots growing damp with sweat, his legs trembling on the rocky ground. *Fucking man up and put them down.*

He trained the iron sights on the leading man's open mouth, trying his best to ignore the shattered cries rising from his gaping maw. His fingers slipped over the grips, his aim jarring wildly from left to right as his hands shook with anticipation.

As they closed fifteen yards, he let his first shot fly. A red splotch beneath the man's collarbone answered the first pull of the trigger before his second round found a home deep in the right eye socket. The infected's legs dropped out from under it immediately.

Morgan felled the woman in the red evening gown and her matching male accomplice with two well-placed shots, blood and skull fragments careening through the sky behind them in a crimson mist before their bodies dropped, collapsing to the dirt.

Kerrigan put three shots into the last woman's lace-covered breasts, chuckling under his breath as the fatty tissue tore open. It hung in flaps where the shots ripped through the flesh before Carey put her to the floor.

The firearms grew silent with nothing left to say. Only the birds softly chirping and the wind through the trees amid some distant cries of the ill tangling in the breeze through the oaks. A soft whimper rose behind him, the teenage tones of a scorned student arriving home past curfew.

Carey turned to Keila, rucksack clenched to her chest, sitting in the dirt, weeping over the drab green fabric.

"What the fuck was that?" Carey asked quietly, shocked and appalled at his group's performance. Two of them had done the work another had started far more effectively than the sole idiot who instigated it all.

"You have to drill them in the head," Morgan chided Kerrigan, hitting his shoulder roughly with her free hand as the blood rose to her face. "You know that," she finished, brushing the hair from her eyes with an air of frustration.

"Ah hell, there were only a few," Kerrigan quipped, loading his third magazine of the morning.

Carey beheld the anger, white hot and pulsing, rising to the surface once more. For the hundredth time in forty-eight hours, he considered drawing his sidearm back from its holster and silencing Kerrigan once and for all. He had some redeeming qualities, like being able to lift very heavy things and... well, that's all he could think of, but he was trying to be generous. *Just wait until you get stuck under a rock,* Aaron laughed, mocking his logic. *I'm SURE he'll pull his weight then.*

Whatever, Carey thought, drawing the pistol. As much as his gun-finger yearned to put a round between the big blonde bastard's eyes, he settled for pretending to examine the action, to ensure it was free of debris. Careful to engage the safety once more, he slipped it back where his temper couldn't slap the trigger without him knowing. It hung heavy on his leg, but not all that reassuringly any longer.

"What happened, Kei?" Carey asked, trying the best he could to keep the arrogance out of his tone, though self-righteousness drifted through his words. *Shit.*

"I-it was too fast," she peeped, still not looking up from the pack clutched in her arms. "They came too f-fast," she said, shuddering.

"Right," Carey sighed, doing his best to stay even-keeled.

Digging in the hoodie draped over his vest, he pulled out the extendable baton. It had served him well and though he hated to part with it, Keila without a weapon was worse than no Keila at all. *Be careful what you wish for. She lost her gun, not her humanity,* Aaron warned, very much stepping on his mental toes.

"Here," Carey breathed, the steel cylinder sitting on his outstretched palm.

"Why?" she mused, seemingly taken aback as her eyes finally met his. The locks of blonde hair soaked with sweat hung in her face like a mask, almost hiding her intent.

"So you at least have something if shit goes bad," he calmly said, like he was explaining toilet seat operation to a toddler.

"I have a gun, though," Keila stated slowly, as if it were the most obvious thing in the world. *What?*

Unzipping her sack, she pulled out a faded fatigue jacket of unknown origin and a scratchy green blanket.

There it was.

A beautifully oiled, well-maintained, fully loaded and ready to rock SIG Sauer P220 Assault Model.

Sitting zipped the fuck away in her bag.

"What the hell were you going to do with it there?!" he snapped, snatching the handgun from her bag. Even the safety was off. "You could've killed yourself, even if *they* didn't get you!" he roared, losing the battle to his self-control.

"Fucking retard!" Morgan barked, fists quivering by her leather-clad sides.

She stared up at him, her meek eyes leaking salty apologies like a scolded child. His breath rattled in and out of his shaking chest, muscles tense and screaming fury. Her gaze drifted to Morgan for a moment before taking the pistol from Carey's white-knuckle grasp. His grip loosened immediately as if it glowed white-hot with her touch. Like she had a communicable disease that was a-catching.

"Look," he sighed, regaining a semblance of peace under some difficulty, "if we can't work together and carry our shares of the load, I might as well go on alone. I'm no more a soldier than any of you, but you have to use your heads. If we start infighting, we're done. If we start slacking off, we'll be food."

His voice was distant; instructional. It bore none of the emotion his mind raced with, none of the crushing doubt threatening to drive him to the dirt.

"Right," Keila peeped, zipping up her pack once more. She held the handgun by the barrel, the sight of which almost sent Carey into a fury.

"Like this," he cooed, knowing the slightest spark would set the bitter tinder of the day ablaze if he weren't careful. "Just like that," he continued, adjusting it in her hand to the proper firing position.

With his correction enacted, her spine got a little straighter. Her shoulders a little more rigid. Most importantly, her chin rose up rather than sinking into the field. She appeared confident and capable, save the tears still rolling down her cheeks.

Feet crunching the dry underbrush once more, they made the tree line quickly. Sparing a quick glance over his shoulder, only the few renegade wanderers in the distance were in sight. Nothing close. Nothing pressing. Nothing to cause them to break apart in earnest with another near-failed engagement. *Thank god.*

The forest was old growth, the trunks around him larger than his arms were wide. Their gnarled limbs wove together high above him, creating a shroud of canopy the sunlight barely filtered through. The day cast down in mottled specks, dust motes stirred from the bare earth and needles beneath them swam lazily through the air. The lack of undergrowth allowed them to see uninhibited, but the landscape wasn't as agreeable.

The barren, sandy dirt between the trees rose and fell like overgrown moguls, creating blind areas in every direction, pressing in claustrophobically from all sides. The dead foliage crinkled and snapped under their feet like a merrily crackling Yule log, but everything else was silent. Deathly silent, though he hated the expression with a passion at the moment. Death, these days, wasn't silent at all.

As they quietly, slowly paced over hill and dale, soft moans, hindered by the landscape called out for them in the morning air. Dispersed by the strange acoustics of the forest, they came from no direction in particular but from everywhere at once, even seeming to filter down from above.

Infected in the trees. Wouldn't that be a fucking sight, he thought as he pictured broken fingers nimbly scratching over grizzled bark. *Thank merciful Christ himself that's unlikely.*

The terrain passed slowly under his hard boots, every breaking twig sounding like a bottle rocket's finale in his ears. Every single one was the one *before* the fatal misstep that would bring the sick descending on them from all sides, trapping them, backs against the long rooted cedars.

Morgan, pacing the earth to his left, seemed to grow more irritable by the second. Her cheery disposition, appearing so damn impenetrable on their outset, was deteriorating with every passed hill. She dragged her feet on the ups, morosely sauntering on the downs. Her pack would snag on a broken branch and behaved like the tree had done it intentionally, slapping and kicking at the dead sticks until she pulled free. It was frightening how quickly her mood was falling. He didn't want to see what she'd be like in a few klicks. At this rate, likely blowing whatever came in her path away with that tiny Liberator indiscriminately. *Probably better I didn't call her after the Glenfiddich night. Christ, what a bitch.*

Kerrigan was holding his own, blessedly. Though his head was down, he carried his heavier pack like a mule. He had three hundred extra rounds of ammunition for the pistols in his sack, plus another two water jugs strapped to the side for drinking. Though sweat poured down under the pits of his red cutoff tee, cords of sinew rising out on his shoulders, he didn't complain. He didn't offer a solitary peep. It was a moment of quiet redemption every time he crested a hill, carrying what could be their survival on his back without accosting them all for his burden. Somehow, very un-Kerrigan, but he wasn't about to debate it.

Keila, in the same vein, hadn't raised her serpentine tongue in a while. She plodded on, pistol dangling from her fingers — held correctly at least — without so much as grunting as she humped the pack over each rise. He had expected with her being the physically weakest of the bunch they'd have been taking turns with her bag by now, though it had been assembled with the lightest gear. Despite the slightly less heavy load, her posture remained straighter than his own, seemingly happy to simply be walking, though her face was a cryptic rune. Completely illegible, but not entirely devoid of beauty in its own right.

Ahead of him, grabbing each tree for support as she climbed, Morgan stopped and spun around so abruptly Carey's heart burst into a staccato symphony. His head whipped from left to right, dead set that an infected must have latched onto his pack and he'd missed it under his own duress.

"I have to pee."

"*Fuck,*" Carey hissed, urging his blood-pump to resume normal operation with a few blows of his fist on his chest. After cycling into overdrive, it felt like it'd rather stop than get back to basics.

"No, I said pee," she quipped through grated teeth, aiming for humour but losing the touch.

Her eyes were tired, hollow somehow. Like she'd aged a thousand years since he'd last looked. It was disturbing, the tiny crows-feet around her eyes as she squinted at him, brow screwed up in concentration. *Must really have to hang one, I guess.* She had been pounding back the *aqua* since they made the forest, after all.

Human functions droned on no matter how stressful the situation may seem.

"Sure," Carey mused, secretly relishing the opportunity to shuck the pack from his back and hang it on a nearby tree.

He felt like Atlas unseating the world from his shoulders, instantly revitalized with fresh vigor. He doubted it would last once the bag went back on. *Live for the moment, buddy boy.*

"I could use one of those too," Keila quipped, clearly taking advantage of the situation while she had the chance.

"Sure," Morgan echoed after a slight hesitation. "Not like I can stop you."

Trudging a short ways from the group with the three in tow, Morgan found a natural basin of sorts carved in the hollow at the base of a tree.

"Guys?" she snapped irately, banishing them with a wave of her hand. "A little privacy might be nice as well, it's the only luxury I have left after busting that fucking pack from here to Tijuana," she added another dismissive flick of her fingers towards Keila.

"Uh, sure," Keila stammered, apparently hurt at her exclusion. *What, you wanna hold her hand?*

After a cursory glance of the area ruled out any infected stumbling upon them for the moment, Carey busied himself thumbing rounds into the empty space of his clip. It was only a few bullets short, but it was a helluva lot easier doing it while he had the chance, than with broken teeth clacking at his neck. The thought sent a cold bolt down his spine, but he kept his face steely. No sense rousing them into hyper-vigilance just yet. There was a time and place.

With each *click* of a bullet admitted into the magazine, he felt that much more comfortable. If the same situation applied, he figured it would feel like a goddamn orgasm to slide a few shells into the talisman on his shoulder pocket. Save the one bullet, he'd do as much good feeding the heavy piece of shit to a zombie in its current state. *Thirty-eight calibre doesn't do well outside of a hundred feet. New military doctrine says that's too damn close,* the doctor's voice echoed in his ears, sending another brutal shiver down his back. *You've had enough luck for one day,* Aaron advised. *Let this bad mutha rest.*

Though he hadn't enjoyed the thought of one of their number out of sight for any length of time, the quick bathroom break brought Morgan back to them safe and sound, seemingly leaving behind her poor attitude with her excretions. *Romantic,* Aaron crooned.

The poison leeched from her body, the added years seemed to have been swept from her face, once again the fresh twenty-two year old beauty he knew so well. *Knew so well? Alright, met before.*

Oh yeah, just met. Just friends too, right? Aaron laughed, a hearty chuckle reverberating off the walls of his skull. *Just fuckin' friends. Literally.*

Keila took her appointed round with the makeshift latrine and they re-shouldered the packs. If the others felt anything like he did, he hoped they'd keep their opinions to themselves some more. He wasn't sure how inspirational he could get. The way the weight of his ballistic vest and the pack seemed to multiply off each other until it felt like he was giving a sumo wrestler a piggyback.

Carey cast his gaze back through the trees, the rolling landscape hiding any sign of the field behind them. On one hand, there was more cover here. It felt safer, more secure. On the blood-soaked other hand, he had no idea which way to go. Not to mention the infected lurking behind every tree. *Shit.*

"How much farther?" Carey probed, trying to keep the tone of an impatient ten year old on a road trip out of his voice. It almost worked.

Morgan chuckled, pulling the map from her pocket once more. It was far from the most encouraging thing he'd ever seen.

"Few hours, at best," she concluded after a cursory glance at the page. "We're only two miles out, if that."

Carey fought the cloying urge to insist she double check. It had felt like ten miles had passed under his boots, halfway to China — not halfway to the corner store.

Setting back out along the unmarked path of Morgan's choosing, the four muscled over barren hill and dale, the day's light barely reaching them beneath the canopy. *Just be glad you don't run on solar,* Aaron mocked. *Thanks.*

Approaching a ridge, his hand firmly wrapped around the rough bark of a dead sapling, he heard it. A rasping hiss, like the largest snake ever created having the worst day of its life. It echoed over the ridges, but it was close. Too close to mistake it for anything else. Whatever it was, it was alive. Or halfway there.

Carey held up a hand, praying anyone behind him was paying attention. Footsteps staggered, then stopped behind his pack, indicating his shitty sign-language had hit home. Thankfully.

Slowly crouching as he neared the hill, his pack bore down on his legs as he sauntered slowly up the rise. His boots were too loud in the dirt, his breathing the racket of a truck downshifting on the highway. The haggard rasping continued, like two giant pieces of sandpaper passing over each other impatiently beneath the hands of Goliath.

He drew the pistol from its hidey-hole on his thigh, feeling the safety slip to the off position under his thumb. The click reverberated in his skull like a broken bell, his gun finger finding the trigger guard a silent thief in the night. A tree just over the ridge bobbed slightly, each dip sending pure, unbridled adrenaline coursing through his tired frame. He was reinvigorated, but the shaking in his fingers threatened to dispatch bullets like rain into the dirt if he wasn't careful.

Steady, he thought to himself, holding his breath as he crested the hill.

A long rope, thick as a child's arm, hung taught from a branch overlying the gulley below. It was a sharp drop to the bottom, falling off at a near ninety-degree angle. Just the kind of setting a lynch mob dreamed of, stealing their desperate captive away in the fading light.

The trailing end of the rope hung in a perfect hangman's noose, the epitome of human cruelty refined down to an art. Swinging from the branch, vertebrate protruding through the skin, hung what once had been a proud member of the Canadian Forces. The savage hiss came from the half-breath rattling in and out of his crushed larynx, feet kicking and arms outstretched towards Carey, begging him to waltz into the grave with the poor soul above the crag.

It's only a short way down, don't mind the drop, his infected eyes seemed to cry out to Carey. *We can move in three-fourth time for all eternity. Now come give poppa a hug.*

His fatigues — so similar to Carey's own — were stained a blackened scarlet around the collar and under the armpits. His still-hitching face was crisscrossed like a street map of New York with blackened veins, standing out in stark contrast to the translucent skin. *His vest is missing,* Carey thought bitterly as he stuffed the P220 back into the holster. *Please God don't let it be the one on my shoulders.*

"Come on," Carey called out quietly as he turned back to the group, their terrified eyes standing out like craters on the moon as they awaited his findings. "We gotta go around."

"Is it..." Keila asked, miming the clacking teeth of the sick with her fingers, her jaw working up and down in similar fashion.

"Yeah," Carey mused distantly, his thoughts far away from the journey ahead. *That poor bastard.*

He'd likely remain strung up there until the rope rotted and snapped. He'd spend the rest of eternity at the bottom of the gulch, watching the clouds go by.

Apparently secure in their ignorance, the rest of his downtrodden caravan resolutely followed him in an arc around the depression. Not a single one turned their heads back to see Pvt. 1st Class Hal Midden's final eulogy to the world.

Though Carey couldn't have known it, the images of the soldier's wife and child leapt out at him as he traversed the rocky ground between the trees. A blonde girl with pigtails, likely still receiving a congratulatory star sticker from her mother every time she made it to the potty. A woman with glimmering hair, standing in a white mermaid wedding dress at the altar, just waiting for a ring on her finger from his cold, dead hands.

The soldier wasn't that person anymore and never would be. It didn't change the fact he left those behind who would never be able to bury a body. Never find closure when the time came.

Lost in the world of the nether, he almost didn't notice the forest was behind him until his boot scraped over the tarmac, sending a rogue bottle skittering across the pavement.

"Ha! Told you fuckers I'd get us out!" Morgan cried jubilantly, bouncing up and down on her toes like a maniacal jack-in-the-box. "Fuck the non-believers!"

"Yeah, yeah," Kerrigan muttered, his formerly-red shirt sopped brown with sweat. "Now get us the rest of the way there."

"One frivolous step at a time!" she replied, waggling the compass in her hand. "Just follow the goddamn leader!"

Her enthusiasm was a little unsettling in its vigor, but Carey couldn't help but become a little elated himself. The forest had been claustrophobic, but even with it lining the straight road in the distance, it felt a million miles away. The shoulders were still lined with close-cropped grass, the public service workers having given them their final haircut not long before. It wouldn't be long before they grew as wild as the Amazon, but that was another thought for another day. *More pressing issues at hand, kid.*

Ahead on the right, a hazy grey column of smoke rose from the smouldering remains of a service station. The soot-caked sign proclaimed it to the world as the *Ellisburg Stop & Fill. More* stop *and less* fill *these days.*

Feet scratching over the pebbled road, Carey at once filled with relief for the too-heavy vest constricting his movement. If his last experience with a gas station had proved anything, it was that underground gas reserves were not to be taken lightly. He didn't know what the shrapnel rating was on the ballistic fibres, but the trauma plate riding over his heart made him breathe a little easier, just in case the burned-out shell of a fill station was actually a slumbering dragon in disguise.

"If we're lucky, we may all get a refill," Morgan mused, her over-the-top excitement abating from her voice. "We gotta pass right by it, anyhow."

Drawing near the station, it was evident either some bold business owner didn't want his fuel reserves plundered, or some looters had been a little reckless trying to fill up by firelight. Either way, the pump island was a snarled mess of winding charred tubes and half-melted nozzles. The burnt plastic was nearly drowned out by a lingering, sweeter smell of raw diesel.

Somehow, it reminded him of the sugar cookie-scented candles his mother liked to light around Christmastime, leaving them burning on the oven when she wasn't busy pretending to bake. The image of Rosslyn busily wrapping presents in the kitchen, strands of scotch tape dangling from the hem of her blouse, almost stopped him dead. *She won't be doing that anymore. Not again. Not ever.* A staggering thought, one much harder to bear than merely knowing she was gone. It brought gravity to her passing, something measurable. Something horrible.

"Might as well check it out," Keila opined, her eyes tracing dizzying circles over the snarled coils of the island. "Anything at all that could help us, we may as well take. I have lots of room in my pack," she trailed off, rosy Tindall blood rising to her face.

"Sure," Carey agreed, snapping back from the painful memory. "But no sparks, no flames."

"Thanks for that," Kerrigan quipped. "Any other tidbits of wisdom you feel like sharing? How about we light a bonfire just for shits and giggles?"

Though his suntanned skin creased in a smile, Kerrigan's eyes remained fully untouched by the expression. It was like watching a wax mannequin melt in the afternoon. Carey merely nodded with a small pasted-on smirk and followed them towards the small building.

The glass door hung ajar, its panes blackened and streaked with residue from the flames. A single handprint, no larger than a child's, was the only clean spot in the matter. It sent a chill down his throat a dip in the Arctic Sea couldn't rival, but he kept his speculations to himself. Demotivation was contagious and there were enough bugs going around.

The shelves, previously stocked with colourful packaging to entice even the tightest purse-strings into opening on impulse stood bare and empty. Not a single pack of Twizzlers, not a solitary bottle of antifreeze remained. Even the shitty no-name *GREATEST OF:* CD's were gone. Where the lighters, swaddled in beer logos and arbitrary patterns once sat, only the drab, black holders remained.

Checking the register — drawer still hanging open like a dead man's mouth — he was unsurprised to find it laden with cash. Whomever had made this final clearing run of the store must have been attuned to the writing on the wall. *Or the handprint on the door.*

"Shitty buzz," Morgan observed, as she flipped open the shutters hiding the would-be packs of cigarettes below. Ontario had some strange regulations when it came to tobacco sales, but Carey always thought that one took the cake.

Watching her open the blinders in turn, Carey couldn't help but think back to Roman. Roman, who would've been the first to check them himself. Roman, who would have merrily made space in his pack for Belmonts and Podiums rather than space blankets and purification tablets. *The water's gonna kill me before this shit does anyway,* he could almost hear him say. *Too bad I didn't bring an extra can of lighter fuel — Hell, I may even try lighting them by friction alone before this trip is done!*

"It's like he was here before us," Keila said quietly, barely above her breath, echoing his thoughts. "It would've been the first place he checked too."

While the others accepted this bizarre statement as a matter of course, Carey fought the urge to scream at her to get out of his head. It was dizzying, the way their thoughts still aligned. The way her eyes traced over the empty rows of Zippos and BICs the same way his had. He settled for placing a tentative hand on her shoulder, flushing with relief when she didn't pull away.

Kerrigan was rooting through the freezers in turn, apparently checking for any treasures left underneath the melting bags of ice. Carey didn't have the heart to tell him anything frozen would be utterly useless to them within a few hours, holding his tongue with his teeth instead. *Live and let live. That's better, Cardinal.*

He could've stayed that way, the light contact with Keila under his palm sending soothing waves of solace through his arm and into his chest.

Could've, if the window hadn't smashed into a trillion glittering points of failure under an infected man falling through it.

His moan rose high and loud as the sharp, jagged shards still clinging to the weather stripping tore into his puckered skin, opening channels in his scalp beneath the SUNCORP trucker hat. The barely-visible badge on his charred coveralls announced his name as *Hank*, the blackened ichor painting its former blue writing a stagnant, murky brown.

Hank's arms reached out at them, his pursuit of their still-warm frames completely uninhibited by the vicious lacerations tearing deep into the muscle as the glass tinkled onto the floor.

"*NO! ROMAN!*" Keila screamed, the pistol in her hands barking hatred at Hank's empty eyes before Carey could draw his own.

Hank's forehead dissolved in a spray of blood, bone and grey matter as round after round penetrated his skull, knocking holes through his cranium one after the other as large as nickels. Keila's finger was a blur on the trigger, squeezing shots off in rapid succession, the booming *cracks* reverberating off the walls, pressing in on Carey's ears until he was dizzy.

"Fuck!" Morgan cried, hunched over and clawing at her ears. The blasts were deafening on the open field, but in the closed-in tiled confines of the gas station, they were nearly as lethal as the speeding lead itself.

Tick. Tick. Tick.

Though the magazine was dry and Hank slumped motionless half-in the window with the top of his head mostly erased, Carey could still hear the firing pin dumbly slapping the chamber in her handgun. The slide had snapped back with no kinetic force left to drive the action, but she still tore at the static trigger, eyes wide and wild.

Hazy, blue smoke drifted from the now-quiet Sauer clutched in her grasp, a small gurgle echoing from Hank's putrid lungs as blood pitter-pattered down the wall onto the floor.

Slowly, gently; Carey took the gun from her shaking hands, her grip protesting at first but gradually allowing him to retrieve the toothless snake. Sliding an arm around her shoulders, the Amazon battle mistress dissolved into tears against the hard Kevlar of his vest, her back hitching and yawing with every gasp. He could feel her tiny fingers rubbing at her ears, her bony elbows jostling his stomach unabashedly, but he couldn't give two shits. He breathed in the smell of her long-forgotten conditioner, now only barely-there after days without a real shower, but it was all the same to him. The smell of desperation mingled with the acrid odor of burnt gunpowder.

"We have to get a move on," he heard Morgan remark slightly coldly, looking up to see her pulling on her earlobes. "That's going to bring 'em in from far and wide and the last thing we need to do is get stuck here with no supplies."

"Yeah," Carey agreed, softly pushing Keila away before pulling a fresh magazine from the side of his pack.

He dropped the spent clip, taking care to stow it in his jacket before replacing it with a fully loaded mag, racking the slide and arming the safety before handing it back to her tear-stained hands. The salty beads carved clean tracks in her grimy palms, reminding him all too much of the handprint on the door. *Time to go.*

"It's going to be dark soon, so we may as well get the flashlights out while we have the chance," Morgan observed, drawing a pack of cigarettes from a zippered pocket of her leather jacket.

"Sure, who's got them?" Carey asked, shaking his head in the efforts to clear his ringing ears.

Kerrigan's gaze moved to Morgan's. Keila's to Carey's. Morgan's to Keila's. Carey's to Kerrigan's. The Mexican Standoff from Hell.

"Anybody?" Keila gasped, voice still thick with lingering sobs.

"Well *fuck*," Morgan concluded, raising a butt shaken from the pack to her lips, lighting it with her Zippo. "I guess I better save the fluid after this. I was saving the pack for zero-hour — which won't come, good lord willing — but I may not get the chance if I have to light the way with it after the sun goes down," she remarked with a shake of her head, blowing a billowing cloud into the room. It mingled with the residual haze of the spent shells before flying out the window above Hank's mostly-removed head.

As if on cue, a low moan carried on the wind into the desecrated gas station.

"Well if that's our signal, we gotta run," Carey observed, adjusting his pack on his back before walking outwards through the door.

"Better late than never," Morgan agreed.

XIV

The other three walked ahead of her, but she wasn't afraid of bringing up the rear. Wasn't scared of being left behind.

In her mind, she'd never left the basement.

The longer she trudged down the road behind Kerrigan, the less he looked like a man and more like a mountain. A living, breathing, towering statue. How *foolish*. How *tepid*.

She'd never received the talks from a mother that most girls her age would've had long ago. Her father had made the cursory observations about the things she already knew, but he'd tried his best. All her knowledge had come from Tarryn and there it had flowed back when she had the chance.

She never thought it would twist her mind the way it had.

Pregnancy. Sexually transmitted diseases. Rape. Rohypnol. She'd heard about all the risks. She thought he had a clear head for dealing with it when the time came.

She never thought it would take part of her sanity along with it.

She didn't want a hand to hold, or another arm to slip so delicately around her shoulders. There was a time and place for that. A wedding. A funeral. A bridal shower. Not now, when the closest thing to friends she had were a pair of men who toyed with her and a woman who she thought wouldn't even bother to stoop to pick her up from the ditch if she fell.

Her mind swam with expectations, shattered hopes. This wasn't the way her sixteenth year was supposed to be. She was supposed to ace her grade eleven finals, opening the doors of pre-university courses before making the rounds with her glistening application. She wasn't supposed to have her dead brother on her conscience. She wasn't supposed to be worrying that her father was likely in the same place.

Though her blonde hair fell in her eyes, she made no move to brush it aside. The tickling on her nose as the strands played back and forth was a sign she was still walking. Still breathing. Still *living*.

It was something she'd never appreciated. It was something Roman would never again have to worry about. For that reason, she let it bother her. She let it pester in her vision. It was just another constant reminder she was alive.

Her boots rubbed terribly at her ankles, two sizes too large and built for a man twice her size, but she didn't care. Her pack jostled uncomfortably on her shoulders, but she couldn't give a rat's ass. So many out there had to watch their bodies tear the living apart with their teeth, unable to control their actions or inhibitions. They were powerless. At least she could still feel the painful throb of her toes. Anything was better than that.

Hank.

His nametag had branded him as *Hank*. Not *Roman*.

No matter how many times she replayed it in her head, it was her brother's name scrawled in looping azure thread across the coverall's breast. It was her brother's vacant stare sizing her up. It was her brother's desire to rip her to inconsequential shreds, just so he could dance forever with her in the wasteland.

She hadn't seen Hank.

She had seen Roman.

And she'd put eleven rounds from the SIG Sauer P220 Combat's extended clip into the space where his strawberry-blonde hair should have fallen. It was his face she'd blown into scraps of a visage. It was Roman still slouched, unmoving over the broken window.

Neil. They were after Neil, so said Carey. After the head of the Cardinal family, jovially tramping from hither to yon through the remnants of a fallen world. After a man that Carey was so goddamn obsessed with finding that he'd completely neglected to realize she was still alive. That *she* had a father somewhere out there. That if Neil had managed to escape, that was just dandy— forget about kindly ol' Bennett and his silly little lighting store.

Forget about him, Keila silently cursed at Carey's back. *Let him rot. Let him eat cake.*

She had been so kind as to keep her reservations about the journey to herself. So damn *kind*. She had left the first place she felt she truly belonged in since her home, striking out past the sentries at the gate on a fool's errand. So fucking *foolish*.

She didn't doubt her father was still alive. She would have felt it if he wasn't. She would have suffered the same, never-ending scratching at the back of her skull like a starved rat desperately trying to gnaw its way out of her mind. She would have felt her world bend to the breaking point before snapping off as cleanly and bloodlessly as the glass pane Hank... or Roman, had fallen through.

It wasn't right.

None of it was right.

It wasn't all Carey's fault, but she couldn't help but harbor her resentment against him. She longed for Tarryn now, more than she had in her entire life. A friend to confide in. A friend to help untangle the horrid web that had silently woven itself between them all, appearing from nowhere but remaining all the same.

In the tent with Carey, that was supposed to have been it. When he had his hand on her hip, his breath on the nape of her neck. That was the moment that passed them by. The moment she could clutch at with failing fingers for the rest of her quickly-passing days, but never recover. *That* was *it*.

She couldn't talk to Morgan about it, their gender binding them together in ways indescribable or not. The way she clung to Carey? That was off-limits. Not that she wanted to, anyway.

What was it about Morgan, anyway? Was it her leather pants? Who shows up to the end of the world dressed for S&M, anyway? Keila couldn't quite place her finger on her, no matter how she tried. The way she degraded, growing bitter and mean until snapping back as if nothing had happened.

She could see it in her older face, the way the creases formed at the corners of her eyes until she seemed to view the world through slits. The way her lips puckered like a sour taste ran rampant in her mouth. The way she hauled on her cigarette, seeming to desire something more in the tobacco than the smoke was giving her, always slightly out of reach.

Keila wondered if her mother had been like that.

More or less, ravens of that feather are pretty much all the same. Assuming her suspicions were correct.

The thought of her mother sent another blinding spear of hatred through her tired mind as the metres of tarmac passed slowly under her boots.

Why did I have to tell him right then and there? She could have carried the secret of her mother's shame to the grave, much like she had her own. Because of her, Roman likely left the world thinking nothing but terrible things of the woman who brought him into it. And it was *all* her *fault*.

She could have told him about her uncle's misgivings in his childhood long ago. She could have cured him of his affliction before it manifested itself in vicious headaches. She was the cause of his downfall. She was the reason he would never walk by her side again.

A firm blow to her face tore her from her thoughts, her grasp tightening on the pistol clutched in her hands.

"Whoa," Kerrigan mused, chuckling. She had walked directly into his pack, broadsiding the canvas with her cheek.

"You okay?" Carey smiled, obviously holding back his own laughter despite his *caring* inquiry.

"Fine," Keila muttered, loosening her grip on the handgun.

The path had come to a cross, another road intersecting their current at a right angle. Four sun-bleached stop-signs stood mocking them with no traffic left to direct. The forest still grew as tall as it had when they'd left it on either side of the shoulder, the small declines down to their level hiding everything below the branches. She could almost imagine the infected stumbling over the undergrowth just out of sight, staying quiet without the stimulus of her scent.

"It's a right, my friends," Morgan grunted.

The colour had begun to drain away from her face again, leaving her cheeks pallid and the hollows of her eyes dark. The same too-old creases furrowed her brow, making her look like a overworked stripper long due for greener pastures in the leather *ensemble*.

Casting her gaze in all directions, the roads were empty. No cars with doors ajar to hinder her view. No wandering zombies just waiting for her to draw closer. No buildings, save for the still-smoking gas station far off in the distance, only the haze from the long-dead fire still in sight.

As they rounded the corner, she could see the forest to their right swathed in fetid water, very unlike the tree line they had previously emerged from into the clear. The smell of rot and decay flooded her nostrils as they strode down the road, organic and putrid.

Keila marveled at the lack of infected they'd seen, furtively casting her glare about to see the one she knew she'd missed.

There *had* to be more of the sick than this, but they hadn't seen any since Hank/Roman had rudely interrupted her private séance for her brother.

Looking down at the swamp, she envisioned them stuck in the mire, up to the waist in the brooding filth. The water sucking them down like quicksand, doomed to forever snap at passing turtles with their yearning jaws until the world burned up in the sun.

Horribly, the mental image of the sick in the marsh transformed, the faces swelling and growing until they all resembled one man.

Her father.

Stuck in the swamp, bleeding but unable to die. Purple rugby sweater soaked with putrid grime and decaying leaves. Glasses hanging from one ear, the lenses smashed and useless to his bloodshot, sightless eyes. Pencil-thin moustache caked with long-dried blood. Some his own. Some not.

A series of howls tangled on the wind blowing in her face, reminding her that not all nightmares remained solely in her mind. Some were right here, walking the forest beside her. *Be careful what you wish for.*

"Sounds like we've got company," Carey observed, scanning the narrow horizon up ahead, hand held up to shield the overcast light from his eyes. "Everybody locked and loaded?"

A few small murmurs responded to the affirmative, but nobody seemed to want to further break the silence. Keila knew very little about the twisted walking corpses, but she knew better than to make more noise than she had to when they were around. Like rotting moths to the flame, it seemed like all you had to do was clap your hands and they'd rush like children at the school bell.

Carey cast a small smile at her under the brim of his hat before turning back to the road ahead, fingers waggling over the pistol strapped to his leg.

What happened to you, she thought, mind racing with empty hopes and less graceful premonitions. *Where did you go. What happened in that goddamn tent?*

She wondered what would happen if she fell. Tripped, busted an ankle. Would Carey rush back to her, carefully splinting her wounded leg to the best of his ability before carrying her in his arms? Or would he let her know just how bad he felt for her, before walking away arm in arm with Morgan, leaving her as Kerrigan's mess to collect?

It didn't really matter. Kerrigan, still walking in silence just ahead, he was alright. He talked to her like an adult, not down to her like a fucking *kid*. Like a *burden*. He listened when she had something to say. When they had been cleaning up bodies in front of the camp, he had made her put down more than one slinker — what the military boys had taken to calling the downed, but not dead, infected.

The ones with vertebrate snapped and glistening in the morning sun. The ones with legs torn clean off, still leaving a snail's trail of blackened fluid behind them, tendons trailing along like cans from the car of a newly married couple.

He'd made her take the swings with her shovel. Made her smash their skulls to pieces with the sharp edge of the blade, hacking until her arms burned and the blood flew like mist.

He said she had to face her fears.

He said she had to learn to take care of herself.

He was right.

Carey would've covered her eyes, gently reassuring her that everything was okay — as if she didn't know any better. As if she were a toddler, thinking the world went away when she covered her eyes. What if he had stayed that way with her, always shielding her when things went bad? What would become of her once he fell himself? At least Kerrigan was thinking ahead like a realist should.

The distant cries on the wind, anguished tones of the afflicted, grew more numerous. It was better than trudging through the forest. She couldn't tell how far they were, but at least she could tell the direction. Unfortunately, it was somewhere entirely too close to dead ahead down the road they were marching like prisoners of war.

"Shit," Morgan grumbled.

Already, Keila could see Morgan's boots beginning to drag again. She could see her knees beginning to lock and pop like a broken robot, seriously in need of servicing. There was no way she needed a pee again — she'd barely touched her canteen since they started walking and so much for saving those cigarettes. The way she lit one off the other reminded her all too much of her brother. All too much of someone combating the illness.

The one that took you somewhere worse than death.

"What's up?" Carey asked, blinking hard at the road ahead.

"Good news is, we're not far from Camp Robinson," Morgan observed, her teeth grinding beneath her cheeks as the map bobbed with every step.

"Don't tell me there's bad news," Kerrigan muttered, cracking his knuckles and rolling his eyes.

"Course not," Morgan quipped, "Unless you count the fact those moans are coming right down our road. I don't know if you've been paying attention, but somewhere over there, there's a fucking welcoming party just dying to meet us," she mocked with a wave of her hand towards the forest on the left. *At least it wasn't the swamp.*

And let me guess, you have to pee.

"Might as well use the rustic little girls room before we run into the shit," Morgan observed. *Right on cue.* "You guys mind?"

"Hell no, I gotta hang one," Kerrigan barked. "You can have that side of the street, but this one's mine!" he joked, sauntering down the shoulder down near the swamp before disappearing out of sight.

"Yeah, I'm due too," Carey remarked with a grimace, obviously not all that pleased to spend some quality time with Kerrigan. "You two watch out for each other. I hear gunshots and I'm coming running, fly up or not."

"No worries, cowboy," Morgan said with a smirk, though her formerly overflowing well of enthusiasm seemed to have hit a drought. "You cool?" she probed at Keila through half-lidded eyes, turning away to the opposite embankment without waiting for a response.

Yeah, dandy.

Keila waited until Morgan disappeared behind a large old oak before she moved. She didn't want to scare up the crows just yet.

She eased her pack off her shoulders, laying it gently on the smooth tarmac road. Carefully, she picked her way down the embankment, following in Morgan's footsteps, making calculated steps to avoid breaking any twigs.

Twenty seconds that felt like a century later, she stood before the tree. The one Morgan had disappeared behind. *Just do it*, she told herself. *Get this done once and for all. If she's infected, they need to know. We can't do this again.*

Standing there in the brush by the side of the Ontario highway, it hit her. She didn't fear a grey, twisted hand shooting out from between the branches to tangle in her hair. She wasn't holding her breath because the infected may hear the low rattle in her chest.

It was Morgan. She was the one making her fingers tremble. Making the fine hairs on the back of her neck stand erect like regimental soldiers on display for inspection.

Painfully slowly, she stepped around the tree, her heavy boots as light as feathers on the dry forest floor. Leaning against the gnarled old sycamore, she peered around the breadth of the trunk.

Morgan sat at the foot of the tree, perched between its aged, sturdy roots with one sleeve rolled up to her bicep, the leather crinkling where it bunched around her shoulder. Where Keila expected to see a blackening bite mark — the brand of the damned — she saw virgin, white skin.

Standing out amidst the track marks spiraling up and down the inside of her forearm, a single needle filled with a murky brown substance sat in the crook of her elbow up to the hilt. Morgan's hand shook as she slowly, methodically pulled lightly on the plunger, her blood mixing with the substance in the vial like a drop of ink in a bathtub.

She could hear Morgan's breathing hitch in her throat as the plunger descended slightly, forcing the brew into her veins.

Until she slipped.

Her balance, so reliant on the tree for support, cast wildly off centre as her boots fought for traction on the needle-strewn ground before falling on her side into view.

She could see Morgan's eyes jump open in slow motion like cellar doors as the entire contents of the syringe slammed home into her venous system.

"*Fuck!*" Morgan gasped, ripping the needle free of her arm.

Blood welled up in a single spot on the bend of her arm, all so similar to the way it had leeched through Barbara's skin in the apartment so many days ago.

Keila let out a whimper, wondering what would become of her folly. She sat up, brushing the debris from her shoulder as she fought to gain her feet.

"Are you alright?" Keila asked in a panic, her voice young and quavering like startled doves.

"That junk was supposed to last me the whole trip!" Morgan hissed, raising her hand above her head and flexing her fingers. "A little at a time to stave off the shakes, but that's not what I had in mind."

"What is that?" Keila asked, feeling like she already knew the answer. She was looking her mother in the face, after all.

"Black tar heroin mixed with a little blow," she mouthed, breathing sharply.

Already, the colour was draining from her face, her eyes fluttering as she nodded forwards before catching herself.

"Shit," Keila whispered, her knowledge on the subject limited to the cursory discussion in grade ten health class. "Are you going to be alright?"

"I think so," Morgan breathed, blinking hard at the quiet light of the forest. "I don't think it was that much. Dumbed it down with a lot of water. You can't fucking tell a soul about this, though," she stabbed, eyes ceasing their strange movements to narrow straight at Keila. She looked more like a predator than a woman.

"Course," Keila agreed quietly, eyes playing over the empty syringe sitting amidst the twigs. So bloody unremarkable.

"I'm gonna start getting sick again if we don't make it to the camp soon, though," Morgan observed, rolling her sleeve down with restless, pale fingers. "That was supposed to keep the process at bay until we got there. Morphine should do the trick if we can get it."

"Sure," Keila agreed again, wondering how the hell the situation had turned from a *she* into a *we*. Keila wasn't the one with a dependency problem.

"You know if you tell them, it'll just tear us apart, right?"

"What do you mean?" Keila asked, playing the fool she knew Morgan to take her for.

"Carey, Kerrigan. They won't believe you. Not gonna find your daddy all alone out here in the world if they think you're a *liar*," Morgan elaborated, the last word dripping poison more lethal than she put in her arm.

"R-right," Keila agreed a third time.

Though she tried to sound calm and collected, the statement hit home to a place too familiar. Too recent. No, the two men didn't give a shit about Bennett, but here Morgan was, flying the tattered flag in her face. And she was right.

The idea gripped her like a funeral march, her heart banging out every beat of the sombre symphony. *She's fucking right.*

"Come on, we gotta beat feet back up to the road, or they're liable to come looking," Morgan muttered, buttoning her sleeve and reshouldering her pack. "Loose lips sink lesser souls, right?"

"Right," Keila mumbled weakly, brushing the remains of her fall from her side before following her back towards the road.

Loose lips sink ships.

Loose lips leave me all the hell alone.

A moan, guttural and clotted, hailed out amongst the constant undertone of toneless cries of the day from somewhere nearby. Somewhere up the road. Somewhere Keila's shaking legs had no desire to take her.

"Good thing the camp's close," Morgan remarked brightly, rejoining the men standing on the centerline of the old highway. "No more than an hour now if my calculations prove correct."

"Good," Carey remarked, adjusting his hair as he reset his hat. "Cause whatever the hell *that* is, we need to hurry up and pass it by," he finished with a broad wave of his hand towards the left of the road.

"Mmph," Kerrigan groaned, chewing his lip as his eyes passed over Keila once more. The hungry way they had ever since her *second* night in the tent-city.

"Well then, off we goal," Morgan cried.

She danced a little before striding off to lead the group with a stage walk — knees pulled high to her chest before kicking her boots one by one at the air before her.

"Goal?" Carey asked, rubbing the back of his neck before walking after her.

"Whatever."

The foursome trod down the hard pavement, once again moving towards their ultimate destination. Safety, security and a warm meal — just around the corner. *As long as she makes it,* Keila thought to herself, her nails digging into her palms.

It wasn't three minutes of steady pacing before she noticed it. Morgan, leading the merry band, began to drag her feet.

It wasn't like she had when she had obviously been gripped with withdrawal symptoms, her toes barely scratching the tarmac to show her discomfort. Her boots became affixed to the road, her legs merely shuffling one foot in front of the other.

"You alright?" Carey asked to her left, eyes fixed on the source of the loud, grating rasp as she walked.

"F-fine," Morgan stammered, not turning to face the rest of the caravan.

I have to tell them.

They'll call you a liar, Morgan's threat echoed in her head.

The ball bounced back and forth like a pendulum within her skull, banging the empty hollows of her bones.

Morgan stumbled from the left to the right of the road in perfect synchronicity with her inner argument, pitching wildly under the weight of her pack.

Tell them.

Liar.

"Maybe we should hold up for a second," Keila voiced quietly, hoping to be heard, yet wishing to be ignored all at the same time.

"No... gotta go," Morgan mumbled thickly, her black hair waving as she met obvious resistance to her steps. Her boots slowed, sending stones skittering madly onto the shoulders.

"This... this would be a good time to take a second," Keila tried again, speaking a little more loudly. The others paid her no heed, Kerrigan and Carey too busy exchanging confused glares at each other to take notice.

"This..." Morgan peeped, feet stopping pigeon-toed on the asphalt, halting steps finally coming to rest.

She turned to face the three in a deathly pirouette, her eyes bloodshot and wide.

Her face was a ghastly white, her eyes blacker than a starless early morning. A fluffy opaque foam clung to her quivering lips like misplaced lamb's wool and turned pink at the edges from the incredulous lipstick still clinging to the skin.

"Morgan?" Carey asked quietly, hand twitching next to his pistol.

"This is it," she finished.

The sound of her vomiting, retching blood between her feet before collapsing to the road would be a sound Keila would never forget.

The image of her limbs trembling on the tarmac at a runaway pace would stay with her until the day she died.

XV

No.

"Morgan!" Carey cried, rushing to her side.

He knelt on the road beside her, the asphalt digging into his bony knees. Her arms jittered at her sides, the froth and blood dripping from her lips. Her eyes rolled into the back of her head, only the horrid whites visible under her fluttering eyelids.

"What happened to her?" Carey pleaded, entirely beside himself.

I'm not losing another. Not another one. God damn it, no.

"What's wrong with 'er?" Kerrigan croaked, walking to stand over her on the opposite side.

"No... she's," Carey whispered, the finality of his next word hovering in the balance between light and the nether. "She's sick. Please, for the love of God, tell me she's not infected."

Carey's fingers leapt to Morgan's jacket, unzipping the leather swathing her chest and pulling up her shirt to reveal the smooth, white skin beneath. Although her abdomen was only a small part of her body, he saw no marks. Nowhere teeth had carved through her perfect, flawless skin, injecting her with the horrible illness. Condemning her to the walking grave.

"No... she's not," Keila said quietly behind him.

"She must be," Carey snapped dismissively. "This is just like Barbra. Just like... you know," he trailed off, unable to speak her brother's name. Unable to bring the painful memory into the already gut-wrenching present.

He pulled up her sleeves, tugged at the hems of her pant legs, but there was nothing. Some bruising, some scrapes, but nothing that solidified her as finished. Nothing that spoke her eulogy before she finished breathing. Her jaw worked, the muscles standing out in tight cords under the soft skin of her face. Carey wiped her lips, already dreading the saliva bred rife with cancerous contagions.

You don't know that, Aaron observed cooly. *Make damn sure.*

"Well, we know what has to happen," Kerrigan said from above.

Carey craned his neck up, only to come face to face with the business end of a SIG Sauer P220 Combat. Its infinite black eye stared him dead on, unblinking.

"Don't," Carey instructed, trying to keep his voice level. "We don't know for sure."

I just have to prove it. Prove it and he'll have nothing to go on.

"Look," Carey urged, doing his best to ignore the sidearm all too close to his head. "Help me check her down, she can't have been bitten. Someone's been with her the whole time," he pleaded, trying to ratify the justification to himself as much as to Kerrigan, his eyes narrowed and nostrils flared.

"No point," Kerrigan replied, never wavering the pistol off of Morgan's head. "By the time we strip her down, she'll get us all. I'm not about to have been a packhorse for no reason. Just step aside so you don't get sprayed."

Kerrigan sounded nothing like his former self. The previous Kerrigan would have muttered something macho about slaying undead and praised the gods of rock and roll for letting him do it. No, this was someone else. Someone Kerrigan had hidden from them. The blonde bodybuilder had been an idiot, but he hadn't been cold. Not like this.

"Just help me out, okay?" Carey tried again desperately, looking from Kerrigan to Keila for someone to hear him out.

Keila watched on with anxious eyes, her lip pursed in her teeth, but said nothing. Empty howls continued to ring out in the overcast day, only adding to Carey's anxiety. They were too close for this shit. Too close to finishing their run. Too close to putting this leg behind them.

"Last chance," Kerrigan observed, trading the gun back and forth between his hands as he shook off his backpack, keeping the barrel on target through a bizarre juggling act somehow beyond words.

"*Don't,*" Carey begged, feeling the sting of bile shooting up his throat.

Not another one.

Not another friend.

click

As soon as Carey heard the safety on Kerrigan's SIG snap off, his whole world went red.

He brayed as he rose to his feet, not feeling the pack weighing him down as he spiraled a fist up to Kerrigan's jaw like a viper's strike. *Time to party,* Aaron laughed, clearly enjoying himself.

"*Ack!*" Kerrigan spat, a wad of blood following the trail of saliva down his chin before lunging at Carey.

A single blow from Kerrigan's cinderblock right hand to Carey's temple sent him reeling. Within a moment, Kerrigan had pounced, so much more agile without a loaded rucksack to encumber him.

Carey hit the pavement on his back hard, his sack relegating him to a half-propped position like a turtle on its shell, before Kerrigan's knee dropped onto his sternum. Hard.

"*Stop!*" Keila cried shrilly, waving her hands in the air like her hair was on fire.

Had he been in a less compromising position, he may have even laughed. *Yeah, a real snap dangler,* Aaron chuckled in his head, the voice doubling from the blow to his skull.

The blow pinned him to the road, driving all the wind from his lungs. Carey let out a small cry of astonishment, releasing the last of his breath under the crushing pressure. Kerrigan's handgun leveled on his forehead, the cold steel pressing into the space above his eyes.

"Fuck off, already," Kerrigan hissed, blood trickling in earnest from his mashed lip where his front teeth had pierced the flesh.

Carey could already hear the moans in the too-close distance intensifying, as if their noise had fanned their flames. Somehow, despite the moment, he could almost picture them listening closely for their sounds, numbly triangulating the best way to intercept them like rabid attack dogs.

Kerrigan raised a single finger to his lips, wiping the blood from his mouth before regarding it with a laugh.

"I fucking knew I'd have to go it alone before long, without your whiny ass bringing me down," he chuckled, licking the blood from his finger before wiping the spit off on his pants. "If you're so hell bent on watching her turn, be my guest. Talk to me nicely and I'll just put one in your gut so you'll be awake to watch the show."

"You asshole," Carey mouthed breathlessly, struggling to take in air under the weight on his chest. "You goddamn asshole."

"Maybe, but at least I'll still have Kei-Kei to see me through. You can have the stripper, she was a shitty piece of work anyway," he laughed, his perfect bleach-blonde hair having fallen into disarray, the dark roots beginning to show. "Tough break I had to steal her from you, brother. All's fair in love and war in the end times."

"You did *nothing* of the *sort!*" Keila screamed, her voice crackling as she came into the edge of his vision. "You're the *worst* mistake I've *ever* made!"

She took two further steps before he saw the pistol. She had it leveled from three feet away on Kerrigan's ear. She couldn't miss if she tried. *Careful now, lassie,* Aaron screamed in his mind, the echo rolling and repeating in a maddening chorus. The infected somewhere just beyond the realm of sight cried out in harmony, too numerous to count.

"So that's how it's gonna be, eh?" Kerrigan crooned. He took a moment to regard the sidearm trained at his throat with perfect clarity, his prose returning to the drawl of the uneducated *fuck* Carey knew him to be.

In a flash, the pistol pressed against his head jumped to the right, pointing straight at Keila before a gun blast roared out in the spring afternoon.

"No!" Carey cried with the last of his air, knowing that the girl he swore to protect on a dead man's life was now no longer more than a memory.

Twisting under the mammoth weight on top of him, he craned his head enough to see smoke drifting lazily from the barrel of Keila's P220, her arm unwavering. Her body seemingly untouched.

What?

Carey felt a few droplets strike him in the face, wet and warm, before looking at Kerrigan.

His arm still extended with pistol at port, Kerrigan's gaze had dropped to his chest. A scarlet rose blossomed out from below his left collarbone, a single sanguine pucker defiantly standing out on his shirt.

Kerrigan coughed once, blood spraying in a mist from his lips before rolling off Carey and onto the road. His hands rose off the pavement once before falling still, the gun clattering from his fingers onto the asphalt. The chorus of infected cries rose as if in perfect ecstasy, so horrifically closer than before.

"*Son of a bitch*," Carey whispered, the cool air blissfully rushing into his lungs once more with their hindrance removed.

Drawing his P220, he trained the violent means at his attackers head for good measure before grabbing Kerrigan's handgun off the road. *Jammed.*

The bullet in the chamber hung only half-suspended in the void, dirt and corrosion blocking its proper path to the firing position. *You fucking idiot*, Carey chuckled to himself, still in awe that his pulse continued. He cleared the round, stowing the magazine in his vest pocket before leaving the now-useless piece of steel on the chest of its neglectful former owner.

"You alright?" Keila probed, concern in her voice, drawing to his side as he rose to his feet.

"Fine," Carey remarked, staring her in the face and waiting for the other shoe to drop.

Her realization that she'd just killed a man.

He braced himself with bated breath, doing his best to ignore the broken howls drifting ever closer as he cast a furtive glance down the road. *Still clear. For now.*

A moment passed and it didn't come. No tear dropped from the corner of her eye. No quavering afterword for the man she had obviously thought she loved. She merely rolled her shoulders before staring Carey dead in the face once more. It was the single most beautiful thing he'd seen in his entire life, the way the remorse drained away from her eyes.

"Piece of shit," she spat at the dead man before turning back to Morgan, still prone and twitching on the cold, hard ground.

Morgan. In the moment, Carey had almost forgotten about her. He scampered over to where she lay, again pulling back her collar to check for marks, Kerrigan now no more than a bad taste in his mouth.

"There's no blood welling through her skin yet," he observed, passing his fingers lightly over her throat. She was cool. "No fever either," he remarked, the conclusion too strange to be real.

"I don't think you need to worry about that," Keila sighed, scanning the distance, avoiding his confused glare. "She's overdosing. Heroin. Doesn't mean she's not going to be just as dead if we don't get her help and *fast*."

"*What?*" Carey cried in shock.

It would have been the very last thing that occurred to him, somehow beneath *demonic possession* and *she's turning into a robot*. *Heroin?* It just didn't make sense, but he didn't have time to ponder the matter any further.

The horrid cries in the approaching distance finally came to a head, the source of the commotion boiling forth from the tree line no more than a few hundred metres away.

They were countless in number, falling over each other and scrambling in their slow haste to reach their recently discovered prey. They were too far away to truly make out the individual atrocities of nature, appearing instead as a monstrous pulsing gob of living corpses shambling towards them. All cried hollow victory with their toneless screams, reaching for the trio with hungry jaws despite the distance.

"Grab her!" Carey cried, flooding with panic at the recent unwelcome additions to his peaceful road.

Thanking higher powers Morgan was wearing leather, Carey gripped one side of the overdosing girls pack as Keila grabbed the other and began to drag her down the street, away from the throbbing mob shambling closer by the second.

"Pull hard!" Carey screamed, no longer worried about maintaining a level of covertness given the situation.

His thighs burned as he thrust with all his might, the hundred and ten pound girl feeling heavier by the second. Keila's face flushed as she dug in with her boots, dragging Morgan in tandem with his efforts.

The infected moaned louder and louder until Carey could barely hear his own ragged breathing under the din. There were the low, guttural tone of men. The shrill, crackling shrieks of afflicted women. Underneath, he couldn't help but pick out the mind-wrenching cries of children, their voices weak and empty calling him backwards to take them for a stroll. The wordless choir droned on, his ears burning with the horrid sound of a thousand footfalls gaining ground behind them.

Casting a backward glare, the writing on the wall was plain to see. The infected merely shambled along, but they weren't about to break any land speed records at the moment, either. Regardless, they were closing the distance at an alarming rate — what had been a hundred metres heartbeats ago had decreased by nearly a third.

"Your gun!" Carey screamed at Keila, snatching the weapon as soon as it was offered. He switched his grip on the pack to his left hand, turning to walk backwards and face the horde.

Make them count.

Carey pushed his heels into the asphalt, pulling the ragdoll beneath him as hard as he could as he lined up his shot. A portly man, bare gut shaking and quivering in the April afternoon, stood ahead of the pack. Had he been wearing a blue shirt, Carey could've sworn he'd seen him before at the bridge.

He squared the iron sights on the man's head as he watched him draw past the fifty-yard mark, carefully aligning the notch and post atop the gun with the man's jaw. He squeezed the trigger, the pistol barking in his palm and watched the man crumple. It would have been a moment of elation to make such a shot, had three more infected not stumbled over his corpse to take his place.

"Fuck!" Carey shouted, pulling the trigger again and again as he dragged with all his might.

A few infected staggered before falling, but the screaming horde swallowed up the bodies with their nearing ranks before he could even blink. The pistol leapt and jarred in his hands, but they kept closing the distance as resolutely as before, their numbers not markedly thinned by his efforts before the clip clicked empty.

"Shit, she's all yours," Carey cried at Keila before leaving Morgan to her care. He wasn't at all surprised to see their progress barely slow once his effort was withdrawn, Keila's lips pulled back in a sneer with exertion.

The spent magazine dropped with a clatter unheard under the moans of the closing sick, their arms reaching out for him as he slapped a fresh clip home. *Come dance with us!* Their expressionless faces begged him. *Come down to the swamp and two-step forever!*

Carey squared his stance, stopping dead on the road before the SIG Sauer roared off another four shots into the crowd. They had spread out on the road, numbering easily twelve across on the front line, their ranks swelled with writhing figures behind.

She was right, this is it. Carey felt the sweat from his hands dripping over the grip, the iron sights jarring madly as he cooked off another pair of rounds. An old woman in a beautiful floral print dress met her demise as a slug perforated her left eye-socket, her jaws snapping open to reveal a toothless mouth before falling to the road.

They were no more than twenty metres away, close enough for Carey to smell them. The same rancid meat. The same spoiled milk. It washed over him in waves, his gag reflex barely remaining under his control. He heard every shuffling footstep, every broken bone grinding as they staggered towards him, his resumed shooting bringing down only a fragment of their horrid population.

"Come *on!*" Keila screamed behind him.

She had made it no more than fifteen feet for his efforts. No more than a cripple's stone-throw from where he stood. *Fuck.*

The second magazine clicked empty, the minute *plink* of the firing pin sending his world reeling. Carey clumsily swapped the still-loaded pistol in his holster for the useless piece of *shit* in his hands, thumbing off the safety before bringing it back up to port.

This is the way the world ends. Not with a bang, but with a whimper. He had heard it so many years ago and never thought of it again. *This is the way your life ends — not with a bang, but with a desperate cry.*

Then make it bang, Aaron screamed, seeming to take control of his arms and drop a pair of infected in the forward line. *Make it fucking bang until it bangs no more.*

Nine shots. That was all he had left. *And one in that old piece of garbage on your shoulder if it comes to it, so SHOOT!* Aaron chided.

Eight.

A guido, likely one of Kerrigan's embezzled shirt-wearing brethren from another life, dropped like a stone to the pavement. The round took off a piece of his skull as large as an apple near his hairline.

Seven.

A boy wearing Superman pajamas fell to the tarmac, catching a bullet with his teeth and losing the battle.

Six.

The shot perforated the space beside a man's nose. *That three-piece suit's gonna look downright fucking dapper in Hell,* he thought.

Five. Four. Three.

A trio of infected to his right bit the asphalt, heads hitting the ground one after the other in perfect broken rhythm. *Samba, please. Let's pick up the pace.*

The howling in his ears was deafening, almost drowning out the pitiful *cracks* of his P220, the sound of clacking jaws rounding out the overtone.

Shit, he swore under his breath as he ran back to Keila's side, gripping the pack with all his might before heaving backwards. The afflicted were too close. Too many. The thought dropped like a grenade into the turbulent mirth of his mind, sending the last shreds of his hope splashing out of his head.

Grenade.

This is it.

Squeezing off the last three rounds in his pistol — the ones he had imagined with his, Keila's and Morgan's names emblazoned on the side—he shoved the handgun into the side pocket of his bag. It emerged clutching the solitary grenade he'd brought along for the trip.

"Carey," Keila said softly, breathless and wheezing as she pulled her cargo with all her strength.

Her green eyes peered up at him through the grime, sweat and stray greasy hair that framed her face like two emeralds at the bottom of a mineshaft. They tore into him like blades, but he knew they understood. It was the same unspoken bond that in time would have let them finish each other's sentences as they sat old and grey in rocking chairs. It was the same link that had been forged through the shed blood of everyone they loved.

She knew.

Carey nodded, handing her the munition. It seemed to bob in her hands like the passing of seconds on a clock. *Tick. Tick. Tick.*

The infected roared from a mere twenty yards away, relentless in their pursuit. They could have had a saccharine-sweet final moment together and the sick would've devoured them just the same with their ragged, broken teeth. There was no need to be dramatic. There was no need for a final statement.

Tick. Tick. Tick.

This is it.

Carey reached over his shoulder, drawing the talisman. Drawing what was meant to be in his hands as he breathed his last. Its polished steel smiled up at him as he cocked the hammer, its knowing, empty eye free of judgment, promising only release. The Taurus revolver felt warm in his hands as the infected drew closer, no more than three car-lengths away. It seemed to click in rhythm to the beat of the grenade.

Tick-tick. Tick-tick. Tick-tick.

It would be their final composition, the one they left on the earth.

Staring at the Taurus in his palm, listening to the rolling clatter of the implements mix with the infected soon to breathe down their necks, he almost missed the low whine in the distance.

What?

"*Don't!*" Carey cried at Keila, grabbing the C13 Fragmentary Grenade from her hands before her finger could wrap through the pin. "*GO!*" he screamed, gripping Morgan's strap once more and digging into reserves he didn't know he had to run.

Tasting the blood rising in the back of his throat, the muted rumble broke into an outright roar as a pair of black RG-31 Nyala combat trucks careened into sight above the heads of the mob of infected, their arms only metres away from his face.

The flat-black painted South African-made trucks, layered with bush-bars and headlights, screamed towards them from down the road behind the infected. The remotely-controlled M151 PROTECTOR units saddled on the weapons-mounts hammered 7.62mm fire from its MAG-58 machineguns, the iridescent camera playing left and right as the trailing ranks of the sick were cut down like autumn timber.

"Hot *damn!*" Carey screamed with elation, shoving the Taurus into his over-laden sweater pocket where it rattled against his empty mags, jostling as he pulled Morgan with all his might.

Soldiers dressed in black fatigues, breathing-masks covering their faces, spilled from the doors as they flung open, carving down infected with expert shots. Their C7 Assault rifles cast star-shaped arcs of fire as they ripped down body after body in their midst. They fell into formation outside ten yards, aligning in a vanguard as three similarly-outfitted soldiers rushed at the three hustling away from the scene, Morgan barely gurgling at their feet.

Two of the men grabbed her, doubling her back to the vehicles while the last put a hand on Carey's back, pushing him towards the waiting caravan. Before he could let out a cry of relief, he was thrust in an open door, shins knocking painfully off the iron running boards before the vehicle was moving.

"What the *fuck!*" Carey cried out in dismay, head still swimming with exertion and confusion.

"Any contagious?" the soldier beside him snapped, voice muffled by the breathing apparatus strapped to his face. His brown eyes stared accusingly at Carey, his fingers far from releasing the carbine in his hands.

"No!" Carey screamed, horrified. "She's overdosing... uh, heroin or something," he begged, wishing nothing more than to be believed. For his near-fatal efforts to save her life to be vindicated.

"Check her out," the soldier bearing Master Corporal's shoulder flashes barked to the men in the back of the cabin as the truck jostled over the road. "Start an intravenous and get her stabilized until we can get some naloxone into her. Nice to see you, by the way," he added as an afterthought, directing his attention back to Carey's shaking frame.

"You have no idea," he breathed, still hearing the phantom tick of the grenade in his pocket.

The soldier reached up to his mask, pulling the straps from the back of his head with his gloved hand. With the bug-eyed view windows and heavy circular filter removed, Carey was staring at a ghost.

A spectre, vanished long ago into the night after writing a check his ass couldn't cash to people who didn't like to be fucked with. The guy who he'd worked with at The Stallion until his *penchant* for late nights and nose candy sent him running from town with his tail between his legs.

Chris Eichmann, the prodigal former-roommate, past *confidanté* had returned.

"You've got to be shitting me," Carey gasped, not quite able to wrap his head around the memory made real before him.

His jaw was sharper, his neck broader and his eyes more tired; but it was him. *El Eicherino*, in the flesh.

"Wish I was," he said with a laugh, his voice pure and jubilant. "Been a while, hasn't it."

That was like saying *this was all mildly irritating, this whole infection.* Understatement of the goddamn century. Carey reeled in silence for a moment as the truck bounced over potholes and what he couldn't help imagine were bodies. The trees rushed by on either side of the truck, the weapon on the truck whizzing mechanically as it scanned from left to right at the beckon of the operator sitting on his other side, controls in his lap. The monitor gave nothing away — only a blur of smoke and trees, punctuated by the following truck now and again.

"How... what..." Carey stumbled in spite of himself.

Ninety seconds ago, he was plotting his leap off the mortal coil. Fifteen seconds ago, he stared a man he thought dead square in the eyes.

"Signed up to get away, ended up being pretty damn good at it," Eichmann chuckled, patting the rank insignias on his shoulders. "Got signed up with the best unit in town," he continued, pointing at the badge on his bicep.

It was a black dog, silhouetted against a pine-covered mountain with teeth bared. Beneath it, in white, bold letters, it read 3rd C-SOR — JACKAL — DEATH WAITS IN THE NIGHT. Before, Carey would've thought it was the cheesiest thing he'd ever read, but the words leapt off the embroidery, stunning him into a stammer.

"The Jackals? The Jackals?" Carey coughed, wondering how many more times he could sound like a star-struck schoolgirl before he received a cursory slap to his senses.

"One and only, baby. Best of the best," Eichmann said, beaming with pride, allowing his rifle to dangle by the straps linked to his webbing. "We're set up just a mile down the road. Heard your little party and figured you were idiots from Camp Robinson out for a tour. Can't let those Princess Pat's Regiment guys have all the fun, can we?" he laughed again, exuding confidence. "Went in for a stroll to save some green-necks and walked out with you three, heavens be damned!" he cried, clapping Carey on the shoulder.

"Stabilized, Major," one of the men called from the back, fiddling with the wires they'd strung to Morgan's chest.

She lay on the floor of the truck, her black hair strewn across her face, but she'd ceased quivering like the last leaves in autumn. It wasn't much, but it was more than Carey could hope for.

"Saw some asshole laid out on the road. Was he with you?" Eichmann probed, his eyes becoming serious as if from nowhere.

"Was," Keila piped up, breaking her silence from across the cabin. "Got bitten. Turned. Didn't leave us with much choice."

"See it every day, it seems," Eichmann remarked with a knowing waggle of his bushy eyebrows.

He rose, walking hunched towards the drivers, exchanging unheard mutterings with them at the RG-31 Nyala's wheel. Carey shot Keila a glance, receiving nothing in response. *Could be worse,* Aaron advised, knocking down his opposition to the matter. *Could've spilled. Feel lucky, 'ya jerk.*

The armoured truck took a sharp left turn, angling down a side dirt road off of the main drag. Through the reinforced window, Carey could see snipers in tree stands, perched high in the tall pines flanking either side of the road. They raised hands as they passed, receiving salutes and jeers from the men in the vehicle in reply.

Coils of concertina wire — so much like the setup Carey had seen back in New Braniff — were pulled back from the road to allow their trucks passage, quickly replaced as they passed.

As the vehicle drew to a halt, the doors flew open, the men amicably exchanging pats on the back as they jumped from the truck.

"Is she gonna be alright?" Carey asked as Morgan was hastily loaded onto a spinal board, machines whirring and beeping from all sides.

"We'll see," Eichmann opined, helping Carey from the truck before hoisting Keila to the ground below. "Sawbones in our units are the best around. Last thing the government wants to do is spend money to train our replacements, rather than just patching us up."

Standing beside the enormous black war machine, he saw no rows of tents. No stockpiles of ammunition strewn about in crates for the taking. No cranes and no cherry pickers. Instead, like an accountant's desk, everything had a place and everything was firmly in it. Situated in a treeless grove in the forest, construction site-style fencing bordered the encampment — so much more effective than the hack-job chain link roll-a-fence Base Alexander had erected around their own. Six cover-all quarter-round tents, arranged in perfect symmetry on both sides of the centre of the base, stood resolute as the Pyramids of Giza. Directly in the middle, in perfect irony, sat a small cabin, complete with bivouac tents careening off every side. *If only Roman could see us now.*

"Welcome to Forward-Base Jackal," Eichmann announced with a wave of his hand, putting an arm around Keila on one side,

Carey on his other. "The best, the proud, the don't-get-killed-when-the-world-falls-down," he sang, horribly off-key.

"Jackal," Carey mused dazedly, "We were headed for Robinson from Alexander."

"Ah, up in arms with the Alexandrines, eh? Well, you missed your mark by more than a few miles to the east, my friend."

Carey chuckled, shaking his head at Morgan's directions. Nothing but sheer dumb luck had managed to get them this far, though he doubted his own orienteering would've proved much better. At least they didn't wind up in the States, as may have been the case if he held the reins.

"Just as well you showed up here, Robinson's been struggling ever since that helicopter brought every *grey* from here to New Hampshire in on them," Eichmann continued, knocking the dried mud off his boots against the truck tire. "You guys have to get a run-down from the medic before you'll be allowed to go a-wandering through the base, but you look fine to me. Come, friends — you're home!"

Probed, tested and stuck with needles to the umpteenth degree; when Carey Cardinal's head hit the pillow, he was already asleep.

Near-death experiences are draining.

Near-death experiences at your own hand are something else altogether.

XVI

The quiet, constant *ping* of the electrocardiogram hooked up to her chest brought a solace he didn't know possible after what he had witnessed.

Hooked up to more tubes and wires than a first-generation computer, Morgan was alive.

The medic said a little longer and she'd have been done for this world. Said there was still a possibility for irrecoverable damage to her brain function. Said she may not even know who the hell he was when she woke up. If she woke up.

All 'maybes,' and no definite answer. She lay in a deep coma. One where she likely heard nothing. Saw nothing. Felt nothing. *Thought* nothing. He couldn't help but wonder on that last one, whether Keila had received the same speech from Doctor Roberts after his own trip through the nether in Camp Robinson.

Damn, wouldn't that be a laugh.

The instruments measuring her breathing, heart rate and oxygen saturation were the only light in the dark, empty tent; devoid of other patients. Too much like Robinsons, the beds were vacant. Save for him; she was alone.

Waking up after a short but needed rest, he'd found Forward Base Jackal clad in darkness, the light of the day long gone. He had no idea what the time was, but he didn't give a shit. Sleep was time he spent in *that* world. He needed to use all the time he had left *here*.

Keila had been softly snoring when he left, her deep breathing calmly reassuring. He'd let himself out for a piss, only to sneak like a would-be paramour in the night to the medical tent. To her side, where he stood mesmerized by the green line bobbing up and down in time on the EKG's readout.

That was almost it.

He didn't know how long he'd been here, but his mind had been playing the same circular game since he'd clandestinely stolen past the canvas doors and propped himself on the nearest cot.

Guilt, some would call it. He couldn't help but think it ran deeper than that. Spinning endlessly like a merry-go-round with a sleeping operator at the controls.

Before pulling the grenade from his pack, before showing resolution to his fate against overwhelming odds; he'd almost pulled the trigger. That *other* trigger.

The one that would have left her all alone. The one that would have let her be overtaken by the ravenous horde, torn apart by broken fingers while she lived in the fever-dream. The one that would have left Carey and Keila utterly alone in the woods, likely walking in that same fever that gripped the population, wandering the swamp with their sightless eyes half-cocked to the sky.

I almost left you.

He knew she would thank him for saving her. Thank them both for being her walk-on-water sent-from-Jesus saviours, bringing her safely to a place where she at least had a shot.

Really, if not for her, they wouldn't be here.

Wouldn't be alive.

In the conventional sense, anyway.

"Thought I'd find you here," a gruff, kindly voice accosted him from behind.

"Eichmann, I've never doubted your superior intellect," Carey mused, half-joking without turning.

Ask him three weeks ago where Chris Eichmann was and he'd likely answer *in the bottom of a coke-filled grave.* My, how the times change.

"We need to chat," the soldier said with apprehension in his voice, hesitating for a moment before taking a seat beside him on the cot.

"Oh?" Carey remarked, not taking his eyes off the cardiogram. *You're the reason we're here. I only hope to get to thank you.*

"Camp Alexander has a problem," he said after a moment. Carey could hear Eichmann's hands wrenching as he spoke. That sandpaper sound of hard-earned callous on callous.

"You don't say," Carey replied, completely uninterested. Nothing could take the place of that little, jumping green line in his mind.

"Let me clarify. Camp Alexander has a problem. With you."

"No shit," Carey chuckled, eyes tracing the emerald readout.

"Captain abandoned ship. Captain Meyers, that is."

"That's not quite right, is it," Carey muttered, beginning to grow tired of the interruption of his séance.

"Before he left, he had wanted to send a platoon after his lost messiah. A certain helicopter technician, who bears an uncanny resemblance to you. Wouldn't you believe it?" Eichmann observed with a small prod with his elbow. "They weren't up for losing men on a fool's errand, so he left to find you. Thought you were worth it or something. Has somebody been telling porky-pies, amigo?"

"Perhaps," Carey replied, a sinking stone settling directly in his gut. *Fuck.*

"Yeah, figured. Now Base Alexander wants you court-marshaled, since you turned up safe and sound *here*, rather than *there and* you've got a decided lack of knowledge they so crave."

"You don't fuckin' say," Carey mumbled, rubbing his neck.

The *ping* of the EKG seemed to turn against him, its tone more accusing than reassuring. *Ping! Ping! Liar! Ping! Thief! Ping-ping!*

"Lucky for you, the radioman owes me a favour and agreed *not* to relay that onto the commander *here* until daybreak."

"Fortunate. So I have a bit of time to consider my fate before I'm strung up the nearest tree," Carey grumbled, the prospect of death feeling more like an inconvenience than a true threat. *When you've seen one Reaper, you've seen 'em all.*

"No," Eichmann corrected, "You're fortunate that you're coming with me to Robinson. Some old bastard apparently went nuts, spraying around with a shotgun before running off into the woods. Made off with a kid or two as well, so I hear. They want a little divine retribution, so they want the Jackals to come check it out, strapped for men as they are."

"Oh, how the mighty have fallen," Carey observed, considering the prospect.

"Indeed," Eichmann agreed, rising to his feet. "Grab your things and meet me by the trucks in an hour. I'll have gear for you, since you're going to have to blend in to get the hell out of here."

"What about them?" Carey urged, a bolt of terror running through his chest.

His own death would be an inconvenience. Keila or Morgan suffering for his failures would be something else altogether.

"I'll handle it, just be there," Eichmann stated, patting him firmly on the back. "We've got work to do."

Work, Carey thought.

Better bring a jacket. It's cold out there, Aaron laughed.

END